W9-BWH-470

PRAISE FOR MATTHEW FARRELL

What Have You Done

"A young crime writer with real talent is a joy to discover, and Matthew Farrell proves he's the real deal in his terrific debut, *What Have You Done*. He explores the dark side of family bonds in this raw, gripping page-turner, with suspense from start to finish. You won't be able to put it down."

—Lisa Scottoline, *New York Times* bestselling author

"A must-read thriller! Intense, suspenseful, and fast paced—I was on the edge of my seat."

—Robert Dugoni, *New York Times* bestselling author

"One hell of a debut thriller. With breakneck pacing and a twisting plot, *What Have You Done* will keep you guessing until its stunning end."

—Eric Rickstad, *New York Times* bestselling author

"A must-read thriller! *What Have You Done* is a roller coaster of a novel that grabs hold and refuses to let go. Fans of Meg Gardiner and Mark Edwards will find lots to love in this debut. I can't wait to read what Matt cooks up next."

—Tony Healey, author of the Harper and Lane series

I KNOW EVERY THING

OTHER BOOKS BY MATTHEW FARRELL

What Have You Done

I KNOW EVERY THING

MATTHEW FARRELL

THOMAS & MERCER

Text copyright © 2019 by Matthew Farrell
All rights reserved.

Published by Thomas & Mercer, Seattle
www.apub.com

Amazon, the Amazon logo, and Thomas & Mercer are trademarks of Amazon.com, Inc., or its affiliates.

ISBN-13: 9781542044974 (hardcover)
ISBN-10: 1542044979 (hardcover)
ISBN-13: 9781542044967 (paperback)
ISBN-10: 1542044960 (paperback)

Cover design by Rex Bonomelli

Printed in the United States of America

First edition

For Mackenzie and Jillian:
I can write about strong women because I live with
strong women.
I'm so proud to be your dad.

PROLOGUE

Although the darkness was too thick to even see his hands in front of his face, he knew the two bodies were with him in the room. A mother and daughter, killed within minutes of one another, each death an escalation in rage and fury, then desperation and futility. The lights had been on then. He'd seen every second of what had unfolded, heard every sound that had echoed in the brick-and-concrete chamber they'd been trapped in, but at the same time, it had felt like a dream. Even now, the sounds were only a whisper of recollection, growing faint as each minute passed.

The wounds from the shotgun blast appeared to be life threatening. He'd be dead soon. Of that, there was no doubt. No one knew where he was, and at this point, he wondered if they'd stopped looking. In the long run, it wouldn't matter. He'd be nothing more than a third body on the cold concrete floor, next to the woman and her daughter. This would be his end, his fate. This dark basement would be the last world he'd ever know. He was ready. In fact, he was looking forward to it.

The heavy chain that connected him to the wall pulled on his wrist and weighed on his right shoulder. It jangled when he moved and sounded loud in the quiet space. He stopped, listening for the man up in the house, hoping the noise hadn't been loud enough to warrant a visit.

Footsteps above.

He could hear the man's boots walking across the floor. He waited for the inevitable sound of the basement door swinging open and those boots thumping as they made their descent down the stairs. But this time things were different. The footsteps walked straight above him, then turned back in the opposite direction. The man was walking quickly, almost running, from one side of the house to the other.

A shotgun cocked.

The footsteps halted.

Silence.

He stayed as still as he possibly could, listening for something—anything—that might tell him what was happening. He was waiting for that basement door to open, but there was only the complete quiet that enveloped the house. The chain on his wrist jangled ever so slightly, and he caught it in his left hand. It was too dark to see even a hint of anything. All he could do was wait and die.

A door crashed open upstairs. Men's screams exploded in the quiet, one after the other.

"Police!"

"NYPD!"

"Come out now!"

He listened as he leaned against the wall, instinctively trying to protect himself against the fury in the voices that called out. His breathing was growing weaker. He didn't have much time left. The stampede of movement continued thundering above.

"Get your hands up!"

"I got him here! In the kitchen!"

"Drop your weapon!"

A shotgun blast exploded and was immediately followed by return fire that came so rapidly he thought someone might've had a machine gun. And as soon as it began, it was over. The house was silent again.

He could smell the gunpowder and fought the urge to vomit. He tried to stand, but his legs would no longer hold him. His throat was dry, choking off the ability to call out for help. He had no idea what was happening.

The basement door opened.

A light came on.

It was a bare-bulb socket that hung in the center of the room, strong enough to illuminate the space. The sudden brightness hurt his eyes, and he shielded himself with his forearm. Someone crept down the steps, each tread moaning under the weight.

"Anyone down here?" a voice called. "NYPD."

He could see now. In every sense of the word, he could see. He could see the two bodies across from him lying almost side by side. He could see the concrete floor below them a shade darker, stained with their deaths. He looked down at himself and could see the wound from the shotgun blast that had torn apart his stomach and chest. There was no way he'd be able to survive such carnage. Then he saw the dried blood on his hands and arms and knew what he'd done. That blood was not his. He could see his weakness.

A thin cloud of smoke followed the police officer into the basement. The officer, in his dark tactical gear and helmet, looked like a specter, like the angel of death coming to take him away to pay penance for his sins. And that was okay. He deserved whatever punishment was coming. He was weak, and he was a sinner.

He was ready for hell.

He'd already lived it.

1

Randall Brock adjusted the monitor so everyone would be able to see. He took a breath, then picked up the remote and pressed play, easing himself against the wall, watching as the session began to unfold on the video. He knew what was coming and knew how things would end. It wasn't good.

On the screen, Dr. Peter Reems leaned back in his chair, much the same way the real Peter Reems was sitting now, staring at the monitor, observing the monster inside the man. "Go ahead, Jerry," he said on the video. "You can begin."

The patient, Jerry Osbourne, squirmed in his seat, trying to get comfortable, his eyes cut into slits as he repeatedly wiped at the perspiration on his brow. "You sure you wanna hear this?"

"Yes. It's okay. I'm right here. You and me. I want you to close your eyes and tell me everything. Just like we talked about."

"But I—"

"It's okay. I promise. Close your eyes."

Jerry did as he was told, and his body began to relax, shoulders slumping a bit, chin hovering just above his chest.

"Good. Now tell me."

A final sigh. "It's dark. Not the kind of dark where it's just nighttime, but real friggin' dark. The kind where storm clouds come in and cover everything: the moon, the stars. Everything. Like a giant blanket over the sky. That kind of dark makes the shadows even thicker, you know? And it makes the places that do have light seem safe. But safety in a darkness like that is fake, and you can't trust nothing fake. When it's dark like that, the light is just a trap. And people fall for it all the time. They run to the light. They'll do anything to get out of that darkness. It's what makes it so easy. All you gotta do is wait in the light with a stupid grin on your face and that promise of safety, and they come to you. They walk right in."

"Who walked in to get out of the dark?" Peter asked.

"She did. But not like you're thinking. She wasn't running from the darkness. She was already in it, stuck there, like she was trapped. I brought the light to her."

"Explain what you mean."

"I saw her when I went in to get my cavity filled. She was this new girl in charge of patient charting or something. She looked smart. Clean. Attractive enough, I guess. But when I tried to talk to her, she blew me off. Not in a polite way either. I introduced myself and stuck out my hand. She looked down at it like I was offering her a dead fish or something and brushed right past me."

"How did that make you feel?"

"Made me feel like a loser. Like a nobody. I was pissed. So I waited outside in the parking lot until the office closed and she came out. I go up to her and ask why she was being so rude, and she said she wasn't, but even as she's denying it, she's being a bitch. I stuck my hand out again and asked her to shake it. She laughed and told me she wasn't interested. I told her I wasn't interested either. I just wanted to be friendly. She said she had enough friends and walked away. She *walked away*. Couldn't take two seconds to shake my hand?"

"What did you do after she left?"

"I went home and chugged a few beers. Watched the game. Had a little fantasy about her. But then all these mental images of what I wanted to do to her started popping up in my head. Not in a sexual way, though. This was, like, violent. I wanted to hurt her. I wanted to end her. I tried to talk myself out of it. I mean, I couldn't really want those things, right? I don't even know where these thoughts and feelings came from, but the more I tried to ignore the images in my head, the more the urges came. They wouldn't leave. I just kept thinking about it. Obsessing about it. I googled to find out what was wrong with me and ended up on all these freaky websites that did nothing but feed the urge. I was a different person, just like that. But then I figured a person can't change just like that, so it must've been in me all along, growing like a weed or a cancer that I wasn't aware of. And for whatever reason, this girl brought it to the surface. I think it was her laugh. The way she laughed at me made me realize she was living in this darkness, and she couldn't escape from it. I had to bring her the light. Simple as that."

Peter nodded, jotting a few notes. "What happened next?"

A thin smile crept onto Jerry's lips. "I spent the next few days following her everywhere she went. Work, home, the movies, the food store. I watched her when she walked her poodle and knew what her shifts were at work. I even knew when her breaks were."

"Tell me how you brought her the light."

"I cut the hose to her transmission fluid. I knew how long her commute home was and how long she'd last before the car would give out, and I just followed behind far enough so I was out of sight. The fluid empties, she pulls over, and I drive up to save the day. A light in the darkness. Safety. Or, like I was saying before, the illusion of safety.

"That part of the road has the lake on one side and the woods on the other, so it was pitch friggin' black. She took one look at my truck heading over the crest of the hill with my yellow emergency lights twirling, and I could see her relax. The damsel in distress had found her knight driving a tow truck. What a coincidence, right? When I pulled up and rolled down the window, she couldn't really see me. I asked if she needed a tow, and she said she did. Said she wasn't sure what happened and that she was so thankful. Figures. Only thankful and friendly when she needs help. Otherwise, she couldn't give a rat's ass about anyone."

"What did you do?" Peter asked.

Jerry shrugged. "I got out, hopped down from the truck, and before she could make heads or tails of anything, I knocked her in the side of the head with my tire iron. Didn't kill her or anything. Just had to make it quick. I got her up in the truck and drove about two more miles so I could pull off into this small clearing I knew about from when I used to go hunting there. I shut everything down and carried her into the woods. Walked about half a mile. She was coming to toward the end, but with the darkness being so dense and her head being all squirrelly, she didn't start to panic until I was putting the zip ties around her ankles."

"How did you feel when you were tying her ankles?"

"In control. Like I was the boss. She feared me, and that's what I wanted. She needed to understand the consequences of her actions, and nothing teaches consequences like zip ties around your wrists and ankles."

"What happened after you tied her up?"

"At first she kept looking around, like she couldn't figure out what was happening. She was yanking on the zip ties, trying to get her arms and legs free. I guess after a few minutes everything finally dawned on her because this tiny whimper came out. It was starting to get louder, like she was going to scream, so I slapped a piece of duct tape over her mouth. When I got close enough to put the tape on her, she got a good look at me. I could see the recognition in her eyes. That was awesome. That was exactly what I wanted. In that second, she understood everything that was going to happen."

"You could have stopped right there. What was the point in pushing things further? She would've learned her lesson. Don't you think?"

"No, I had to do it. I had to. She had to pay, and she had to pay with her life. That's the deal. I didn't make the rules."

Peter shuffled in his seat behind his desk, his eyes fixed on the screen. From where Randall stood next to him, he could see Peter's finger tapping nervously on his thigh. Randall realized he was doing the same. The tension in the room was thick.

"Who made the rules, then?" Peter asked on the video.

"I don't know," Jerry replied. "But I didn't."

"Okay. How did you make her pay?"

"First, I dumped a can of gasoline all over her. The fumes made my eyes burn. As soon as the gas hit her, she started freaking out. I guess that was reality slapping her in the face. She was flailing around, trying to kick out of the ties, screaming behind the tape, crying. I loved every second of it. I told her how she could've lived if she'd just been nice to me. But this was her fate, I guess."

"Did you ever think about letting her go?"

"Aren't you listening? I couldn't let her go. Wasn't allowed. I lit a match and told her that I had enough friends too. She was trying to say something through the tape when I dropped the match onto her lap. Man, her entire body went up in seconds. It was crazy how fast she caught. And her screams, even through the tape. I watched for a bit, but then the bushes around her started catching, and the leaves on the ground were lighting up. I had to split before someone called the fire department. I started whistling as I walked back to my truck. You wouldn't think so unless you tried it, but the whistling and the screams actually played off each other nicely. It had a certain melody to it. I guess you could say that was our special song. Written just for the two of us."

2

The room was silent. Randall shut the video off and laid the remote on the desk. He folded his arms in front of him as he watched the other two men, trying to gauge their reactions.

Dr. Lienhart, the head of the Psychiatry Department at Quarim University, stared at the blank screen. His expression was unchanging, his body completely still except for his head, which shook back and forth ever so slightly.

"I thought you said we were making progress," he said finally.

Peter rubbed his hands on his pants over and over, carefully choosing his words. "We are. But understand this entire experiment is going to have some ups and downs along the way. A patient's road to wellness is never a linear thing. I'd surmise that Jerry has at least eight to ten more sessions to go before we see more significant changes. But we're getting there."

Dr. Lienhart, who'd been sitting with his back to Peter and Randall, slid to the edge of his chair and turned to look at them both. He absently scratched at the liver spots on his forehead with long thin fingers. "What I just saw was a patient who had been making progress suddenly revert back to his violent fantasies. How do you expect me to go to the board for more funding when we have nothing to show for the funding we've already received? This isn't advancement. This is a step back. A rather large one, if I do say so myself."

Peter stood up from his seat and walked around to the front of his desk. "We are making progress overall, sir. With everyone in the study. Jerry, as you know, is patient number three. He's highly intelligent. He's a loner. No friends. No family. His father died when he was eighteen, and his mother two years prior to that, which is the same family dynamic as the other two patients in the study. When I was first introduced to him, I saw clear signs of psychopathic tendencies that were on the verge of acting out. His fantasy about killing the records girl involved rape and torture. He talked about dismembering her, beating her, choking her right up to the point of death, then letting her live so he could do it again. There was no remorse or reflection. Just anger and the need to control."

The old man glanced at Randall, who remained silent. "He's sick. And what I saw before was a man who I thought was getting better. Now he's back to burning his fantasy girl alive again. I can't go to the board with this."

"What you just saw was my twenty-first session with Jerry," Peter said. "That means twenty times previously he's told me he wanted to kill the records girl and then explained how he was going to do it. Without my prompting or leading, Jerry began to alter the details of his fantasy, and what was once a personal and violent act—the act of him raping her and placing his own hands around her neck, feeling her skin on his, squeezing the very breath out of her—has become a distant fantasy, as if he's watching a movie instead of starring in it. He's removed the personalization. Now he ties her up and backs away. He hardly touches her. He dumps the gasoline over her body. He lights a match and throws it. He's no longer directly responsible for her death. It's the fire and the propellant that kill her, not him."

"But the last two sessions before this one, he'd decided not to kill her at all." Lienhart folded his hands across his chest. "You came to me with the theory of curing psychopathic behavior by forcing subjects to talk through their fantasies. You said that if they talked about them in as much detail as possible, they would subdue the need to actually act out. And I admit at first it seemed to work. But if the subject is going to revert back to the violence, then it's all a waste of time."

"The fantasy will continue to abate. This is just a hiccup. He'll continue to distance himself from the intimate act of murder until there is no more fantasy. One day I'll ask him about the records girl at the dentist's office, and he'll simply change the subject. There will no longer even be a kill fantasy."

"And what if he *does* act on these stories?" Lienhart asked. "What if this experiment is more hope than fact? For all we know, we could be planting ideas that make it easier for him to go out into the world and kill someone."

Peter shook his head. "No," he said. "That's not how this works. I'm not planting any seeds to change the fantasy. I'm simply asking the patient to tell me, in detail, how they want to kill their victim. The patient naturally changes their own story. There's no leading. It's completely organic. That's why we will have setbacks every now and again. Jerry is treating himself. Each patient will take their own path."

Dr. Lienhart looked back and forth between the two men, unconvinced. "Tell me about the others. Where are we with them?"

"Patient number one, Stephen Sullivan, has no fantasy anymore. He balks at the slightest hint of hurting his ex-girlfriend, and we're at the point where Stephen might leave us altogether. He won't even talk about his ex anymore. In his mind, he's moved on. Patient number two, Jason Harris, has no kill fantasy anymore but still shows anger around the subject of his father. We're working through that."

"So of the three patients or subjects or whatever you want to call them, two are still showing violent signs, and one of those two just regressed. That's hardly a success worthy of a McKeen Cattell Fellow. You'll have to do better."

Peter nodded. "I understand."

Randall raised his hand. "Sir, if I could just interject for a moment. I've been with Dr. Reems from the beginning of this study. I'm telling you, he's onto something. This could change the way we treat this kind of psychosis. This could change everything. The scientific community will stand up and take notice. I guarantee it."

Dr. Lienhart struggled to get out of the chair. He straightened his jacket, pulling on the bottom hem. "I think you very well may be onto something here," he said. "But I can't go to the board with this as it is today. You'll have to continue with the funding you've already been given. That's the best I can do at this point."

Peter's shoulders slumped a bit. "I understand."

"Get me a full report with session notes on my desk when we get back from holiday break, along with your detailed plans regarding the next few phases of this treatment. We'll give it until the end of the second semester. If I see real progress . . . I mean real progress, gentlemen . . . we can talk about a five-year grant. But if I see more of what I saw today, we might have to move on. I know you don't want to hear that, but you're not the only ones around here working to further their cause."

Peter shook Lienhart's bony hand. "The entire case study package will be waiting when you get back."

The old man opened the office door and nodded toward Randall. "Plans for the holiday, Dr. Brock?"

"Just work," Randall said.

"No family visits or Christmas celebrations?"

"No, sir. Just my wife and I this year. Nice and quiet. Nothing planned other than that case study package you'll need."

Lienhart stopped halfway out the door, turning to look at the two men one last time. "I know you've been working hard on this, and I know this could be nothing more than a minor setback in the grand scheme of things. But if we're going to offer a cure for violent psychosis, we have to be one hundred percent right. These people are too dangerous. I want you to remember that. A life you think you've saved could end up taking many more lives if you're wrong. This has to be perfect."

Peter followed the old man and gently shut the door behind him. He leaned his head against it and closed his eyes. "That went about as expected."

"Maybe we shouldn't have shown him the video," Randall said. "We could've said Jerry never showed up for the appointment and we had to reschedule."

"We can't do that. We can't start hiding things or manipulating outcomes in order to get funding. That's not how this works."

"I know how it works, but I also knew this would happen. We've come so far. I knew a setback like that would make Lienhart nervous. He hasn't liked this study from the start."

Peter pushed himself off the door and looked at Randall. "What happened?" he asked. "How could we go from making such incredible progress to Jerry reverting back to violence again? What made him do that?"

"I don't know."

"Well, think."

The frustration in his friend's voice was apparent.

"I don't know," Randall repeated. "Like you said, this isn't a linear thing. We got thrown a curveball."

"We have everything riding on this study," Peter said. He walked back over to his desk and flopped down in the chair. "You realize we could change the way homicidal tendencies are recognized and treated, right? We could alter how law enforcement acts in the face of these potentially violent people. We could change how the prison system views violence. What happened to your brother would never have to happen again. We could change that."

"This has nothing to do with Sam," Randall said.

"I know. I'm just saying." Peter began snatching papers from the top of his desk and putting them in binders. "You better get a move on if you're going to make Amanda's ceremony. Her husband can't be late for her big night."

"I'll see you there?"

"Wouldn't miss it."

Randall took the stack of papers that was closest to him and walked them over to the groups of binders on Peter's desk. He watched his friend clean, a look of defeat written on his face. They were working so hard.

"We're close," he said. "Don't give up. We'll get there. We just need to keep pushing forward. We can do this. Setbacks and all."

Peter leaned forward, placing his elbows on the desk and folding his hands together. "You better be right," he said, his eyes locked on Randall's. "Both of our lives depend on it."

3

Randall scanned the expansive ballroom of the Bear Mountain Inn and surveyed the clusters of people filling the space. They were talking in their own tight circles, smiling and laughing, every piece of them a lesson in perfection. Tuxedos were tailored with the precision only money could buy. Gowns glistened in the overhead lighting. Dazzling jewelry dangled from every woman's wrist and ear while diamonds hung from many of their necks. He looked down at himself and placed his hands on a belly that could have been firmer if he'd hit the gym with more dedication. His pale Irish skin almost matched his graying hair. His shoes were polished, and his tuxedo fit as it should have, but he still couldn't help feeling a sense of irrelevance. The people who had come to the inn to celebrate his wife were heirs to generational money. This was the kind of money that involved trusts for children who had yet to be conceived. This money owned estates that would be passed down for the next millennia and required teams of lawyers, accountants, managers, and financial advisors to be at their beck and call. This money sat on boards of Fortune 500 companies, ran multinational conglomerates, influenced elections, and had just about anyone you could think of in its back pocket. These people who had come were the real players. They were the ones who made the world turn, and Randall, having been raised in a working-class family by a farmer and a housewife, felt insignificant around them.

He and Amanda had been married for two years now. They'd met at a bar, of all places. She'd been with a group of donors after a fundraising gala, and he'd been alone. Their paths had crossed at a jukebox under the soulful voice of a crooning Ray Charles, and within minutes of shaking hands and making small talk, she'd said she knew beyond a reasonable doubt that they were soul mates. He couldn't agree more. Her sense of humor played so effortlessly against his seriousness. His concern balanced her carefree nature. She dragged him out of the house on days when he wanted to stay in, and he introduced her to introspection on nights she wanted to dine with friends. They were the perfect yin and yang, meant to be together, and only just now lucky enough to get that chance.

Amanda's father, Clifford Sturges, had been a mergers-and-acquisitions superstar on Wall Street during the 1980s and '90s, raking in tens of millions of dollars and growing all of it into a family fortune that would last generations. Clifford had been either the lead banker or part of the lead team for some of the biggest mergers in history. There was the Capital Cities–ABC merger of 1986, the Sony-Columbia merger of 1989, the Viacom-Paramount merger of 1994, and the MCI-WorldCom merger of 1999. But Clifford couldn't have it all. He died of a massive heart attack in the spring of 2001, and Amanda, already active with the philanthropic community on Manhattan, took half of her father's fortune and started one of the largest nonprofit groups in the country. The other half went back to her since she'd been his only daughter, and her mother, who lived on the West Coast, had been out of the picture for over thirty years. Everything she and Randall owned had been paid for by Amanda's inheritance. But what they shared in their relationship was priceless.

He buried himself in a corner, grabbing at the collar of his dress shirt, which was both too tight and too starched. A warm glass of red wine occupied his other hand. He checked his watch. A few more hours to go before he could get back to the office, which weighed heavily on his mind. He had so much still to do, and the holiday break was hardly enough time. He'd see Amanda receive her award and make her speech, and then he'd head to the campus.

Peter was making his way across the room, drink in hand, tuxedo looking just right on his toned frame. They'd met at NYU as freshman roommates and had been like family ever since. Even though Peter was the same forty-five years of age as Randall was, he looked decades younger. His hair was still full and brown. His blue eyes always turned ladies' heads, and his smile made them smile. He'd married out of college and was still with the same woman after twenty years, and although he'd strayed a few times over the course of two decades, their marriage was a happy one. Randall and Peter had spent too many summers together, too many internships competing for a coveted spot on a psych staff, and they knew too many of each other's secrets. It was a friendship that was deeper than any he'd ever experienced, even with Amanda. Peter Reems was his rock.

"Dr. Reems," Randall said, raising his glass.

Peter acknowledged his friend by raising his glass in return. "Dr. Brock."

"Thanks for coming."

"Are you kidding? I wouldn't miss it."

"I know, but the way I left you today. I wasn't sure if you'd be buried at the office after what happened."

"Nope. Not tonight. This is more important."

"Thanks." Randall took a sip of his wine. "I'm sorry for what happened with Lienhart."

"Don't apologize," Peter replied. "In fact, I'm the one who should be apologizing for getting all depressed and panicky after the old man left. It wasn't your fault we had a setback. That's what case studies are all about. This is a work in progress, and we have no idea how each subject is going to respond. I know that, and I should've known that earlier. That's on me. Jerry threw us a curveball today, but this entire thing is experimental, so what were we expecting? Things like today are going to happen. I was wrong with my reaction. It was unprofessional."

"We'll get it to work," Randall said. "The treatment. The case study. The cure. All of it. I know we will. We have to."

"Hey, Randall!"

Randall looked up to find Charles Label and two other men he didn't know working their way toward him and Peter. Charles was one of the regional managers of Amanda's organization, Glass Hearts, and ran four homeless shelters in Yonkers. He was short and thin and had a beard that took over most of his long face.

"Hi, Charles. It's good to see you again. How're things?"

"Everything's fantastic. The kids are getting used to the school, so that's a plus. Everybody is settling down in the new house. We're great."

"Is Mary here?"

"No, she's overseas at the moment. She sends her best, though."

Randall turned toward Peter. "You know Dr. Reems, right?"

"Of course," Charles replied as the two men shook hands. He pointed to the men on either side of him. "I'd like you both to meet Alexander Dellium and Felix Hutchinson. Their foundations are two of our most generous donors. Alex runs a hedge fund in the city, and Felix is in from San Francisco. He's the CEO of a cloud tech service firm out there called Skiez."

Randall took his time smiling and shaking each man's hand firmly, trying to properly represent the husband of the woman who was being honored. Firm handshakes. Big smiles. All for Amanda.

With his thick blond hair pushed back from his face, Alex looked like he'd just stepped off a crew team. He towered over Randall at what must have been six feet three.

Felix was just the opposite. He was shorter, almost on par with Charles, with a gut he tried, unsuccessfully, to hide under his cummerbund.

"San Francisco," Randall said as he shook Felix's hand. "That's quite a trip."

"Your wife is quite a lady," Felix replied. "The work she does for those in need is something I'm constantly in awe of. I wish I had her drive to see some righteousness in this world. Alas, all I can offer is money, so that's what I do. I know she'll put it to the best use possible. She always does."

Charles snagged a glass of champagne as a waiter walked by. "Randall and Dr. Reems here are working on a big project up at Quarim University. Psychiatry Department."

"Is that right?" Alex said. "I've always been fascinated by those who can shape minds. Good for you."

"Do you teach?" Felix asked.

Randall shook his head. "Peter does. Right now I'm assisting him on a research project, and since he has classes, I'm running most of the documentation and data entry for our study, so there's not much time for anything else."

"Tell us about your research," Charles said. "What are you working on?"

"It's clinical work, mostly," Randall replied. "We're studying the behavioral aspects of the mind and how it can play out in the physical world."

Peter nodded and stepped in, always the consummate salesman when it came to their study. "Randall and I are on the cusp of developing a new method of treating people who have homicidal tendencies. We're working to remove that tendency and thus make them regular members of society again. Just like you and me."

"You're removing their homicidal tendencies?"

"That's right."

"Like you would remove a cancerous tumor?"

"That's a great analogy," Peter said, smiling. "That's exactly what we're doing, minus the surgery. This is all done with the mind. Through therapy."

Randall looked around while Peter talked up the project. Peter was a natural salesman. He knew how to give a potential donor or subject or professor or researcher just enough to pique their interest, but not enough to disclose anything of importance. He danced that line as if he were on a high wire. Something Randall could never do.

On the opposite side of the room, a man was leaning against one of the oak pillars that separated the dining area from the bar. The man wasn't moving or smiling or interacting with any of the other guests, and when Randall noticed him and their eyes locked, the man didn't look away. A slight rumble of pain rolled in the back of Randall's head. He closed his eyes for a moment, hoping that a migraine wasn't coming on. Not tonight.

"And it's working?" Alex was saying.

"We're still in the first phase," Peter replied. "Very preliminary."

Randall turned from the man across the room, trying to ignore the pain that was starting to gain strength. "Let's just say we're encouraged by the results we've seen so far. We really can't speak about it in detail, though. I'm afraid Peter has already told you more than he should have."

Felix fished a business card out of his breast pocket. "It sounds like what you're doing could be a game changer. My god, the lives you'd be saving. The people you'd prevent from becoming victims. If it's as significant as it sounds, gentlemen, my interest is piqued. I have lots of people who can open doors for you. Or perhaps, if funding is needed in the future, you'll look me up. I'd love to learn more when the time is right."

Randall took the card. "Of course."

"Honey, you can't hide in the corner all night. This is a celebration!"

The men surrounding Randall and Peter parted as Amanda approached them. She looked stunning in her long black gown with silver sequins that sparkled in the light. Her dark hair hung at her shoulders. Her brown eyes were big, round, always present. She had an athlete's body, toned and firm. Every piece of her was done up with purpose. Makeup, hair, nails, jewelry—it was all so tasteful and elegant. She slipped her arm around Randall's back and pulled him into a half hug.

"I take it Peter and my husband are captivating you with their scientific brilliance?" Amanda asked, acknowledging the other men with a smile.

"Indeed they are," Felix replied. "He and Dr. Reems were telling us about their latest experiment."

"Is that right?"

"It's absolutely fascinating."

"It appears some men just can't keep a secret." She kissed Randall on his cheek. "I hope you had these guys sign an NDA. I wouldn't trust a single one of them with exclusive information."

The group laughed, and Amanda's cell phone rang. She'd been holding it, and she looked at the screen, quickly refusing the call.

"Who's that?" Randall asked.

"No one. A donor. I've been fielding congratulation calls all night. It's one after the other."

Randall caught movement out of the corner of his eye. When he looked, he saw several waiters carrying empty platters back toward the kitchen. They passed, and he noticed the man from across the room again. He was closer now, standing against a wall near the restrooms, staring at Randall, unmoving. He was dressed in a tuxedo like the others, drink in hand, but he wasn't talking to anyone. And that stare. It was penetrating.

"Hey, who is that?" Randall asked, pulling Amanda closer so she could see.

"Who?"

More waiters passed in front of them. When they were clear again, the man was gone.

"Who, honey?"

Randall looked around, that dull throb in his head surfacing. "Now I don't see him. He kept staring at me. First he was by the bar, and just now he was near the restrooms. It was unnerving."

Amanda craned her neck to try and see through the crowd. "What did he look like?"

"I don't know. Just some guy."

"Tall? Short? Hair color? Anything? I'm sure I know him. I can introduce you."

"It was just some guy. Never saw him before. Average height, I guess. Dirty-blond hair? He was wearing a tux, so it's not like he was sticking out, but the way he was staring at me. I didn't like it."

Amanda frowned. "Did he seem hostile? Should I get security?"

Randall shook his head. "No, nothing like that. Forget it. We certainly don't need security. It's nothing."

Amanda looked around again. Her brow furrowed, and she suddenly appeared nervous. "You're sure?"

"Yes. It's fine. I didn't mean to freak you out."

"You look pale."

"I think I might have a migraine coming on."

Three loud thumps came from the speakers that surrounded the room. The crowd turned toward the stage, where an older man stood in front of a microphone.

"Ladies and gentlemen, I'd like to thank you all for joining us," he began. "Tonight we honor Amanda Brock, who, through her Glass Hearts Foundation, has positively impacted the lives of thousands of people who have largely been forgotten by our society. Her countless hours of commitment and her unwavering support have shown us all that kindness, selflessness, and compassion still exist. Tonight we honor Amanda, but we celebrate the lives she has changed for the better."

The crowd erupted in applause. Amanda tapped Randall on his chest, kissed her hand, and placed it on his cheek. "I gotta go," she said. "Are you going to be okay?"

"Of course."

"Get an aspirin or something from the waitstaff. I don't want you on those mountain roads if you're suffering from a migraine."

"I'll be fine," Randall replied. "Now go get what's coming to you."

Her phone rang again. She fumbled to shut it off before it could ring a second time.

"You want me to hold that while you're giving your speech?"

"No, I got it."

"Maybe you should put it on mute, then."

"Aspirin. Go."

Amanda smiled and walked away, palming her phone as she navigated the cheering crowd. He thought he could see a tinge of panic in her smile and wondered who was calling. He really should've gotten an aspirin before his headache got worse, but instead he followed her toward the stage, where she would be presented with her award and give a speech she'd been writing, revising, and stressing over for the last month. As he fell in with the others, he looked around once more for the man who had been staring at him, but there was no one present except for the people who supported his wife and her charities. They were Amanda's extended family, and they were all rooting for her. They loved her as much as he did. And still, even wrapped in that room of camaraderie and support, he couldn't help but think about what Jerry Osbourne had said.

That kind of dark makes the shadows even thicker, you know? And it makes the places that do have light seem safe. But that safety in a darkness like that is fake, and you can't trust nothing fake. When it's dark like that, the light is just a trap.

4

The morning sun hadn't risen enough to lighten the sky. It was still dark but for the headlights that shot up and out from the depths of the rocky valley that connected the side of the cliff to the Hudson River. It had taken the fire department over an hour to navigate the terrain and set up the three spotlights that now flooded the scene. The team had been working since the moment they'd arrived, flashlights in hand, some mounted on helmets as if they were miners digging for coal. The cold was biting, and with the wind coming off the river, the air stabbed at their exposed skin, stiffening the joints in their hands as they worked to investigate the accident and extract the body.

State Police Investigator Susan Adler made her way up and around the boulders, slipping on the icy surfaces where the spray from the river had settled and frozen. She wore a pair of black ski pants she'd taken from the trunk of her car and had two layers of sweaters under her New York State Trooper field jacket. Her thick gloves kept her hands warm but made her motor skills clumsy. It took steady concentration to get a good grip on a rock and pull herself forward in the dark, not quite knowing what her next step would be.

She'd gotten the call when she was at her desk finishing up her report from an earlier arrest. She was supposed to be rotated down on the case list, but since she'd been physically at the barracks when the call had come in, the watch commander asked her to respond as a senior on scene.

The car had been a silver Mercedes sedan. That much she could tell. Beyond that—model, number of doors, year—was a mystery. There was simply too much damage. From a cursory look at the vehicle, it appeared as if it had run off the road some two hundred feet above where she stood and hit the jagged mountainside as it somersaulted down, snapping off tree branches until it had eventually come to rest wedged between two large boulders at the bottom of the canyon. Its headlights—one still on and functioning—faced the sky.

Now that she was within the sphere of the mounted spotlights, Susan could begin to see details. There was blood splattered on the interior of the car and across the hood. The windshield was gone, as were the side windows. The roof was crushed all the way down to the headrests on the seats. Somewhere in that carnage was a body, but this would not be a rescue. It was a wonder the driver hadn't been ejected at some point during the fall.

A younger man dressed in jeans and a state police windbreaker broke free from the Collision Reconstruction Unit and climbed his way over to Susan. "Investigator Adler?"

"That's me."

The man smiled and extended his hand. "Tommy Corolla. Nice to meet you, although I wish it was under better circumstances."

Susan shook his hand. "You're the new guy?"

"Yup."

"What are you doing here?" she asked. "You're supposed to report to the barracks later on this morning."

Tommy shrugged and gestured toward the wreck. "Technically it is the morning, and when dispatch called and asked if I wanted in on your rotation, I told him I'd meet you here. Hope you don't mind."

"I don't mind. Just figured you'd rather sleep on your first day."

"No, I'd rather get in on this."

"It's just a car accident."

"Better than forms from HR."

She could see him a little better in the light. He looked to be in his thirties. He was cute enough. Wavy hair was combed and kept neatly in place with a gel of some kind. Brown eyes surveyed the scene, taking it all in. He was clean shaven and tried to appear calm, but she could tell he was nervous.

"You know what we're looking at yet?" she asked.

"Looks like the car ran off the road up there, plowed through the protective fencing, and landed in these rocks. Driver is DOA. Fire and rescue is trying to cut the body out, but it's wedged in there pretty good."

"Who called it in? Do we have an eyewitness?"

"No. A captain from a tug that was coming down the river from Albany called it. He thought the way the lights were angled looked suspicious and contacted the Coast Guard, who came to have a look; then the Guard contacted us. We have a team from the parks department over at Bear Mountain ready to do a rope climb to see if we can collect anything that might've been ejected, but it's too dark right now."

"Anyone run the plates for an ID?"

"Can't. Front plate came off somewhere during the fall, and the rear plate, if it's still intact, is buried between those two boulders. No checking the registration on the windshield either. There is no windshield. We'll get more when the sun comes up. The CRU team did what they could with the light they have. They gave the okay to get the victim out."

Susan looked up into the night sky at the rock face looming over them. Route 202, known as the Goat Trail, was a twisting road that cut its way up the outside of Bear Mountain, then on through Rockland County and into New Jersey. This section of the trail, about a quarter mile south of the Bear Mountain Bridge, was the most dangerous. It was a road that ran both north and south, its twists and curves the tightest at this point.

"Looks like it could be a two-hundred-foot drop," she said.

Tommy followed her gaze. "Yeah, something like that. Enough to kill you. That's for sure."

"They're renovating the barrier wall up on that section, right?"

"Yeah, that's what some of the guys on scene were saying. They got reinforced fencing up there."

"I thought that fencing was supposed to be as strong as the wall they're fixing."

"It is." Tommy pointed to the mangled sedan. "The guys I was talking to said that fence is the real deal. Reinforced chain link, made out of steel that gives just a bit, but not enough to break. The driver must've been hauling ass to bust through it like he did."

Susan could make out the edge of the cliff with the help of a faint red glow from one of the cruisers that had been stationed up top where the fence had been breached. That had been one hell of a fall. She'd driven that road too many times to count. Her kids liked to look over the edge to try and spot hawks flying below. She knew how tight those turns were.

"Got something!"

Susan and Tommy turned around to see a young trooper emerging from the bushes, sidestepping his way down a steep incline adjacent to where the spotlights had been erected. He held his flashlight out in front of him, carefully balancing his way over to where they stood.

"We found this about fifty yards up the west end," the trooper said as he handed over a black leather pocketbook. "Must've gotten thrown out on the way down."

Tommy grabbed the pocketbook and rubbed dirt off the leather casing. "So I guess our driver is a female."

Susan took the bag and unzipped the top. Tommy shined his flashlight inside while she rifled around, eventually coming away with a matching leather wallet. She opened it and held it up to the light.

"Okay," she said as she studied the driver's license. "Looks like we can ID our victim after all." She leaned in to see more clearly. "Driver is Amanda Brock. North Salem, New York."

5

Randall knew that the effects of stress on memory could impact a person's ability to evoke the details of certain events. During times of stress, the body reacted by secreting stress hormones into the bloodstream. An excess of these hormones could impair the ability of the hippocampus to recall memories. Randall knew this because he'd read it in the *Journal of Neuroscience* decades earlier during one of his first internships. It was ironic that he could remember the factoid, even cite the work he'd taken it from, but couldn't recall the exact events leading up to him sitting in the county morgue.

The scenes came to him in flashing images. The knock on the office door. The look in Peter's eyes as he stuck his head in. The woman in the navy suit who came in behind Peter. The ride in the back of a black Ford Taurus. The scraping concrete sound the door to the morgue made when it opened. The silence of the tiny room they'd placed him in. The ticking of the clock on the wall, counting the seconds.

You have been alone for one . . . two . . . three . . .

He knew the woman was sitting behind him, against the wall, but he refused to turn around. Inspector something. Investigator something. He knew she'd shown him her badge back at the office, but he couldn't remember her name or exact title. She was just as quiet as he was. They were waiting, but for what, he wasn't entirely sure.

Your life is changing in one . . . two . . . three . . .

The small, windowless room was tucked somewhere inside the morgue. The door finally opened, and a middle-aged woman came in carrying a folder. She had a white lab coat on, and round glasses magnified her eyes.

"Dr. Brock," she said quietly. "I'm the county medical examiner. Dr. Nestor."

Randall nodded.

She's going to deliver some really bad news in one . . . two . . . three . . .

Dr. Nestor sat down in a chair across from him. "As you've been made aware, we believe your wife has been in a fatal car accident, and we need you to identify the body that was recovered at the scene. I know this comes as a shock, and I'm so sorry you have to go through this. I want to let you know that the identification of a loved one is not like you see in movies or read in books. There's no big reveal, and you don't have to see the actual body to confirm." She placed the folder onto the table and slid it toward him. "There is a picture of the deceased in this folder. All you have to do is open it and let us know if it's your wife. Can you do that?"

You're going to be a widower in one . . . two . . . three . . .

"Yes."

"Good. The picture you'll see is only of the deceased's face. Other than her face, she's covered in white linens. There's some bruising, and a small laceration, but nothing graphic."

"Okay."

"I'm going to take my hand off the folder, and you can open it when you're ready. It doesn't matter how long you want to wait. You take all the time you need. I'll stay here with you until you're ready."

Your life will become unrecognizable in one . . . two . . . three . . .

Dr. Nestor let go of the folder and sat back in her seat. Randall pulled it closer toward him, staring at it, rubbing the top of it gently with the tips of his fingers.

"I don't know if I can do this," he said as tears began to fill his eyes.

"I understand. You take however long you need."

"I mean, if I open it and it's her, then that makes it real, you know? If I don't open it, I can hang on to the chance that you're wrong, and Amanda's not dead. Maybe she was just running late after the ceremony and didn't get home yet. Maybe she went out to celebrate with friends, and the battery on her phone ran out. As long as I don't open this folder, I can hang on to those thoughts, as silly as they might be. But if I open it, and it's her, it becomes real."

The room fell silent again. Randall concentrated on his breathing. It couldn't be her. It couldn't be Amanda. But he wasn't a fool. They wouldn't have him here if they had any real doubt. They'd found her car. They'd found her purse. It was her. His wife was dead. The clock on the wall continued to mark the seconds.

Everything changes in one . . . two . . . three . . .

He opened the folder, and a sound escaped his throat that he'd never heard himself make. It was a combination of a sigh and a howl. It sounded animalistic, inhuman. It was the sound of his heart breaking.

Amanda.

There was a cut on her forehead, and her left eye was swollen. Her nose looked as if it had been broken, and there was some general bruising on the right side of her face, but it was her. Of that he had no doubt.

"That's Amanda," he whispered as the tears came. "That's my wife."

Dr. Nestor closed the folder and took it back. "I'm sorry for your loss."

"So what now?" he asked. "What happens now?"

"We need to determine what caused her to run off the road, so we'll need to do an autopsy. Once that's complete, we can return her body to you. If you can let us know what funeral home you'd like to use, we can send her there. Shouldn't take more than two days."

He nodded, and Dr. Nestor got up from her seat, leaving the room at the same time the inspector/investigator woman who was sitting behind him got up and took the medical examiner's place at the table.

She looked at him, and he stared back at her. Her skin wasn't as white as his, but she still had that Irish paleness with tiny freckles dotting the bridge of her nose and under her green eyes. Her dark hair was pulled back in a ponytail. She wore no jewelry and hardly any makeup.

"My condolences to you and your family," she said. "Do you have any children?"

"No. We've only been married for two years. Got a late start. Kids were never really a consideration."

"Anyone we can call for you?"

"No. I'll be okay."

The woman paused for a moment. "Dr. Brock, I'm going to need to ask you a few questions about last night so I can complete my report. I know this is sudden for you, and I don't want to seem callous. We just need information so we can put this all together. Is that okay?"

Randall looked at her, trying to place her name. He was totally blank. It was the stress. His hippocampus was drowning in stress hormones. "I don't mean to be rude," he said, "but who did you say you were again?"

"Investigator Adler of the New York State Troopers," she replied. "I'm in charge of the case involving Amanda's accident."

"Right."

Adler leaned forward. "Can you tell me about last night?"

Randall sighed and struggled to think through the events of the previous day. "We were at the Bear Mountain Inn. She was being given an award for her philanthropic work. Amanda runs a large nonprofit organization that funds a bunch of smaller charities. They were giving her a humanitarian award."

"Who was?"

Randall chuckled. "I can't even remember. The board, I think. Through the national chapter of her organization. It's called Glass Hearts."

"Were you with Amanda the entire night?"

"No. I left early because I had to work on some things back at the campus where you found me this morning."

"What time did you leave the event?"

"Around ten, I think. Got to the campus about a half hour later."

"And what time did the ceremony end?"

"It was scheduled to go until midnight. I'm sure people hung around at the bar afterward."

"Did you hear from Amanda after you left?"

"No. I called her on her cell to see if she got home, but it went to voice mail. I left her a message to call me, but she never did. I guess I fell asleep after that and didn't wake up until you and Peter came for me this morning."

"What time did you call her?"

"Probably around twelve thirty? One, maybe?"

"Is there a chance she could've been drinking before she got behind the wheel?"

"I doubt it. I'm sure she had a glass or two of wine or champagne, but Amanda was adamantly against drinking and driving. If she was too tipsy, she would've gotten a lift or called a cab. She takes that stuff very seriously."

"Was she on any medication?"

"No."

Adler finished writing in her notepad, then stood from her seat. "I think that's all I have right now. This appears to be an unfortunate accident. I truly am sorry."

"Thank you."

"I'll take you back to your office so you can get your car. I'm sure you have a lot to take care of."

Randall pulled himself up from his chair. He looked around the plain white room one last time and wondered how many people before him had been forced to open that folder when all they wanted to do was keep it shut. How many people would have to do it after he left? How many lives were irrevocably changed the moment they stepped through that door and sat with nothing but the clock on the wall ticking away the seconds?

Life as you know it will end in one . . . two . . . three . . .

6

The sky was a brilliant crystal blue—the kind of blue that only came with cold weather in the Northeast. The light snow that had fallen overnight was gone. The temperature on Susan's dashboard had said it was thirty-eight degrees, and although the sun was shining, with the wind coming off the river from the west, it felt ten to fifteen degrees cooler.

She made her way to where Tommy was standing, looking out over the cliff. He'd stayed behind and supervised the scene while she'd made the next-of-kin notification. While she'd been gone, a construction crew had set up large plastic barriers topped with yellow strobe lights to act as a temporary substitute for the fencing. A trooper car remained, its lights and hazards still flashing, warning those traveling south to lower their speed and heed the curves.

Tommy spun around when he heard her approaching, the loose gravel crunching under her feet.

"You know you're going to have to get down to HR one of these days," she said, smiling. "Hiding out at an accident scene isn't going to make the paperwork go away."

Tommy laughed. "My supervisor ordered me to stay on. It wasn't my place to refuse that order."

She joined him on the far shoulder, pointing at the barriers. "Road crew set things up pretty fast."

"Yeah, they were in and out. Left about fifteen minutes ago. You get the positive ID?"

"Yup, it's her. Husband confirmed. I just dropped him back at his office. He's a professor up at Quarim. About a half hour north of here."

"This is a helluva thing to have to deal with right before the holidays."

"It's a helluva thing to have to deal with at any point in the year." Susan walked to the edge of the road and looked over. Troopers and fire personnel were still below, working in and around the car, breaking it up into smaller pieces so they could haul it out. The Collision Reconstruction Crew also remained. They'd taken out their total workstation and cameras and were in the process of trying to reconstruct the second half of the accident, after the Mercedes had driven off the cliff. She could hear their voices echoing in the canyon but couldn't make out exactly what they were saying. "My mother lives in the next town over. Cold Spring. I can't tell you how many times I've taken this road. Scary to think about going over like that."

Tommy joined her at the edge. "Look how far she landed. I mean she must've been doing sixty, seventy miles an hour to get that kind of distance. It's impossible to go that fast on these roads. They're too windy. You could never get up enough speed without having to downshift at the next curve."

"Doesn't look like she did downshift at the next curve."

"It's still crazy to think how fast she must've been going."

Susan leaned over and looked straight down. "Anyone rappel down the cliff yet?"

"No, not yet. Now that there's daylight, I'll get someone moving. The other guys are cleaning up the primary scene now; then we can take a look around the perimeter."

"Excellent. I put in a request for her cell phone records. I'd be interested to know if she was talking on the phone when she went off the road. Could've been distracted."

"Maybe." Tommy pointed toward the orange mesh fence. "I think I found something and need a second opinion."

"Show me."

Susan followed him back toward the road. He stopped when they got to the section of the fencing that Amanda Brock had crashed through. He bent down and motioned for her to come closer.

"I was looking at the fence before when I was waiting for the road-crew guys to set up the new barriers," he explained. "Didn't make sense that a sedan could just plow through specialized reinforced fencing like this. It wasn't like it was a half-ton pickup or commercial vehicle. It was just a car. So I started poking around at the impact point. Look at this."

Susan knelt next to him and examined the edge of the fence that had been breached.

"You're in your car going, let's say, sixty miles an hour. You lose control, run off the road, and slam through the fence so hard and get so much distance that I'm guessing you didn't have time to apply the brakes."

"Okay."

"How do you think the fence is going to bend at its breaking point?"

Susan thought for a moment. "I guess the metal would stretch a bit, then break outward, toward the river. Toward the direction it was being torn."

Tommy nodded. "Exactly. Now look."

Susan bent down closer. The edge of the chain link where the car had burst through was flat. The metal wasn't stretched at all, and the edges weren't torn or bent either way.

"That's odd," she said. "It's like they've been cut."

"Pretty much what I was thinking. Both sides of the hole are like that. The only part that's bent the way you think it should be is the top. Otherwise, this thing flapped out like a doggy door. No resistance whatsoever. Drove right through it."

Susan stood back up. She made her way across to the other side of the hole and examined the fence. The point at which the chain link had given way there was also straight. "You think someone cut it to gain access to the cliff? Maybe do some hiking or rope climbing? This could've been cut months before last night happened."

"If that's the case, Mrs. Brock is the unluckiest person on earth. You mean to tell me she hits the fence at the exact spot it was cut so there's no reinforcement to save her from going over the edge?"

"Unlikely."

"Yeah. Unlikely for sure."

"Okay," Susan said. "Have a couple of guys walk the rest of this fence, and let's see if there are any other breaches. Any cuts through the steel of any kind. And let's find out what kind of tool you'd need to cut through something like this."

"Ten-four."

The wind picked up, and Susan had to turn her face away from the loose gravel and dirt flying around. As she turned, she looked at the road. Drivers passed them on their way down the mountain, staring to try and see what was going on.

"No skid marks or treads of any kind," she said. "She never stopped."

"CRU came up last night with the drag sleds, but they had nothing to compare it to because she didn't brake."

"Why wouldn't you instinctively brake?"

Tommy shrugged. "Either it was suicide, she was asleep, or she was dead. Any other explanation just doesn't make sense."

7

Amanda had fallen into his life by way of a half-empty bar, twenty-five cents, and the magnificence of Ray Charles.

Randall had been sitting on one of the stools at the bar, watching sports highlights on a television perched in the corner. The place was tiny, tucked away mostly for San Francisco locals, and the usual crowd wasn't due for another hour. A small group of well-dressed men and women caught his eye when they walked in. He could see them reflected in the mirror that stretched behind the bar. Three women and six men. They were laughing and happy and seemed glad to be in each other's company. They pushed two tables together in the corner, away from everyone else. Randall watched them until they sat down, then turned his attention back to the television, pulling his beer closer and gripping it as if it might run away.

"Your turn," the old man next to him slurred.

Randall looked up to find the old man pointing at the jukebox that had been set up next to the restrooms. He hadn't noticed the song finish. He got up and made his way toward it, fishing in his pocket for his last quarter of the day.

"Make it a good one," the man called out.

Randall ignored him. He leaned over the glass display, reading from a never-ending list of songs that seemed to cover every genre ever constructed. He slid his quarter into the coin slot and traced his finger to make sure he had the right number for his selection.

"So what are you thinking?"

One of the women from the group was standing next to him, peering over his shoulder at the song list. His breath caught in his throat for a moment, and he found himself unable to reply. She was dressed in a tailored blue sweater and black slacks. Heels and a red scarf tied around her neck completed the outfit. Her hair was pulled back with a headband, accentuating her eyes. When she looked at him, it was as if everything else in the world stopped.

"I'm always good for a classic eighties song," she said. "But no techno. Brings back too many memories I like to keep buried."

"I was going for 'Georgia on My Mind.'"

She smiled. "Ray Charles? Yeah, that could work. But how about something more upbeat? 'I Got a Woman' or 'Leave My Woman Alone'? Those would work."

"You know your Ray Charles."

"Indeed I do. So how about it? Upbeat?"

Randall shook his head and looked away. "I'm not really in an upbeat mood."

"Oh. Well, then." She nudged him out of the way, found the track, and plugged in the associated number. The strings of the orchestra began, followed by Ray's sultry voice streaming through the speakers. "There you go."

"Thanks."

"I hope you find a better mood soon because I have a purse full of quarters and I'm not afraid to use them."

"I'll try and adjust."

She paused for a moment, then held up a laminated name badge that was hanging around her neck. "I'm Amanda, by the way."

"Randall." He extended his hand, and she shook it. He could feel her smooth skin and wanted desperately to hang on and pull her close. He didn't know why, but there was something about her that made him want to lose himself when he looked at her. Her eyes. That smile.

"You don't sound like you're from around here, Randall. East Coast?"

"Jersey."

Amanda's smile grew larger, and she clapped her hands. "I'm from New York. Just in on business. You?"

"Been out here for a few years. Planning to stay."

"I see." She began swaying to the music, lip-synching some of the lines, watching him. "You know we can't tell anyone we met at a bar, right? It's too cliché."

"Who would we tell?"

"People."

"Like who?"

"I don't know. People."

Randall nodded. "So then if we can't tell them the truth, what should we tell them?"

Amanda let her head rock back on her shoulders to think. "How about we say we met while listening to Ray Charles? They'll assume it was a concert, and we won't correct them."

"Ray Charles died in ninety-four."

"Oh." Amanda laughed, then placed a hand on his shoulder. "Okay. How about we just say we met in San Francisco and leave it at that?"

———

Flurries began to float from the sky as Randall navigated his BMW around the curves of the North Salem farm roads, heading toward home. He passed miles of fenced land, the green acres slowly turning white as the snow dusted the area. In the distance, beyond the second hill where the horse stalls were kept, he could see the large red barn and old rusted weathervane that marked the center of his gated community. If Norman Rockwell had an image of an America that would never cease to exist, North Salem farm country was it. It didn't get much prettier.

Randall passed the two stone columns at the entrance to his development and turned in. The houses here—part of an eight-acre working farm—were massive. Five to seven bedrooms, three to five bathrooms, square footage that started at over three thousand and topped out at six. Four-car garages, in-ground pools, private tennis courts, wraparound porches. There was no end to the bravado of these homes, and there was no way he could be living here without the help of his beautiful and talented wife. Now she was gone. He couldn't believe it.

He pulled into the garage and shut off the engine, sitting in the silence of his car, thinking about the picture of Amanda the medical examiner had shown him and comparing that to the woman he'd met at that bar. Amanda had always been so full of life. Her carefree nature was what he'd loved most about her. How would he be able to go on living without her by his side? He didn't want to go back to the man he'd been before they'd met. He couldn't be that person again.

His phone buzzed in the cupholder next to the gearshift. He picked it up and read the screen.

Incoming Call: Peter Reems

Randall declined the call and slid his phone into his coat pocket. After a few moments, the device buzzed one final time. Peter had left a voice mail. His third of the day.

The driver's door opening and closing was the only sound in the three-car garage. In the bay next to him was the two-seater convertible she'd gotten him on their one-year anniversary. Just something to play around in. The third bay was empty. Randall suddenly realized that Amanda's silver Mercedes would never be parked in that space again. No one else was coming home.

He shut the garage door and made his way inside the house, leaving his bag and briefcase in the back seat of the BMW. The house was bigger than they needed, but he loved it like it was a one-bedroom cottage in the middle of the woods. Something about it just made it feel like home. The smells, the warmth, the furniture that didn't really match but somehow worked together. Kind of like the two of them. It had been perfect. But now everything seemed different. In fact, everything was.

He walked down the same hall he'd walked down the night before and turned into the same kitchen. Nothing was out of place. A plate and empty glass sat in the sink. The flowers he'd gotten Amanda to congratulate her on the award remained in a vase in the center of the kitchen island. Their calendar was still pinned to the corkboard near the pantry, all of their plans meticulously laid out over the next few months. But now those plans would never come to fruition.

The house was dark but for a lone floor lamp Amanda had left on in the living room the night before. Randall took off his coat and draped it over one of the kitchen chairs, then staggered into the family room and collapsed onto the couch.

He had gotten her number that night. She waited until the bar was about to close, and when he got up to use the restroom one last time, she placed a business card under his glass. She was gone by the time he came back. They traded phone calls and emails in the months that followed and grew closer despite the distance. By the time she came back West for another round of fundraising, they were friends. By the time she left, they were lovers. After a year together, she convinced him to move to New York, and he convinced her to marry him. He didn't know how wealthy she was until after they got engaged. It was never about anything other than love for the two of them. They were meant to be together, and now, the love of his life was dead. They hadn't been given enough time. It simply wasn't fair.

Randall sat up and pushed his hair out of his eyes. He snatched the house phone from its docking station on the end table next to the sofa and looked at the screen. Nine voice mails. He hit the command to play them back.

"Hi, Amanda, it's Ruth. I left you a message on your cell too. Just wanted to wish you luck tonight. So sorry Bruce and I can't make it. We'll have a private celebration at my house soon, I promise. Good luck! I'm so proud of you."

"Giirrrrllll, it's Luis. Why aren't you picking up your cell? Text me back or something."

"Hi, guys, it's Sebastian. Not sure anyone even checks home voice mail anymore, but I think Amanda's cell phone is off or something. Wanted to drop a quick message about how lovely tonight's event was. Amanda, your speech was perfect. Not sure what you were stressing over. It went off without a hitch. Anyway, you did great, and it was nice to see you both."

"Hi, it's Gina. Where are you? We were supposed to have coffee at the café. I'm sitting here alone like an idiot. Sleeping it off? Call me. Oh, and check your cell. I think you have it off."

Randall listened to each message, then deleted them. He placed the receiver back on the docking station and thought about the daunting task of calling relatives and friends with the news. Amanda had known so many people. How could he get to them all? He supposed he could handle it strategically and call a handful of people he knew would be willing to spread the word. For reasons even his scientific mind couldn't figure out, people loved gossiping about tragedy. If he could call the right four or five people, he knew they'd be more than happy to reach out to the rest of Amanda's network. That would leave her relatives, which would be his responsibility. There was no one alive in his family to call.

The wind blew several tree branches against the bay window in the family room, causing him to turn toward the noise. As he looked out at his expansive property in the back, he glimpsed a figure standing just inside the stone wall that marked the end of his yard and the beginning of his neighbor's. The figure was covered in a long black coat, semi-hidden among a cluster of adolescent pines that hadn't yet reached their full height and girth. He couldn't see the person's face—an oversized hood hung over their head. There was no way to know if it was a man or a woman. The only other thing he could see was this person's breath from beneath the hood clouding in the cold December air.

He stood up from the couch and walked toward the window. The figure didn't move. It remained still, as if it were a tree itself, and for a moment he thought that his mind could be playing tricks on him, making him see a person who wasn't there. But the closer he got to the window, the more apparent it was that there was no mistake. This person was breathing. They had gloved hands, ten fingers. Two feet protruding from beneath the oversized coat. They didn't move. They simply faced the house and waited. Watching.

The phone rang, and Randall jumped. He let out a small cry of surprise and spun around, quickly grabbing the receiver off the end table.

"Hello?"

"Randall, it's Gina."

"Hi, Gina."

"Can I talk to Amanda? I've been calling and texting all day, and she's not calling me back. She was supposed to meet me for coffee this morning and never showed. I'm guessing she's wiped from last night, but still. Is she there?"

Randall turned back toward the window. The figure in the oversized coat remained, unmoving.

Can he see me in here? Is he looking at me?

"Will you hang on a minute?" Randall asked.

"Sure."

He put the phone down and walked to the patio doors, which led to a sunroom. He opened the doors, crossed the sunroom, and stepped outside onto the deck.

The figure remained.

"Can I help you?" Randall called as he leaned over the deck railing. "You there! In the pines. Can I help you with something?"

Steaming breath. In and out. In and out.

"You're on private property. I need you to leave, or I'll have to call the police. Please."

The figure waited for a few more moments, then slowly turned around and walked into the thicker section of pines until Randall could no longer see him. He went back inside the house and grabbed the phone; then he walked into the different rooms, checking the windows around his property. No one was there.

"Randall?"

"Yeah, sorry. I'm back."

"So can I talk to your wife, please?"

The request came with such innocence. She wanted to talk to Amanda. He knew as soon as he told her the truth, the cascade of news wouldn't stop for weeks. Not in a small town like this. Not with the friends Amanda had.

Tears that had been absent for most of the day suddenly came rushing forward. Randall thought about Ray Charles and that jukebox in San Francisco as he slid down onto the kitchen floor, the phone pressed tightly to his ear.

"Are you okay?" Gina asked.

"No, you can't talk to my wife," Randall heard himself barking through thick sobs. "Not anymore. I'm sorry, Gina. Not ever again."

8

"Mommy!"

Susan walked through the front door and was instantly attacked by little arms wrapping themselves around her waist. She dropped her bag and ran her fingers through two sets of platinum-blond hair.

"Hey, guys!"

The twins, five-year-old Casey and Tim, looked up at her with identical smiles. They both shared her freckled nose and green eyes. Their almost perfectly round heads came from their father.

"Mommy, we haven't seen you since forever," Casey said. "Was work hard?"

"Yes, honey. Work was hard."

"Did you catch the bad people?" Tim asked.

"I'm trying." Susan slipped off her coat and hung it on a rack next to the door. "So how was everybody's day?"

"Today was good," Tim said. "I painted you a picture in school. Look!" He scurried down the hall and swiped a large piece of construction paper off the dining room table, returning with it outstretched in his hand as if he were running with a flag.

Susan took the picture and studied the multicolored lines and circles, trying to figure out what it was before she had to admit she didn't know what she was looking at.

"It's a dinosaur with flowers!"

"Of course it is. I love it! Thank you." She looked down at Casey. "What about you, sweetie? What'd you make?"

Casey played with her bangs, which hung in front of her eyes. "I didn't have to make a picture. I played puppets instead."

"I see."

"Tim got paint on his new shirt."

"It was an accident!"

"I told him to play puppets with us, but he wanted to paint, and then he made a mess."

"Tattle!"

Susan ushered them farther into the house. "Don't be a tattle, honey. I'll wash the shirt. It's fine. Go play, and I'll fix dinner in a minute. Baths tonight."

Casey stomped her foot and arched her back to get in proper whining position. "Baths? But I—"

"No excuses. Baths. Tonight. Go."

Casey was about to say something further but instead ended the conversation with a huff. The twins climbed the stairs and ran into the spare fourth bedroom she'd converted into a playroom after her ex, Eric, had moved out. She could hear the pattering of their feet on the carpet, accompanied by the faint sound of conversation.

Susan's house was a seventeenth-century colonial that had once been part of a large swath of land in Fishkill but had been subdivided and then subdivided again until it was whittled down to a half-acre lot. The wood planks that spanned the floor were original, as were the exposed beams in the ceiling. The fireplace in the living room had been reconstructed in the 1970s, and the kitchen had been renovated more than a few times over the centuries, but the bones of the old home remained intact, which was one of the things she and Eric had fallen in love with.

"Mom?"

"In the kitchen!"

She'd been officially divorced for a year now, but she and Eric had been separated for almost two. The kids were just reaching the point where they understood their father wasn't going to ever be living with them again, and they'd finally stopped asking for him each night. They seemed to accept the every-other-weekend plan the judge had set up, and she did what she could to make life as normal for them as possible. If it weren't for her mother, she didn't know what she would've done for childcare. For one, twins in a day care would be unbelievably expensive. Second, her shifts were always rotating, and when she was on a case, there was no punching a clock. Her work took her wherever the evidence pointed at whatever time it happened to point. Her mother, living only a half hour away, had been a godsend.

The kitchen smelled of garlic and oregano. Beatrice McVey, wonder woman and mother of the decade, stood over the stove, stirring sauce in a pan. She was short and plump with jet-black dyed hair that she kept longer than most women her age. She was a widow going on ten years now but had handled the loss like most Irish did. She'd cried, celebrated the good times she'd had with her husband, and moved on. She was the toughest and smartest woman Susan knew.

"Hi, honey," Beatrice said without turning from the pot. "Wasn't sure when you'd be home, so I started dinner."

"Thanks."

"Did you even come home last night?"

"No, I'm beat."

"I didn't think you did. What'd you catch?"

"First it was a pursuit that ended up being a kidnapping. I was at the barracks filing on that when we caught a car accident. That's at least cut and dry. Should be cleared by tomorrow." She walked over to the sliding door and flipped on the outside light. "How're the chickens?"

"I think they're all in."

The lights mounted on the back deck illuminated the yard, and Susan could see the chicken coop Eric had made the last year they were together. He'd been on some kick about organic food and eating things that were all-natural. At the time, he'd had big plans, but chickens were

49

as close as they'd come to being organic farmers. She had six of them and got fresh eggs every morning.

"You make enough to stay and eat with us?" she asked.

"Sure. I got nowhere to be tonight."

"You can sleep over again if you want. I'm sorry it has to be two nights in a row."

"Don't be sorry. I'm fine. But you must be exhausted. Eat what I got here, and go take a shower. I'll help with the baths, and then we can all go to bed nice and early."

Susan plopped down on a kitchen chair. "Sounds like the best plan I heard all day."

She'd never imagined being a single mom with twins, but that was life, right? Expect the unexpected. She'd envisioned having four children, all two to three years apart, running around the house, laughing, fighting, and sticking up for one another at school and on the playground. She'd been an only child and had never experienced the camaraderie of siblings. She'd dreamed of family game nights and the Adler crew setting out on Halloween in one big mass of costumes and goody bags. She'd envisioned the annual chaos involved in trying to settle everyone down for their Christmas picture, and the satisfaction she'd feel when the card came out perfect. The twins had come first. Two in one shot. They were already halfway there. But then she'd discovered Eric cheating with a coworker who was just out of college and a little too eager to climb the corporate ladder. They'd separated for a while, and then Eric filed for divorce, saying that he'd simply fallen out of love with her and didn't see any future together. What was she supposed to say to that? Was there an argument to be made? Was she supposed to beg him to stay? Screw that. She got the papers drawn up, took the child support, and told him to shove the alimony up his ass; and here she was, thirty-eight years old, exhausted, and unloved by anyone younger than seventy-two and older than five. This was the unpredictable adventure of life. Her life, at least.

Susan's cell phone rang in the bag that was still by the door. She hopped out of her chair and walked down the hall, snatching it before it sounded off for a third time.

"This is Adler."

"Susan, it's Emily Nestor from the ME's office."

Susan sat on the landing of the stairs. "Hi, Emily. What's up?"

"So we're done with the autopsy on Amanda Brock, and I found some discrepancies that I thought you should be made aware of."

"What kind of discrepancies?"

"I can show you better if you come down to the office tomorrow, but just to give you the gist of what I'm looking at, I found a couple of things that were inconsistent with a car accident."

"Like what?"

"First of all, the victim's blood had already coagulated prior to the crash and had started to settle."

Susan shot up from the step and walked into the living room. "Are you saying she was dead before she ran off the road?"

"It appears that way," Nestor replied. "I also found evidence of blunt-force trauma to the back of the victim's skull. Now I want to be clear that the trauma could've happened during the crash itself. Her body took quite a beating rolling down the cliff like that. But this particular wound is a bit inconsistent with the randomness of the other wounds caused by the accident. This one looks like someone was aiming for the base of her skull and was successful. That coupled with the blood, and I'd put time of death an hour to ninety minutes before the crash itself. No other sign of foul play. Tox screen was clean. Looks like she had some champagne, but BAC was well under the limit. No signs of a stroke or heart attack that might've caused her to lose control of the car. Other than suicide, I can't find a reason why she'd just run off the road like that."

"We thought about suicide, but how would that explain the blow to the back of the head and the blood coagulating?"

"It wouldn't."

"So she's in the car, already dead, and someone ran it off the road to make it look like an accident."

"I can't say for sure, but that looks likely at this point."

"I'll see you tomorrow."

"I'll be here."

Susan hung up the phone and stood quietly in the living room, her mind racing.

She was dead before the car ran off the road.

Unpredictable lives. It looked as if everybody had one.

9

Randall sat in the empty office, staring at the monitor, watching the session play out on the video. Patient number two—Jason Harris—sat forward in his seat, his fingers nervously pulling at his jeans.

"How have you been since we last spoke?" Peter asked on the video. "Anything happen this week that you'd like to discuss?"

"No, not really. Pretty regular week. Starting to get cold, so work is busier. People tend to get to things like new tires or snow tires when they feel the weather turn. This cold blast got a lot of people to the shop. I like being busy, though. Makes the day go by faster."

"And how's everything at home?"

"The same."

"How's your mother?"

"Useless, as usual. I don't get how you could live the only life you got waiting hand and foot on someone else, taking all their crap, all their put-downs and complaining, and consider that a life fulfilled. But, hey, that's her, not me. I think it's slavery, but she's not going nowhere. Been putting up with him this long. She'll keep doing it until one of them dies. She don't know any other way to live."

"Are you talking about your dad?"

"Who else would I be talking about?"

"How are things going with him?"

"He's still an asshole, if that's what you mean."

"Explain."

"So my mom's been battling this cough for like three weeks. Up all night, coughing all day. I think it's bronchitis or pneumonia or something like that, but she won't go to the doctor. Says she can't afford it. I offered to help pay, but she still refuses to go. Won't take my money. Instead, she buys this over-the-counter crap that isn't working. I talk to my dad about it, and he just waves me away like I'm wasting his time. One night the coughing gets so bad he kicks her out of bed and makes her sleep on the couch so he can get his rest for work the next day. He's a prick like that."

"How did that make you feel?"

"How do you think? He's a terrible, selfish man. Just bring her to the doctor, get her the prescription she needs, and he won't have to deal with the coughing anymore. And she won't have to suffer through it. But he says it's too expensive. Maybe if he had a job that paid regular benefits, she could get what she needs."

"Have you talked to your father about helping to pay?"

"He keeps telling me to shut up and mind my own business. So I do. But the other night I come home and she's in the kitchen scrubbing mud off the floor that my father tracked in from the site he's working at. All he had to do was take off his boots on the porch, but no. That would be too much. He walks in, makes a mess, and now my mom's on her hands and knees, scrubbing the floor, coughing and spitting up. You know where he is? On the couch with a beer, watching the game on TV."

"How did that make you feel? Specifically."

"Angry."

"Angry how?"

The camera captured Jason, his hands clenched into shaking fists, his chest rising and falling.

"I wanted to hurt him."

"What did you want to do?"

"I wanted to punch him as hard as I could. Right in the nose. I wanted to hear the cartilage break, and I wanted to knock him onto the muddy floor. It would've been nice to wipe up the mud with his face. I would've really enjoyed that."

"What else?"

"I wanted to take my mother and run away. Leave that son of a bitch on the floor and just take her away. She stays with him because she has to, and I throw up my hands because she ain't never gonna change. But really, I'd love to take her away. Show her a better life."

"Thank you, Jason. Thank you for sharing."

———

Randall stopped the video and finished transcribing the interview on his computer so he could add it as part of the case study file. Thus far, Jason was looking to be their second success. If they could get him all the way to having no more violent fantasies about his father, that would be a true win and could stem a negative reaction to Jerry Osbourne's regression. When Jason was first introduced, his kill fantasy had involved cutting out his father's tongue so he couldn't order his mother around anymore. He then wanted to remove his father's eyes so he wouldn't be able to look so disapprovingly at him whenever they were in the same room together. Once the eyes and tongue were gone, Jason had fantasized about cutting off his father's hands so he couldn't hit his mother anymore. Then he would sit next to his father and tell him all the ways he hated him until the old man bled to death.

He and Peter had worked hard, regurgitating the fantasy repeatedly, until, over time, little details began to change. The tongue was cut out, but the eyes remained. Hands were not cut off, but fingers were. Eventually, a knife wasn't involved at all, and there was a gun instead. At one point, Jason talked about shooting both of his parents, which, as with Jerry, had been an unexpected turn. He'd never fantasized about killing his mother before, but as the murders became more distant and less personal, her weakness gave him the motivation to end her life as well. But that quickly passed, and the focus was back on only the father. One day the gun disappeared, and although the punishment became close and personal again—Jason physically beating his father up—the endgame was not death but pain. This was a significant turn. Now they worked to get Jason to the next phase—a disregard of anything violent and a desire to simply move on, accepting what was and leaving his father's house altogether.

Randall got up from the desk and sat on the edge of the windowsill so he could look out over the quad that linked three other buildings with the Science Department. The morning sun was just breaking over the trees near the freshman dorms. He was alone, which was, most definitely, the plan. The evening before had been exhausting, starting with the phone call from Gina, who'd been hysterical, then calmed down and offered to call Amanda's other friends to let them know.

Amanda had been an only child, and the lone living parent was her estranged mother on the West Coast. He had no way of getting in touch with her, so he'd called her aunt in Florida and her two cousins in Colorado and Mississippi. More tears, as well as promises that they would come and make things as easy for him as possible. They'd offered to help spread the news to the rest of their small family, and he'd agreed. Email addresses had been exchanged, and Randall had promised he'd send details about the funeral as soon as he could get his head around everything. It was all so overwhelming, a tidal wave of grief and responsibility crushing him into the surf. Amanda was dead, and now he had to bury her.

The grassy promenade that was usually filled with students was empty. He loved the energy on campus when school was in session. The youth, the expectation of success, the optimism. It was addictive. It would be another few weeks before the students returned from their holiday break. He wondered if, even with their energy, he could ever feel optimism or promise again. He couldn't imagine ever making himself completely whole.

"Dr. Brock."

Randall almost fell off the sill as he spun around. A man stood in the doorway—about his height, a bit younger, but too old to be a student. Messy hair hung just above his eyebrows, and dark stubble covered most of his face. His eyes seemed darker in the shadows from the hall. He was wearing a long black coat.

"You were at my house yesterday," Randall said. "I recognize the coat."

"Yes, I was."

"And Amanda's party. You were there. I saw you. But your hair was a little different."

"We need to talk."

The man walked into the office and crossed the room, easing himself into one of the two chairs that Randall and Peter used to conduct their sessions. A camcorder was set up on a tripod, but the power had been turned off. The man fell back against the chair and let his coat fall open as he crossed his legs, revealing an outfit that was simple enough: a pair of jeans and a white button-down dress shirt.

"I called out to you from my porch," Randall said. He remained leaning against the window behind the desk.

"I heard you, but it wasn't a good time. I shouldn't have come then. Not with everything going on with Amanda. You'd just gotten home after you found out. That was my mistake."

"How do you know that?" Randall asked. "How do you know about Amanda?"

The man stared at him for a moment. "Do I look familiar to you?"

"No, not really. I know you from the party. That's it."

"We've been in many of the same circles over the years, but I don't think we've ever officially met. You can call me Sam."

Randall was quiet.

"Of course, that's not my real name. It's important I remain anonymous for the time being, so I chose the one name that I knew would connect us. I chose your brother's name."

Randall felt light headed, his feet heavy as he crossed the hardwood floor.

"I know what you're asking yourself," Sam said, a thin smile creeping across his face. "Or at least what you should be asking yourself. If I know about your brother, what else could I possibly know?"

"What do you want?"

"I'm here to help you."

"I don't need your help."

Sam stared up at Randall, his eyes fixed on his host. "You and little Sam used to play on your father's farm. It wasn't often your father gave you time to horse around. Chores on a farm are a serious thing, and you had responsibilities. Even as a young man, your help was crucial. But that day, you had time to yourself. You cherished that. But then there was always Sam wanting to be part of your world. He looked up to you, and yes, he could be annoying at times, but aren't all younger brothers? You didn't look at it that way, though. To you, he was just another chore, and watching him was another task on your list. So when you went into the woods that surrounded the dairy barn, he followed you, but that was your time to be alone. You didn't have any more chores, so you ignored him. Too bad. It seems tragedy has a way of finding you, doesn't it?"

Randall was stunned silent. He eased himself into the chair opposite his visitor.

"You were supposed to be Sam's protector. He was your brother, not an item on a chore list. You were the one who was supposed to be looking out for him."

"How do you know this?" Randall asked, his voice no more than a whimper.

"You're missing the real question," Sam replied, leaning forward. "It's, What else could I possibly know?"

Silence hung between the two men. Randall tried to hide his trembling hands by crossing his arms in front of his chest. A headache was coming on, quickly gaining strength. His vision was beginning to blur at the edges. He knew immediately that it was a migraine, stronger than the one that had threatened at Amanda's ceremony. This one was going to be bad.

"You need to leave," Randall said carefully, forming each word to ensure his voice wouldn't crack and give away the fear that was mounting.

"But first I need to tell you something. I need to tell you the secret that brought me here."

"What?"

Sam lowered his voice to a whisper. "Amanda was murdered, and I know who did it. I saw the whole thing."

Randall shot out of his chair and stormed across the room, the shroud of guilt and remorse falling to his feet. "That's nonsense!" he cried, suddenly full of energy. "My wife died in a car accident."

"No. She was murdered."

The possibility seemed ridiculous. Randall closed his eyes for a moment as his headache intensified. "Okay, then tell me who did it. You said you were there. You saw it. Tell me, and we'll go to the police."

"That's not how this is going to work."

"Did you do it? Did you kill my wife?"

"No."

"Then if she was murdered, tell me who's responsible."

"In time. Not yet."

"I'm calling the police."

Randall fumbled for the phone on the desk. He picked up the receiver and suddenly felt a hand on his shoulder, spinning him around so he was face to face with this strange man.

"No police," Sam said. "This is between you and me. I can help you, but if you involve the police, you'll be implicating yourself and be forced to share secrets you're not yet ready to share. You know I'm right. I'll help you find the truth about Amanda. And I'll help you see your own truths too." He took Randall's hand and placed an object in it.

"What is this?"

"It's Amanda's phone. You'll find her first truth there. But no police."

"How can you have her phone?"

"We all wear masks," Sam said, ignoring Randall's question. "Some wear them better than others, but we all wear them. Life is nothing but a ruse. You never really know someone. Not in the true sense of the word. You didn't know Amanda, and she didn't know you. But I can help you see what you need to see."

"In exchange for what?"

Sam let go of his shoulder and backed away toward the door.

"In exchange for what?"

Sam pulled the hood up over his head, and Randall watched as he ducked back into the hall. He stopped at the threshold. "I know more than you can imagine. No police. I know everything."

The man disappeared. Randall hung up the phone and collapsed against the wall, sinking to the floor as his migraine slowly spread across his skull, crushing him from the inside out. He cradled Amanda's phone in his hand, confused and scared, rubbing its smooth surface with his thumb over and over until the pain swallowed him whole.

10

Peter paced the length of the office. "So do we call the police?"

"What am I supposed to tell them?" Randall asked. "A man came to visit me and told me Amanda's accident was actually cover for her murder? I don't know who he is. I don't know where he came from. I've never seen him before. Not until the award ceremony. I'm sure of it. And he told me not to involve the police."

"Of course he did. He probably wants to extort you or blackmail you or something. He knows about your brother, which means he knows more than he should. And it probably means he knows Amanda's accident just made you a very wealthy man. It makes sense."

Randall was seated in the same wingback chair he'd been in earlier with Sam. "Look, I'm obviously going to let the police know. I just don't know what to tell them yet. What if they start asking too many questions? What if they track this Sam guy down and he starts talking about things we don't want to talk about?"

"Then we deal with it."

Randall shook his head. "No. I can't. I think it makes more sense to take a few days and try and figure out who this guy is and what he wants. That'll give us a better idea of which direction to take."

"How did he know about your brother?"

"No idea."

"Does he know about William?"

Just hearing the name sent a bolt of lightning down his spine. Randall stood and faced his friend. "I don't know, but I'm going to find out. I just need a few days."

"Amanda will be buried in a few days." Peter stopped pacing and perched himself on his desk. "If she really was murdered, then there could be evidence that needs to be collected from her body. We need to tell the police now."

Randall was quiet, thinking.

"I'm also wondering," Peter murmured, "if this isn't . . . something else."

"It's not," Randall said. He met Peter's eyes. "It's not."

"Your wife just died. You're overwhelmed with grief . . ."

"I'm fine."

"Okay. Then you need to tell the police."

"I will. I'll make it as broad as I can so they don't ask more than they have to. But I'll tell them."

Randall sipped his tea and glanced at his reflection in a mirror hanging across the room. His migraine had dissipated after he'd called Peter in a panic, but his mind was still cloudy. When he'd tried to describe what Sam looked like, he couldn't quite conjure up enough detail. It was all so frustrating.

Peter walked behind his desk and reached into a small refrigerator he kept hidden. He took out a soda, peeled the tab. The carbonated hiss was loud in the quiet office. "You don't need to be here for a few days. We have time. I don't want you thinking about Stephen Sullivan or Jason Harris or Jerry, got it?"

"How can I not think about them? Our study depends on them."

Peter's eyes began to well, and he wiped them with his hand. "I'm not worried about the case study. I'm worried about you. Amanda's dead, Randall. I can't wrap my head around that, and I can't imagine what you must be going through. I get that you want to hide here and use the study to take your mind off of what happened. I'd probably do the same thing. But the case study shouldn't be your focus right now. You need to grieve. You need to come to terms with everything."

"I know."

"Tell the police about this Sam guy."

Randall nodded and looked at the mirror again. He stuffed his hand in his pocket and felt the smooth edges of Amanda's phone, knowing he should tell Peter about it but quickly deciding to keep it to himself for now. Showing him would only lead to more questions and more pressure to talk to the authorities. "I'll call the woman from the state police tomorrow. Right now I just want to go home. It's late and I'm tired." He studied his reflection and saw a man who was drained, his heart shattered. The stranger's words echoed in his mind.

Amanda was murdered, and I know who did it. I saw the whole thing. I can help you.

11

Susan and Tommy followed Dr. Nestor down a long corridor that connected the lobby of the medical examiner's office to the autopsy rooms. Inside, there were two stainless steel tables set up in the center, with a sink and supply closet on one end and a six-body mortuary refrigerator next to a desk on the other. The aroma of pine air freshener wafted through the space, but Susan could still smell the unmistakable scent of salt and sugar combined with the bitterness of rusted metal that always made her nose crinkle. It was the smell of blood.

Amanda Brock's body was positioned on the table closest to the refrigerator. She'd been placed on her stomach, her face poking through an attachment on the end of the table as if she were about to get a massage. A blue sheet covered her up to the shoulders. Her hair had been parted and pinned back with metal clips.

Dr. Nestor made her way over to the small desk and pulled a file from on top of it. She motioned for Susan and Tommy to join her at the body, turning on the spotlight over the table.

"So like I said last night on the phone, there's a chance this neck injury could be from the accident itself, but it's just too perfect. I find it unlikely to be anything but premeditated." She put on gloves and pointed to a heavily bruised area at the base of Amanda's skull. "You can see that the bruising here is an almost-perfect circle. Pretty difficult to do that randomly."

Susan looked at the bruise. "So it was a foreign object."

"I'd say so. Something like a bat or a pipe. Something that had weight at its edge and was rounded. A golf club or something thin like that would be unlikely. It would have to be thicker."

"How about a rock or a boot to the back of the neck?" Tommy asked.

"Doubtful." Nestor opened the file she'd taken from the desk. She hung a set of x-rays up on a light board next to the instruments table. "We took these after I discovered the bruising. The top eight bones in the spinal column make up the cervical vertebrae. You can see here that her C3 and C4 have actually been broken, and upon autopsy we were able to determine that the blow was so fierce that the part of the spinal cord these vertebrae protect was actually cut. My report calls this the main cause of death. Her spinal cord was torn, which led to a sudden loss of nerve supply to the body. Heart and blood vessels began to shut down, her blood pressure dropped rapidly, and she died. Based on what we're seeing here, I'd conclude death was fairly instantaneous."

Nestor snatched the photos from the light board and put them back in the file.

"Normally, to get this kind of damage, you'd need to have a great deal of force behind it. Close-contact trauma, like a blow with a rock or hitting her with the butt of a gun, wouldn't build up the force needed. It's possible stomping on her neck could produce an injury similar to this, but in that case, I don't think the bruising would've been so precise. I'd say bat, pipe, fire poker, if it was thick enough. Maybe even a heavy branch from a tree. Something someone needed to swing to get the right energy behind it. Does that make sense?"

"Absolutely," Susan replied. "Your findings here and the fact that the blood had coagulated and started to settle in the body are clear evidence she was dead prior to the car running off the cliff."

"Yes. I would agree."

"Plus we have the fencing cut before the accident," Tommy said. "That's premeditated if I ever heard it."

Susan nodded. "Looks like we're going to be ruling this a homicide."

"I'll email you my report by the end of the day," Nestor said. "We're going to release the body back to the husband if that's okay with you."

"Yeah, that's fine as long as we have everything we'll need for an investigation." Susan looked at Amanda's body lying facedown on the table and wondered what could've happened to make someone want to kill her in such a manner. Killed, then discarded off a two-hundred-foot cliff to cover it up. She'd seen her share of homicides over the years, but when murder was committed with such maliciousness, it always made her second-guess the point of humanity. This woman hadn't deserved such an end.

"Is there anything else you need?" Nestor asked.

"No, I think I'm good. This'll do for now."

12

Randall pulled off the road and into his development. He passed the massive houses in his complex, each one adorned with holiday lights and decorations, each neighbor trying their hardest to outdo the other. Under normal circumstances, this display of Christmas bravado would've made him feel festive and jolly, perhaps even a bit competitive himself, but in his current state, all he could feel was numb. The lights and the decorations no longer represented anything good. Only a reminder that he'd be spending the rest of his holidays alone.

As he crested the hill of the driveway, he saw a sedan sitting next to the garage doors, lights on, exhaust pumping from its tailpipe. Wipers intermittently cleaned a misty rain that had been falling for the last hour. He approached slowly, trying to see who it was, figuring it to be a grieving neighbor who'd stopped by to offer condolences and share stories about Amanda he didn't want to hear. He really wasn't in the mood to smile and thank them for coming. *Yes, Amanda was perfect. She was the best. Yes, I know how much she loved you, and I know how much you loved her. No, I'll be fine, but thank you for offering. That's very kind.*

As he approached, he had the fleeting thought that it could be Sam in the car. He pulled around the sedan and stopped, realizing now that he could see better that it was the Ford Taurus he'd ridden in the day before. He rolled down his window and felt the mist gently kiss his skin.

The Ford Taurus's passenger's-side window came down, and the dome light inside the car turned on.

"Can you spare a few minutes to talk?" Adler asked.

"Sure. Come around front, and I'll let you in. Give me a minute to put the car away."

Randall pulled the BMW inside the garage. Once the door had shut behind him, he grabbed Amanda's phone, which was sitting in one of the cupholders, and stuffed it in his pocket. He snatched his briefcase and went inside.

Why is it freezing in here? Because he'd forgotten to turn the heat on before he'd left that morning. It was something Amanda usually did. She liked it cold at night and warm in the day, so she was always fiddling with the thermostat. He turned up the heat, then let the investigator in through the front door.

Adler walked into the foyer and looked around. "Wow, great place."

"It was Amanda's dream home. Something big enough to accommodate guests and the countless dinner parties she loved to throw, but nothing so big that it was obnoxious and wasteful. She lived here alone before we were married, if you can believe it. All this house just for one person. But as I understand it, her father would've built a house three times this size and only used twenty percent of it just so he could let everyone else know how wealthy he was. Apparently, he was that kind of guy."

"But not Amanda."

"Not a chance."

"She did a great job. It's beautiful."

"Thank you." Randall ushered her into the family room. "Can I get you anything to drink? A coffee or hot tea? I'm sorry it's so cold. I forgot to turn up the thermostat before leaving for the office."

"No, I'm fine," Adler replied. She held up a manila envelope. "I just came by to let you know that the medical examiner's office is making contact with the funeral home you picked and will be transferring Amanda's body tomorrow morning. I'm sure you'll get a call."

"You didn't have to come all the way here to tell me that. You could've called."

Randall took the envelope and watched as the investigator examined the floor-to-ceiling windows, which looked out onto rolling hills and endless forest. She passed the first sitting area and eased herself onto the edge of an antique armchair that had been set up with its mate next to a large stone fireplace.

"I was going to call," Adler said. "But then I figured I'd take a ride. I like it up here."

"Yes, it's pretty, isn't it?"

"I was waiting out there for a while. Wasn't sure if you were coming home."

"I'm sorry. I went to the university just to get away for a bit. I spent last evening making calls to family and friends about Amanda, and it ended up being a long night. I needed the distraction at the office."

"I get it. I'd probably do the same thing."

"Are you married?"

"Divorced. Twins."

Randall nodded. "I sometimes wish Amanda and I met earlier in life so we could've started a family. She would've been a great mother. She was so caring. She touched so many people. I can't believe she's gone. It feels like it's not real."

Adler was quiet.

Randall wiped tears that were just beginning to form and forced himself to smile. "Yes, so that's why I wasn't here. I'm sorry you were waiting."

Adler reached inside her bag and came out with a small notepad and pen. "I know this probably isn't the best time, but I need to tie up a few things for my report. Do you mind if I ask you some follow-up questions from when we met previously?"

"More questions? I thought you had your fill at the medical examiner's office."

"Yes, just a few more to file it away."

Randall sat down on the sofa across the room. He could feel the temperature warming up and took off the vest he'd been wearing. "It's fine. Go ahead."

"It sounds like you two had a good marriage. Is that the case?"

"It is. We had a fabulous marriage. Two years seems short, but being with her felt like we'd been together for decades. She completed my life. She gave me what I never realized was missing. I was a whole person with her."

"Couldn't have been bliss the entire time."

"Wouldn't be called a marriage if it was. We fought, sure, but at the end of the day it was just the two of us being completely unafraid to express how we felt toward one another. She brought that out of me. She made me see that expressing ourselves was healthy, and our arguments never lasted more than a few hours. I can't recall ever going to bed angry. That's just the way it was. We said how we were feeling, and we dealt with it together. Communication is the key to any marriage that's going to last. Being comfortable with that communication is what true love is really about."

"Do you know if Amanda was going through anything?" Adler asked. "Maybe with her foundations? Any struggles she was having? Monetary? Friendships?"

Randall shook his head. "If you're suggesting my wife drove her car off the road on purpose, that's ridiculous. But for the record, no, Amanda wasn't going through anything, and her foundation was fine. No money issues or friendships ending. I can get you the foundation's financials if you'd like. You can have our tax returns as well. Nothing to hide."

"Thank you," Adler replied. "I'll take whatever you can provide." She made a few notes. "What about enemies? Did Amanda have any enemies?"

"No. I've never known Amanda to have enemies." Randall cocked his head to the side and stared at the investigator. Sam's words were in his head again.

Amanda was murdered, and I know who did it. I saw the whole thing. I can help you.

"If I may," Randall said, "is there something I should know? About the accident?"

Adler closed her notepad and placed it back in her bag. She stood and extended her hand. "Nothing you need to be concerned about. These are routine questions to close out the file. Thank you for your time. I appreciate you sitting with me."

"These questions seem anything but routine."

"They are."

Adler walked through the family room, out into the hall, and into the foyer. Randall followed and opened the front door. She stopped as she stepped out onto the porch.

"I am sorry for your loss."

He watched as she walked down the flagstone path toward her car. Amanda *had* been murdered. Sam was right. He knew Adler was hiding this fact from him, and for a moment, he wanted to call out to her and tell her about his encounter earlier that afternoon. She needed to know because he needed to find out who killed his wife. He opened his mouth but choked on his words, suddenly understanding that disclosing anything at this point would be a mistake. Let them investigate on their own. He was in no position to volunteer anything.

He closed the door when he heard the engine start and pulled Amanda's phone from his pocket. He pushed the power button, but an icon appeared indicating the battery had run down. He had no idea where the charger was, so he ran up the stairs and into his bedroom, where the power cord for his phone was sitting on his nightstand. He plugged the phone in and watched as the green battery icon came to life and the lock screen appeared. The wallpaper was a picture of Amanda and a small group of children. Their support home was in the background. He'd taken that photo during a volunteer weekend. They'd painted the inside of the house and planted shrubs in the back. That day seemed like it had just happened.

When the phone connected to the Wi-Fi in the house, buzzes and chimes began to sound as notifications popped up on the screen, one after the other. Four new voice mails, seventeen emails, eleven texts, and nine missed calls. Six of the nine missed calls and eight texts were from someone named Pooh.

Randall knew he only had a few attempts at her password before the phone would freeze and would need to be reset. He tried Amanda's birthday, their anniversary, his birthday, and the date her father had died. Nothing worked. A message came on the screen.

One attempt remaining before lockout.

The phone buzzed in his hand. Pooh was texting again, right then and there. Randall waited to see if this person would call, which would then allow him to answer the phone without needing Amanda's password, but no such call came. After a few minutes, he placed the phone on the nightstand to allow it to finish charging and went downstairs for a drink.

He had to figure out how to unlock that phone. He didn't know the password, so it would come down to the fingerprint- or face-recognition software. Either way, he needed to see what his wife was up to. If Sam was to be believed, Amanda's truths were inside that phone. Truths the police needed to know. Truths that could lead him to the person responsible for her death. Truths about a life he might not have known as completely as he'd thought. Everyone had secrets. He was no exception. Neither was Amanda.

13

The Cortlandt Emergency Services Barracks, or Cortlandt SP, sat on the border between Cortlandt and Buchanan, two Westchester County suburbs about an hour north of Manhattan. The barracks was a concrete building that had been constructed in the middle of a large parking lot across from the Cortlandt train station and next to an outdoor roller hockey rink the parks and rec department had built back in the late '90s. On the outside, the barracks looked clean and still fairly new, despite it being almost twenty years old. Inside, however, the structure looked its age. Tight hallways, small interview rooms, and a crowded investigator's unit made getting around a chore during shift change or briefings. The plain beige paint, cinder block walls, and dirty linoleum were in line with other state-funded facilities. This was Susan's headquarters and had been since she had become an investigator ten years earlier. The dank and run-down surroundings were pretty much all she knew.

She walked in from the parking lot through the steel access door and was immediately inside the investigator's unit. The area held four metal desks, a row of filing cabinets, and a bookcase that was stuffed with multicolored binders. A flat-screen television hung on a brown-paneled wall next to a whiteboard that listed the investigators' rotation schedule. Above the whiteboard was a clock, and on the opposite wall near the door to the workout room was a corkboard filled with flyers, wanted posts, advertisements, and random notices.

Susan's desk was in the corner. Tommy was sitting in the desk facing hers. She dropped her bag on the floor and sat.

"You all moved in?" she asked.

Tommy shrugged. "I guess. Not that much to bring. How'd it go with the husband?"

"Fine. Didn't get much. They seemed to have a good marriage. I didn't sense anything that was off. Still early, though. How was HR?"

"All done. Picture, ID card, updated prints, the works. I'm officially part of Troop K."

"Then let me be the first to welcome you to the team."

Tommy leaned forward and played with a pencil that was in his hand. "Hey, I didn't get a chance before, but just wanted to say that I appreciate you taking me on without any pushback. I figured you might be pissed about having to babysit the new guy."

Susan chuckled as she logged into the barracks' database. "You've seen too many movies, Corolla. We don't slam our fists down on our bosses' desks and demand they leave us alone and let us do things our way. We also don't refuse help, because most of the time we're overwhelmed and can use an extra set of hands. So if the trade-off is me showing you the ropes in exchange for some assistance on a case and an extra body to help in the rotation of future cases, that's a no-brainer."

Tommy nodded and tossed the pencil onto the desk. "Got it. Real life is different from the movies."

"See? You've already learned lesson number one. You're going to work out just fine." Susan pulled up her call report and began logging in her interview notes. "So tell me about yourself. Where were you stationed before coming here? Crosby told me, but I forget."

"Town called Wolcott. A few towns south of Oswego."

"Near Lake Ontario?"

"Yup."

"Wow, that's out there. And you decided to come all the way down here?"

"I came for the promotion, but I grew up around here, so it's nice to be back. Really, though, I don't care where they would've put me. I just want to learn as much as I can and make myself a better investigator."

"Where'd you grow up?"

"Long Island. Port Jefferson."

"I didn't know we had a city boy with us," Susan said. "We'll be heading in to see Amanda's office in Midtown. Maybe you can give me a shortcut to beat the traffic."

"I don't know anything about Midtown," Tommy replied, smiling. "I grew up in the 'burbs. I can get you to a couple malls or the Sound. Jones Beach for sure. But I'm useless anywhere else."

Senior Investigator Jasper Crosby poked his head out of his office. "Susan. New Guy. A word, please."

Their boss was sitting behind his gunmetal-gray desk and rocking in his green upholstered chair, his knees sticking up from the desk's edge. He was a large man, a former Penn State lineman from the eighties who seemed almost too big for the barracks as a whole. His white handlebar mustache played handsomely against his dark skin. And when Crosby spoke, his team of investigators listened.

"I need an update," he said. "Are we confirming homicide?"

"Appears that way," Susan replied. "ME's findings point to foul play."

"I'm fine with that."

Susan sat in one of the two empty chairs. Tommy took the other. Crosby had been her boss since she'd arrived as a new investigator, so they had a tighter relationship than a lot of the other staff who had been transferred in. She liked his direct style. Neither of them had patience for bullshit, which she thought was why they got along so well.

"We returned the body to the husband, but we're still in possession of her belongings found at the scene."

"Still no phone?"

"Not that we can find. I'll need you to sign off on a request to get her cell records. Phone could've ended up in the river."

"What about the husband? You like him as a suspect?"

"He's on the list, but I don't know. I just got back from his place. I don't see it. Definitely not cleared yet, though."

"What's his alibi for the night in question?"

"Working alone at his office on the Quarim campus. I'm contacting the school for surveillance footage so we can see when he arrived and left. Make sure the alibi checks."

"What else?"

"We need the why or who. I'm hoping the phone records will get us going in the right direction. We'll also look into her foundations and see if there's a money trace that looks suspicious. The data from the car's computer should show us where she's been over the last few weeks. At that point we go where the evidence takes us."

Crosby turned and grabbed a folder off a credenza. "We got some preliminary data on the fence from Forensics, and you were right. The section of fence our vic drove through was cut on the bottom and sides, leaving the top to keep everything looking intact up until impact. As soon as the Mercedes hit, it popped right through and off the cliff." He handed her a file. "CSI says it looks like bolt cutters, but they can't be more specific than that."

Susan skimmed the sheet, took it from the file, and handed it to Tommy so she could keep reading. "The fence was Investigator Corolla's find. He's the one who noticed it was cut."

"Good call, New Guy."

Tommy nodded. "Thank you, sir."

"But funny you should mention the car's computer," Crosby continued. "When CSI went to extract it, it was gone."

Susan looked up from the file. "The car's computer was gone?"

"Yup. The fuses that power and store all the car's data along with the mini mainframe itself were removed prior to the crash. Whoever did this probably figured the crash would disguise the fact that the items were taken out, but our forensics guys could see that the wires to the fuses were cut too clean and not torn away like you'd see in an accident."

"Unreal."

"I'll get you the cell phone records, but it's going to take a few days. DA has to get to the judge."

"Thanks, boss."

"Keep me posted as things progress."

"Will do."

Susan and Tommy stood up and shuffled out of the office. They walked back to their desks.

"What have you been exposed to up in Wolcott?" Susan asked.

Tommy sat down in his chair. "Little bit of everything. Road watch, drug busts, gang investigations, domestic violence calls. We were the first line of defense up there, so I've seen a lot."

"Murder?"

"Twice. One was a gang hit. Teenage boy took sixteen rounds from a fully automatic weapon walking home from a party. Other one was a murder-suicide. Girl broke up with her boyfriend, and he couldn't handle it. Stabbed her to death in his apartment, then hung himself."

"You know anything about financial crimes?"

"Learned a little about it at the academy, but nothing I ever worked on."

"Well, as we know, Amanda Brock ran a very lucrative nonprofit, and we're going to look into that. Money and murder go together like peanut butter and jelly. I want to get a better understanding of Glass Hearts' financials. Pull your chair around, and I'll show you what I'm looking for. Since 990s are public information, we can get them online and go from there."

Tommy rolled his chair around to join his partner. "Lead the way," he said. "I'm right behind you."

14

Susan snatched her bag from the passenger's seat and walked up the brick steps to her front door. It was already dark out, and her eyes were heavy from reading through Amanda Brock's financials on the computer screen. She longed for a bath and an early night. Maybe something quick to eat.

As she approached, she could hear music and commotion coming from inside. She put her key in the dead bolt and turned the knob.

When he spun around and smiled, the kids hanging off his arms and legs, the laughter reverberating throughout the house, it was as if time had reversed itself. There was Eric, the sleeves of his dress shirt rolled up to his elbows, his tie hanging loosely from his unbuttoned collar, twirling the children around the living room while they screamed and laughed and jumped up and down, begging for another turn. He'd brought dinner for them. She'd have recognized the sweet aroma of Zavaglia's Pizza anywhere. The television was off, and Casey's mini boom box was tuned to Radio Disney, the volume turned up much higher than she'd normally have allowed. But how could she put an end to all the fun they were having? Parental responsibility be damned. It felt good to see her kids like this.

"Hey, Sue," Eric said. He put Casey down and sidestepped Tim, who was about to grab for his turn. "I didn't hear the door."

"Mommy, we're having a dance party!" Casey declared as she leaped up onto the couch, a giant grin plastered on her face.

Susan couldn't help but smile herself. "I see that. You guys are great dancers."

"Daddy, it's my turn," Tim called, his arms outstretched, ready to be picked up. "Spin me."

"I spun you a hundred times already," Eric replied, laughing. He kissed his son on the top of his head. "I need a rest, and we need to eat." He made his way toward the kitchen and looked over his shoulder toward Susan. "I hope you don't mind. I brought something for us to eat."

"Zavaglia's. I can smell it."

"So I did good?"

"You did good."

"I also relieved your mom. She looked tired, so I figured I'd let her get a head start on home."

"Thanks. She is tired. I'm on a new case these past few days, and my hours have been crazy."

She cursed herself for having to admit it, but Eric was looking particularly handsome this evening. He'd let the top of his hair grow out, and it was starting to get that bushy-thick look that hung down to his eyes. As she followed him into the kitchen, she peeked at his ass. Cute as ever. She didn't know if she wanted to jump him because she was horny or slap him for making her think about wanting him in the first place. She hadn't dated anyone since they'd broken up, and Eric knew her better than anyone. But as soon as she considered it, thoughts of that little slut at the office cut through her fantasy, and the horniness faded, replaced by the hunger for the large half-meatball pie that sat on the kitchen table.

"Go wash your hands," Susan said as the twins spilled in behind them. "Hands first, then pizza." She walked over toward the back door and flipped on the deck light.

"How're my chickens?" Eric asked as she looked out through the glass.

"*My* chickens are fine, thank you. All in for the night."

He opened the cabinet next to the stove and pulled out four plates. "You mind if I eat with you guys?"

"Sure." She watched her ex-husband put the plates in front of four empty chairs like he'd done for so many dinners in the past. "Did you call and I missed it or something? I wasn't expecting you."

"No, you didn't miss a call. This is an unannounced visit."

"That sounds ominous."

"I could just be longing to see my children."

"That sounds like bullshit."

Eric laughed again. "I always loved your directness."

Susan grabbed napkins from their spot next to the stove. "I don't mind that you came by, and if you really did want to see the kids, that's great. Just be honest with me. Everything okay?"

Eric slid a slice of pizza onto each plate. "I need to talk to you about Christmas." He said this quietly so the kids wouldn't hear.

Susan's shoulders sank. Suddenly, all of his charm and attractiveness faded. He'd become her ex-husband again. "What about Christmas?"

"I'm so sorry, but I can't take the kids. I just got word that the firm is sending me to Chicago for two weeks, starting December twenty-second. I won't be back until after the new year."

"That's their entire break."

"I know."

"What about the ski trip? And the cabin in Vermont?"

"I know." Eric ran a hand through his hair, pushing it out of his eyes. "I'm sorry, Sue. I am. This is a mega client we're trying to land, and we have to go wine and dine the crap out of him to make it work. They needed to send a senior guy, and they picked me."

"Yeah, I get it. It's always work first, family second."

"That's not fair."

"This was going to be their first Christmas with you, and they were really looking forward to it. They each wrote letters to Santa with the cabin's address so he'd know where to deliver the presents and everything."

"All I can do is apologize."

"Don't get me wrong," Susan said. "I'm more than happy to have my kids with me on Christmas morning. But they're getting older, Eric. They remember things now. They recognize their feelings. They're going to remember this."

"I'll make it up to them. I swear."

Susan grabbed one of the plates. "You better," she replied. "I won't stand for the divorced-dad-making-empty-promises routine. It's been done too many times before."

Eric put his right hand on his chest. "I swear I will reinvent what a divorced dad should be. They'll write books about me. Bestsellers. Oprah's Book Club. The works."

Casey and Tim came running back into the kitchen and hopped onto their chairs. Without either of them directing the other, Eric started cutting Casey's pizza, and Susan cut Tim's. Just like it used to be.

"So is *she* going with you?" Susan asked, not wanting to hear the answer but unable to keep from asking the question.

"No."

"You lying to me?"

"No."

The twins got their plates back and began to shovel the pizza into their mouths. Susan looked across the table at her ex, wondering how things would have turned out if he'd been faithful to her and their children. She thought about what Randall Brock had said earlier regarding communication being so important in his marriage with Amanda. It was true. She and Eric hadn't communicated enough, and their relationship had imploded. She still loved him, but she knew he no longer loved her, so there was no point in trying to find a way to fix things. This was her life now. Their life. Adjust along the way and move on. She wasn't the first who'd had to make unexpected changes, and she wouldn't be the last. It'd be okay in the end. It had to be.

15

The funeral director walked into the parlor carrying a clipboard and a small catalog tucked under his arm. He stood about five feet even with thinning gray hair and drooping skin, tanned more orange than bronze. A thin mustache lined his upper lip, and for some reason, that made Randall hate him instantly. Too many gold rings. A gold bracelet. An oversized watch. It was all so . . . staged? No, that wasn't the right word. Gaudy. Yes, the man was just so gaudy.

"Dr. Brock," the director whispered as he extended his hand. "It's a pleasure to meet you in person."

"Hello."

"I'm sorry for your loss and can assure you that we're going to do everything we can to ensure Amanda is taken care of throughout this process and that you, your family, and your friends feel at peace when this is over."

How many times had he recited that line?

"Thank you. I appreciate it."

"I have some options we can go over," the director said as he pulled the catalog from under his arm.

Randall sat on a couch next to the little man, only half listening to the sales pitch. His mind was occupied with what he'd need to say in order to be allowed to see Amanda's body. He wasn't sure if that was a common request or if he'd be looked upon as some kind of freak.

"The first thing we'll need is pictures. Family photos, group shots, pictures of when Amanda was young. Maybe a wedding shot of you two. Perhaps a picture of Amanda with her foundation work? We'll build a framed collage to display with the flowers so when people come, they can take a moment to reflect on her life."

"Sure, that's not a problem."

"I assume you'll want the full funeral service and burial?"

"Yes. The family has a plot where her father is in Valhalla. Gate of Heaven. She'll be buried there."

More notes. When the director was done writing, he pulled out the catalog he'd been holding. "Do you know what kind of casket you want? Most folks get metal these days, lightweight steel alloy—"

Randall held up his hand, deciding quickly that it would be easier to simply ask instead of developing an elaborate lie. "I'm sorry to interrupt," he said. "I hope this doesn't sound like too odd a request, but do you think it would be okay if I saw my wife?"

The director stopped and looked at him. "I'm sorry?"

"I'd like to see Amanda. Here. Now. I never had a chance to say goodbye, and I'd like to do that in private without all the ceremony around a wake and a funeral. One minute I was with her at the award dinner, and the next, I'm a widower. It's too sudden. I need to say a proper goodbye."

The director smiled and placed a hand on Randall's arm. "I think it would be best if you waited. Give us a chance to make her look pretty for you. We can make her look like you remember her. And at that point, I can give you all the time you need in private before the wake begins. You can say your goodbyes then. When she's more presentable."

Randall shook his head. "I need to see her now. I don't care what she looks like, and I give you my word I won't be more than five minutes. You can wait outside the door. I just have to say goodbye and move on from there. Please. I'm begging you. Five minutes, and I'll buy whatever you need me to buy for the perfect service."

The director closed his eyes and nodded ever so slightly. "Very well. But please keep this to yourself. This isn't the kind of thing we do regularly."

"I won't say a word to anyone."

"Come, then. We have to make this quick."

———

There was nothing grotesque or macabre about the body lying on the steel table. Amanda looked as if she were sleeping, eyes closed, lips slightly parted. Her skin was bone white with traces of dark lines streaking different areas of her cheeks and forehead. The bruising she'd endured during the accident had been covered with makeup in preparation for the wake. A sheet had been pulled up to her neck so all he could see was her beautiful face and nothing more.

"Oh, baby," Randall whispered as tears filled his eyes. He reached down and gently caressed her hair with the back of his hand. "I miss you so much already. What am I going to do without you?"

He wiped his eyes with the cuff of his jacket and looked behind him to make sure he was still alone. The door was shut. The funeral director was outside, in the hall. He'd have to make this quick.

Randall slipped his hand underneath the sheet and pulled Amanda's right hand out so he could see it. Her fingers were cold, lifeless. He held them for a moment, thinking of all the times he'd reached over and snatched her hand in his. Watching a movie, talking over dinner, lying on the couch with the game on, walking along the boardwalk in Wildwood, New Jersey.

"This can't be real. You can't be gone."

He dug into his pocket and pulled out her phone. He took Amanda's index finger and placed it on the home button. It took less than a second for the phone to recognize her print and unlock. After he gently placed her hand back under the sheet, Randall went into the phone's settings, shutting off all passwords so that he could gain access whenever he needed to from here on out. When he was done, he dropped the phone back in his pocket and bent over to place a kiss on Amanda's forehead. He walked away, tears still welling in his eyes as he opened the door and stepped out into the hall.

"Thank you so much for that," he said to the funeral director, wiping his eyes once again.

The director smiled. "You're very welcome."

"Let's go see about the rest of these arrangements. I want my wife to have the most beautiful funeral you can offer. She deserves it."

"Indeed, she does."

16

A cold rain began to fall for a second consecutive day, dotting the windshield at first, then eventually blotting out the rest of the world in front of him. Randall sat in his BMW, engine idling, heat streaming through the vents at a precise seventy-two degrees. Outside, the town looked gray and gloomy. Most of the leaves were gone from the trees, leaving branches thin and barren. The greenery that had blossomed during the summer had succumbed to earth tones: browns and maroons, yellows and blacks.

Randall's hands were shaking as he held Amanda's phone. Part of him couldn't wait to rip into it, to learn what Sam had promised would be the truth about his wife. But how would Sam know what Randall would find? How *could* he know? The stranger's words echoed in his mind.

You'll find her first truth there.

He slid his finger across the screen and began poking around, ignoring voice mails and emails, deciding to go straight to the texts she'd been sending and receiving. He'd start there, and he'd start with Pooh.

The texts from Pooh began with him asking how the award ceremony was going and escalated into a slight panic as the night went on.

Where are you?

Why aren't u texting me back?

Pick up your phone. I called you twice.

Hey, I'm starting to get worried TEXT ME BACK.

Mandy, seriously, text me. I'm getting really worried.

WHERE ARE U???????

As Randall continued flipping through Amanda's texting history with Pooh, his heart sank, and a feeling of nausea came over him. There were photos—so many photos—of a man, younger, rugged, masculine. In more than a few, he was naked.

I want you, babe.

This is all yours the next time I see you.

I can't wait to touch you and kiss you all over.

Amanda had texted back. She'd also shared photos. Bra-and-panty shots, sexy lingerie he'd never seen before, shots of her naked, reflected in the mirror in their bathroom. But the shot of her lying on their bed, nude, legs spread for the camera, was the worst. And she was dirty in her messages. He'd never seen that side of her before.

I can't wait to feel you in me.

I'm so wet for you.

I wish you could take me right now.

Randall tossed the phone onto the passenger's seat and shut his eyes. He suddenly felt the swell of another migraine coming on and fought to keep it at bay. The images from the texts played in his mind.

How could she have done this to him? To them? He'd always thought they were happy. It was like he was reading these exchanges from a stranger. Those pictures. He was certain they'd been happy. Had it all been a lie?

You'll find her first truth there.

Randall thought about the times her phone had rung at her ceremony. She'd seemed startled or nervous, so quick to ignore the call. Had Pooh been calling?

You'll find her first truth there.

He snatched the phone from the passenger's seat and opened Amanda's emails. They were mostly work related with the exception of a lunch invitation from Gina and a few jokes that had been forwarded from employees at the foundation. He closed out of her inbox and listened to the voice mails, but they were mostly just congratulations from those who had attended the award ceremony. He went back and read more texts from her other contacts. There was nothing of significance. Pooh was the person he was meant to find. Pooh was the truth Sam had promised him.

The rain began to pick up, smacking against the windshield. Randall dialed Pooh's number and waited. The line picked up before it had a chance to ring twice.

"Mandy, oh my god, I was freaking out. Where have you been? I've been texting you. Are you all right?"

Randall squeezed the phone.

"Hello? Hon, you there?"

Pooh's voice was deep, and the concern in it was unmistakable.

"Mandy, you there?"

"Her name is Amanda."

There was a long pause on the other end. Randall waited.

"Who is this?" Pooh finally said, his voice more sheepish now, unsure.

"This is her husband. Don't hang up." He took a breath. "What's your name?"

More silence.

"Okay, you don't have to tell me your name. I don't really care anyway. I'm calling to tell you that Amanda died two nights ago in a car accident. That's why she hasn't been returning your texts. I'm sure you—"

The line disconnected. Randall redialed, but it rolled to voice mail. He hung up without leaving a message and returned to the texts.

I'D LIKE TO MEET YOU. I'M NOT MAD. I'D JUST LIKE TO UNDERSTAND WHAT HAPPENED BETWEEN AMANDA AND ME THAT WOULD MAKE HER TURN TO YOU. NOW THAT SHE'S GONE I NEED ANSWERS. PLEASE.

He hit send and placed the phone in his cupholder, wondering if Pooh would call or text back. Probably not, but it was worth a shot. Randall turned on the windshield wipers and backed out of the funeral home.

There were things that needed tending to before he could return home.

17

The office where Wilbur Fitzgerald sat and oversaw the administration of Amanda Brock's nonprofit empire was quite the contrast to the people the programs were supposed to be helping. Two oversized oak doors swung open into an impressive corner suite that had floor-to-ceiling windows overlooking Bryant Park and 42nd Street West. There was a sitting area by the doors with two leather couches and four leather armchairs surrounding a coffee table made of glass and bleached driftwood. Opposite the sitting area was a quaint bar lined with top-shelf liquor.

Wilbur stood from behind his desk when Susan and Tommy walked in. He was a tall man, old and gaunt. He reminded her of Vincent Price in the old horror movies she used to watch with her dad when she was younger. She would bury herself in the crease between her father's armpit and hip, using his bicep to shield her eyes if things got too scary. If she began to whimper, he'd stroke her hair. She'd loved that. Sometimes she'd whimpered when she wasn't really scared, just so he would play with her hair and whisper that there was nothing to be afraid of. Her dad was right there.

"Detective Adler. Detective Corolla. Welcome."

"Actually it's Investigator Adler and Investigator Corolla," Susan replied. "The state police don't have detectives."

"I see."

Susan followed Tommy and Wilbur toward Wilbur's desk. She looked out the window and could see the people in Bryant Park crowding the holiday huts that had been set up adjacent to the seasonal ice-skating rink.

"Quite a view you have," she said, slipping into a seat in front of the desk.

"The view is taken into consideration with the price of the rent, I'm afraid. I always thought this space was a bit much, but Amanda wanted to project a sense of accomplishment for our more wealthy and corporate donors to see."

"Well, I'd say you accomplished her vision. If I was a donor, I'd be very impressed at this setup." Susan crossed her legs and propped her notepad on her thigh. "I appreciate you meeting us. Just have a few follow-up questions regarding Amanda for my file."

Wilbur nodded, turning solemn. "What a loss. Such a tragedy." He tried to smile. "I'm not sure what you'd need to know from me, but ask what you wish."

"How long have you been the director of Glass Hearts?"

"Nine years. I took over after our last director retired. I was the vice president on the board, and they asked me to assume responsibility."

"Was Amanda active with the foundation?"

"Absolutely. Amanda spent every waking minute thinking about less fortunate people and trying to come up with better ways to help and serve them. The actual business of the nonprofit was largely left up to me to run with our board. Amanda was more interested in a boots-on-the-ground approach. She was always off somewhere attempting to make a difference."

"And what is the future of the organization now that Amanda's gone?"

Wilbur's lips tightened for a moment. "We're waiting to hear back from the attorneys, but we believe the organization will automatically convert to shared ownership within the board, in which case we move on and fulfill Amanda's dream of making people's lives better. If there are any other hiccups, we'll work through them. All of this, as you can imagine, is quite shocking. We're just trying to get our heads around her passing at this point. We're letting the lawyers work on everything else."

"Of course." Susan made her notes. "From the different areas of concentration Glass Hearts has, do you know if there was one specific neighborhood or place in particular that Amanda would visit more than others?"

"Not that I know of."

"Do you know if any of the people she helped took a liking to her? Did she become friends with anyone she was helping?"

"They all adored her," Wilbur said. "Amanda was one of the kindest people ever put on this earth. The care she gave was returned with love, tenfold."

"And her relationships here at Glass Hearts were good?"

Wilbur put his elbows on his desk and leaned forward, staring intently at Susan and Tommy. He lowered his voice. "This isn't about wrapping up a file, is it? You think there was foul play involved in Amanda's death. The kinds of questions you're asking. You're looking to see if anyone had motive to harm her."

"We can't really comment."

"Then I won't pry." Wilbur leaned back in his seat. "But if my instincts are true, I feel it's my duty to point you in the right direction. Start with her husband."

Now it was Susan who leaned forward. "What about Dr. Brock?"

"Don't like him. Never did. One day Amanda is traveling the country trying to forge donor relationships, and the next she's getting married. It was all too fast, as far as I'm concerned. But she's always been a woman of action, so I guess I shouldn't be that surprised. Apparently, she met Randall in San Francisco, and they kept in touch until she finally convinced him to move East so they could be together. Before I could make heads or tails of her new relationship, I was standing in a church watching them get married. It happened too quickly."

"Was their marriage okay?"

"As far as I can tell."

"Did Randall ever harm Amanda?"

"Not that I know of."

"Do you have any proof Randall Brock could be involved in Amanda's death?"

Wilbur shook his head. "Just my instinct. If I had actual proof of anything, I would've already called the police. I didn't even know her death was suspicious until just now. But if you're saying her accident wasn't an accident, I'm telling you to look into Randall. He's trouble."

Susan closed her notepad and rose from her seat. "Thank you, Mr. Fitzgerald. I think that's all we need for now."

"Not a problem," Wilbur replied. "Feel free to call me should you need anything else. I'm here to help. Remember that. I owe Amanda everything."

18

He was planning on picking up his dry cleaning, stopping by the supermarket, and heading back to the house to look at dresses for Amanda to be buried in, but instead, Randall found himself immersed in Amanda's phone, searching for clues as to who Pooh might be. He was finally able to identify the man through a picture they'd taken together sitting on a bench in Madison Square Park. At first glance, it seemed like a fairly innocuous photograph. Couple sitting together, smiling for a selfie. No one around them seemed to be paying attention, which was the beauty of the city. You could hide in plain sight, and no one cared to look for you. But something caught Randall's eye. Pooh had been holding a small stack of mail against his chest. All it took was the magnification of the picture and a quick Google search to ensure the blurry, blown-up letters matched what he thought he was seeing, and Randall had his man.

His name was Hooper Landsky, but according to his Facebook profile, all of his friends called him Hoop. Amanda had simply spelled his name backward in her phone contacts to keep his identity hidden. Hoop equaled Pooh. Mystery solved.

Hoop owned his own architecture firm and worked out of a building on East 22nd Street, across from Madison Square Park. Randall wondered how many times they'd met up for coffee or lunch or, perhaps, something else. His stomach turned at the thought. How could he have been so blind?

He knew he should go home and get to work preparing for the next few days, but instead, he drove to Manhattan, contemplating whether he would confront his wife's lover or not. He parked in a garage near the Hammerstein Ballroom and walked over to Hooper's building on 22nd Street. The firm's name was HL Architects. They were on the fourteenth floor.

Randall called from the lobby and asked if Mr. Landsky was in. The receptionist said he was and patched him through, but Randall hung up before the call connected. At that point he left the building, walked across the street to Madison Square Park, and waited, semihidden among the leafless bushes and general anonymity of the city itself, to catch a glimpse of the man who'd been having an affair with Amanda. If he confronted him, what would he say? Was there a point to finding out why she'd been cheating? Was there a point to any of it now that she was gone?

He waited, and it didn't take long before Hooper came out of his building. It was lunchtime, and people were spilling onto the already-busy sidewalks in search of something to eat. Hooper had dark hair, a thick beard, and an athletic build and was handsome. He was wearing jeans that hugged his muscular thighs and a slim-fit black-and-red flannel shirt. Despite the cool temperature, he didn't wear a jacket. Seeing him in person, knowing what he'd done with Amanda behind his back, hurt Randall more than he'd thought it would. He could barely breathe.

Hooper waited on the corner of 22nd and Park with about a dozen other people. He had earbuds in and was swaying ever so slightly to the music. When the light turned green, he crossed Park Avenue. Randall stepped out from behind the bushes and followed.

The shirt was easy to keep track of in the dense crowd. Randall hung back as they crossed 5th, then 6th Avenue. If they stopped for a light, he would turn and face the opposite direction until they started moving again. He wasn't sure how much this guy knew about him or if Amanda had shown Hooper any pictures. It was better to play it safe.

He still wasn't sure if he'd try and talk with the man or if this trip was purely a reconnaissance mission.

As they were nearing 7th Avenue, Hooper finally ducked into a small eatery. Randall waited outside, counted to twenty, then sneaked in and stood in a corner where there was nowhere to sit. The place was spacious by Manhattan standards, with couches and soft chairs on one side and tables on the other. People were working on their computers or talking in small groups. Specialty coffees and a lunch menu were scribbled in colored chalk on a board behind the counter. Every few minutes, a bell would sound as the cook pushed out a fresh plate of something onto a serving tray.

Randall watched as Hooper stood next in line to be served. He could see the attraction someone might have to this guy. He looked like a man's man, but not so much that he couldn't be sensitive too. The messages on Amanda's phone played back in his mind. How could she have done this to him? To them?

He looked down and noticed his hands shaking. He couldn't tell if it was nerves, anger, adrenaline, or fear. It didn't really matter either way. He stuffed them in his jacket pockets to keep them hidden and tried to blend in, but the texts and the pictures kept rotating through his mind. Then something else came. Something darker. An idea. A plan.

His phone rang.

Randall fumbled inside his pants pocket, tearing at the phone as if he'd just been woken from a nightmare. He could feel a small quake inside his skull and turned away from the line, hoping Hooper didn't look toward the origin of the ringing. Luckily, the place was busy, and the general noise of the crowd helped disguise the ringing.

"Hello?"

"You shouldn't be there."

"Who is this?"

"You shouldn't be there. Leave. Now."

Randall cupped a hand over his ear. "I can hardly hear you. Who is this?"

The voice on the other end paused. "I told you to look in her phone. Find her truth. That's all you were supposed to do. Why are you following *him*?"

It was Sam.

Randall glanced over his shoulder. Hooper was gone. He scanned the shop to see if he'd taken a seat but didn't see him anywhere. No sign of Sam either.

"Where are you?" Randall asked. "How did you find me?"

"Hooper already left. I don't think he noticed you."

"Where are you?"

"Close."

Randall ran out of the shop and looked up and down the street before stepping into the flow of pedestrian traffic. He could see Hooper was already crossing 6th Avenue, and as Randall looked toward 7th Avenue, he saw a man standing still amid the sea of moving people. The figure was wearing a long black coat, and an oversized black hood covered his face. He was holding a phone up to his ear.

Sam.

Randall jumped off the steps and ran as fast as he could, ducking and dodging his way past the people streaming at him from every direction. He could see the top of the hood turn from him, but the figure was still too far away.

"Stop!"

When he yelled, the people on the sidewalk moved out of the way so he could pass. He stumbled across the street and just missed being hit by a taxi, horn blaring for him to get out of the way. He sprinted to the corner of 7th Avenue, stopped, and looked around, phone still in his hand, his breaths heavy and ragged. Sam was gone. He waved at an older man who was passing by.

"Excuse me," he panted. "Did you see a guy walk through here? Long black coat? Big hood?"

The man shook his head. "No, sorry."

Anonymity in the big city. A blessing and a curse.

Randall looked at the incoming calls on his phone. Sam's call had come from "Unknown Caller." He redialed but knew it wouldn't go through. He waited as the phone rang countless times, breathing heavily in the cold air. No one answered. No voice mail.

Hooper had made it back to his office. Randall had never had a chance to talk to him. He'd never even had a moment to look into his eyes and search for the reason why Amanda had done what she'd done. Sam had gotten in his way, and Randall knew the man with the hood was out there somewhere, watching him, following him. What he didn't know was why.

Who was this man?

What exactly did he want?

19

Susan came home after the kids had already eaten. They were in the living room watching *Finding Dory* for the hundredth time, snuggled together under a blanket while Beatrice sat in one of the dining room chairs, knitting a bright-red sweater. The yarn extended up from a wicker basket at her feet and danced like a cobra for its snake charmer. Everyone turned when Susan walked in with Tommy trailing behind her.

She made introductions, then moved into the kitchen while her mother gathered her things and called it a night. Casey and Tim were fascinated with her new partner, asking him question after question about where he was from and where he lived now and if he knew whether the video game store at the mall had opened back up yet after the fire they'd had a few months earlier. Tommy took it all in stride, answering everything as best he could until the twins finally settled down and took to just staring at him from the living room. They no longer cared about finding Dory. They wanted to know all they could about Tommy Corolla.

Susan grabbed two beers and placed them on the kitchen table before they began emptying their files on the Brock investigation. "Crosby lets me have some leeway when I'm on a case. He knows I have the kids, so he tries to accommodate. But I can't miss anything on a case, so I take my work home with me most nights."

"Yeah," Tommy replied. "I get it. No worries."

She watched him as he read through the forensic report. She could tell he was one of the good guys, and it felt nice to be leaned on when it came to the job. There hadn't been a true transfer at the barracks in years.

Tommy put the autopsy report back on the pile. "I don't know what we're running all over the place for," he said. "It's gotta be the husband. Fitzgerald told you flat out."

"All Fitzgerald told us was they got married fast. That's not a crime. Besides, Fitzgerald could be covering his tracks and throwing us off onto Randall. You never know."

"How do you figure?"

Susan shrugged. "Maybe the foundation's bylaws say that if the board takes control of the company, each board member gets a payday. I don't know. With Fitzgerald being the president of the board, that could set him up big."

"Maybe. Let's bring Brock in and shake a confession out of him anyway."

Susan laughed. "It doesn't work that way. And what makes you think it was the husband? Other than Wilbur Fitzgerald's gut."

"It's always the husband. Wife dies mysteriously—it's the husband."

"Is that a scientific fact?"

"Might as well be. There are no such things as coincidences."

She took a sip of her beer. "Randall Brock leaves the party two hours before his wife. The party ends later than it was scheduled to end. Randall is supposedly thirty minutes away at the office on the Quarim campus. So how could he get to his wife without being seen by any other partygoers, without knowing the party had run late, kill her, and drive her car over the edge of the cliff?"

Tommy shrugged. "I don't know. Maybe he never went to the office. Maybe he was parked somewhere, and it didn't matter when the party ended because he was staking her out. Maybe she went home, and he killed her there and drove back up. We'll never know because the info system on her Mercedes was taken out. Probably by the husband."

Casey walked into the kitchen holding her cup. "Mommy, I need milk."

Susan took the cup. "There's milk in here, honey."

"That milk is yucky. I want new milk."

Susan smelled the milk and shook her head. "Smells fresh to me. Drink this. I'm not wasting it."

"Are you looking at bad-guy stuff?"

"Yes. For work."

"Can we help?"

Tim jumped into the kitchen from the dark hallway. "It's the husband!"

Tommy laughed as Susan took her kids and guided them back into the living room.

"Sorry about that."

"Don't worry about it. I love it. The boy and I are in agreement."

Susan snatched a pen and pad from the table and started jotting notes. "What I was going to say was that we're waiting on the university to give us surveillance footage to see if Dr. Brock was there when he said he was. I'll also contact the alarm company the Brocks use for their home to see if the alarm was deactivated between the time the party ended and Amanda's death."

"I'm sure the husband covered that trail too."

"And what about motive?" Susan asked. "What's the motive for Randall killing Amanda?"

"She was rich, right? Her money, not his. He killed her for the money."

"But he already had the money with her alive."

"Maybe she was giving too much of it away through her charities, and he had to put a stop to it. Maybe she didn't care about being rich, but he did. Maybe he was just selfish and wanted the cash to himself so he could control it."

Susan shook her head. "You've seen the 990s. The foundation was making six times more money through donations and fundraisers. Her personal giving was a small fraction. In fact, as the foundation grew, her personal donations decreased."

Tommy finished his beer and placed the bottle on the table. "Okay, then maybe he was just screwed up in the head. Maybe there was no grand motive, and he just up and killed her. Any way you slice it, it's him. I can feel it."

"We'll draw up a profile on Randall and see what we can find. In the meantime, we have to keep digging. We can't distract ourselves with a suspect who really isn't a suspect. Amanda's phone records should be in tomorrow. We'll start there."

"Why do you think he's clean?" Tommy asked.

Susan shrugged. "You should've seen him when he had to identify her body. He couldn't do it. You can't fake the shock and despair I saw. If he killed her, his reaction would've been different. I saw real loss. It wasn't an act. Even when I came by for follow-ups the next day, he was in this daze, like he couldn't tell if he was in the real world. I've seen it before. It's PTSD. That's genuine. I don't think he did it, but if he did, it still doesn't matter at this point. We don't have anything that proves anything."

"In that case," Tommy said, "how about another beer?"

"Coming right up."

Susan got up and took another beer from the refrigerator. She popped the top and handed it over.

Tommy took the beer and leaned against the counter by the sink. "Your kids are great," he said. He waved to them, and they dove back behind the couch.

"Thanks."

"Single-mom thing must be rough."

"It has its moments. My mom's a huge help, though. Some days are easier than others."

"How long you been single?"

"Two years. Officially divorced for one." She sat down and began separating papers and documents, putting them in different piles. "How about you? You leave any broken hearts behind at Lake Ontario?"

Tommy laughed. "Me? Nah. Too busy doing what I had to do to get this promotion. Being an investigator means a lot. My father was a detective with the NYPD back in the day, and my uncle was a lieutenant with the Albany PD."

"So it's in your blood. Can't escape." Susan leaned back in her chair and crossed her legs. "What else?"

"What else what?"

"Tell me your story, Investigator Corolla. If we're going to be working together, I need to know your story."

Tommy walked back over to the kitchen table and sat down. "Pretty boring. I already told you I grew up on Long Island. I'm the youngest of three. My brother is the oldest. He's a CPA in a big firm on Manhattan. My sister's married with two girls of her own. She lives just outside of Charlotte, North Carolina, near Lake Norman. Right now she stays home with her kids, but before she got pregnant she was a shipping coordinator for some pressed-steel manufacturer down there. Her husband is an ER trauma nurse."

"You were the only one bitten by the badge?"

"Yup. My parents had me late in life. My brother was already out of the house, and my sister was on her way out. The only ones around to influence me were my mom and dad, and I knew I wasn't going to follow in my mom's footsteps working at the cosmetics counter at Macy's, so police work it was." He took a swig of his beer. "My dad used to bring home old cases that were solved from like the eighties, and we'd walk through them. Suspects, procedures, clues at the scene. It was our version of playing catch in the yard. When I graduated high school, I went to the University of Delaware to study criminal justice. Minored in psychology so I could figure out how these guys think. After that, I was recruited by the state police. I wanted the NYPD like my dad, but now that I'm state, I can't imagine being anywhere else. I did my time in uniform and then got this promotion. The end."

Susan raised her bottle. "Here's to Tommy Corolla, part-time psychologist, full-time investigator. Cheers, my friend."

Tommy held up his beer. "Cheers." He cradled the bottle in one hand and started working the corner of the label with his other. "What about you? What's your story?"

"You already know about the single-mom part," Susan began. "I'm an only child. My dad was a union guy. Pipe fitter. Died a few years ago from mesothelioma. All those years working in the city. All that asbestos in the buildings. It did him in. I miss him."

"I bet."

"I think my mom helps as much as she does to keep her mind busy. She tries to act tough, but I know she's hurting. They were married for over forty years. Can't give up someone that easy when you've been around them that long. So the kids keep her busy, and I get great childcare. It's a win-win for both of us."

Tommy paused for a moment. "I know I said this earlier, but thanks again for being cool with taking me on. I didn't know what to expect when I got down here. You made it easy, and I really appreciate that."

"I'm happy to show you the ropes," Susan replied. "But from what I see, I don't think you'll need much hand-holding for long."

"I'd really like to catch the guy who did this to Amanda Brock. First case and all. It'd be nice to get a win right out of the gate. And maybe when it's over, when we're not partners anymore, you'll let me take you out to dinner to thank you?"

She could feel her cheeks flush and smiled as she looked at the younger man sitting across from her. "Are you asking me out?"

"Maybe," he replied, grinning nervously.

Susan tapped the pile of papers that was sitting on the kitchen table. "Let's catch this guy first; then we'll talk about drinks. Maybe even dinner. Deal?"

Tommy nodded and took a sip of his beer. "Deal. We'll start with the husband."

20

His ride home from the city was nothing more than a blur. Randall was standing in the kitchen, but he couldn't remember actually arriving at the house. He'd been on autopilot the entire way. One minute he was walking along the streets of Manhattan, and the next, it was past midnight and the BMW's headlights were illuminating the workbench at the end of the garage.

The house was quiet. No call from Amanda that she was upstairs. No television blaring from the family room. No music streaming or warm fireplace raging after a tough day in the cold. It was just him.

His stomach rumbled, and he went to the refrigerator, grabbing a Tupperware full of chicken parmigiana one of the neighbors had made the other night. He threw it into the microwave and set it for three minutes.

A light came on in the family room. Randall spun around in shock, almost tripping over his feet. He let out a small whimper of surprise when he saw Sam sitting in the armchair closest to the fireplace, hood up over his head, the shadows from the lamp hiding his features.

"What are you doing here?" Randall demanded once he got himself under control again. He could feel his voice crack, and he swallowed. "How do you know where I live? How did you get in here?"

"Do you really want to know?"

The digital chime of the microwave sounded, but Randall ignored it. He walked into the family room and turned on the rest of the lights.

His heart was beating ferociously in his chest. His breath came in short stutters. "Get out of my house."

"You found what you needed to see in Amanda's phone. Now you know she was keeping secrets. Just like you." Sam lowered his hood and stared into Randall's eyes. "What were you planning to do to Mr. Landsky if I hadn't called?"

"I wasn't going to do anything," Randall snapped. "I just wanted to see him. I wanted to see the man who was having an affair with *my* wife. In person."

"Why?"

"I don't know."

"You wanted to harm him."

"No."

"You wanted to hurt him. Make him suffer for stealing Amanda away from you."

"That's not true."

"You wanted to kill him."

"Shut up!" Randall closed his eyes and grabbed at the bottom of his sweater, squeezing and twisting it as if he were wringing out a wet sponge.

"Do you feel a headache coming on?" Sam asked.

Randall didn't answer.

Sam rose from the chair and crossed the room, his boots thumping on the floor, which creaked under his weight. "I showed you her first truth," he said. "Amanda wasn't the woman you thought she was, just like you're not the man everyone thinks you are. We all have secrets, Dr. Brock. I want you to come to grips with yours."

Randall opened his eyes and gently knocked the back of his head against the wall he was leaning on. "Did you kill my wife?"

"No."

"But you know who did."

"Yes."

"Then tell me. Please. Just tell me so I can go to the police. No more games. Was it Hooper? Is that why you told me about the affair? Did Hooper kill Amanda?"

"I want your truth," Sam said.

Randall rubbed his temples and fought back tears. "My truth about what?"

"You know."

"I don't."

"Yes, you do."

"I don't!"

Sam sighed, his gaze piercing. "We'll start with your brother."

"What about him?"

"I want to know the truth about what happened to him, and I want to hear it from you. I have to hear it from you. This is how our arrangement will work. I'll give you a truth, and you'll give me a truth, until we've uncovered everything about the manipulated and artificial life you're living. Once that happens, you'll never have to hear from me again."

Randall stared at his uninvited guest. He searched for a response but couldn't find the strength to say anything. It felt as if his world were crumbling. The world he'd worked so hard to construct, brick by brick, lie by lie, was falling apart around him. Sam knew. And that was all it took. One person. One person to bring it all down.

"I want to hear about the hike in the woods," Sam continued. "I want to hear about the stream. It was rapid that day. All that runoff from all that rain made the pull of a little stream turn into a monster. What a perfect alibi."

"Go . . . away."

"When you lay down at night, and the house is quiet, and your thoughts start to drift, can you still hear him calling for you? Do you still pretend he slipped and fell?"

Randall leaped off the wall and tackled Sam to the floor, wrapping his hands around the stranger's neck, trying to get on top of him so he could squeeze the life out of him. He wanted to kill this man. He wanted to end him. For a flash of a moment, he saw no other way. If he killed this man, he could keep his secrets. And if he could keep his secrets, he would never have to relive any of it ever again.

Sam grunted once, then pulled his right leg back and twisted it around Randall's neck, instantly flipping Randall off of him and immediately gaining the upper hand. He let their momentum rotate their bodies until he was sitting on Randall's chest, his thumbs digging into Randall's eyes. Randall instinctively grabbed at Sam's wrists and pulled, but Sam pressed harder until Randall cried out from both the fear and the pain.

Sam suddenly pulled away and stood up. "I'm no threat."

Randall rolled onto his side, covering his face, keeping his eyes shut. The pain in his skull was intense. He was afraid he'd been blinded.

"It doesn't have to be like this," Sam said. "A truth for a truth. That's all I want."

"Leave me alone!"

"I will give you Amanda's second truth, but that's all I can offer until we talk about your brother. And Rose. And Lily."

Randall froze when he heard those names.

"I'll remind you one last time. No police. If you tell the police about me, I'll incinerate everything you hold sacred. Your life. Your reputation. What's left of your career. Your friends and their wives and their children and their grandchildren. And then, once you've seen all the death and you know you're the one responsible, I'll kill you. Slowly. But by then you'll be begging me to end you. Like those women begged you."

Randall opened his eyes into slits and watched as Sam turned and left. Footsteps thumped down the hallway, through the mudroom, and out into the garage. He scrambled to his feet and staggered into the kitchen.

A small green envelope had been placed on the counter. Randall picked it up and examined it, flipping the top of the envelope open and sliding a thin copper key into his palm. It was a key to a safe-deposit box.

Amanda's second truth.

A newspaper clipping had been under the green envelope. He unfolded it, reading the bold headline. For a moment he was back there, feeling everything all over again, knowing then that no matter how far he tried to run, how deeply he tried to bury them, his truths would find a way to the surface. There would never be any reprieve. There would never be any escape.

Horror House in Queens!

21

Susan immediately noticed the woman's flat nose and eyes that looked out of place on her round face. Tiny moles dotted her skin from the head down. Her hair was up in a bun, accentuating her puffy red cheeks. "Gina Pellori?"

"Yes. Can I help you?"

Susan held up her badge. "I'm Investigator Adler from the New York State Police. This is Investigator Corolla. We'd like to ask you a few questions about Amanda Brock."

Gina thought for a moment, absently biting her thumbnail. "Any chance this can wait?" she asked. "I'm getting ready for Amanda's wake. It's today at four."

"We'll only be a second."

Gina backed up into the house, and Susan and Tommy walked inside. Their eyes were instantly drawn to the three-story cathedral ceiling in the foyer and the grand staircase that curved its way up to the second floor. The three of them walked into the formal living room, where a collection of modern art adorned the walls. Susan and Tommy sat on a camel-leather couch.

"We ran Mrs. Brock's cell phone records as part of our investigation," Susan began. "One of the numbers she called most was yours. You two were close?"

"Yes. I was her best friend." Gina hugged her bare arms as tears formed in her eyes. "I can't believe she's gone. I really can't. And Randall. Oh my god, I can't even begin to imagine what he's going through."

"How long had you known Amanda?"

"She moved here in oh-six. The entire development was going up then, so it was customary for the people who were already living here to throw a welcome party for those just getting built, and me and Amanda hit it off. She was alone here in the complex for a while, so I kept her company. We've been like sisters ever since. She married Randall two years ago, but he'd moved in about a year earlier."

"Do you know if the Brocks had gotten any work done on their home or were planning a renovation? Something where they'd need an architect?"

Gina shook her head. "No. I'm on the homeowners' board. If they were planning anything, we'd know about it. We have to give permission, interior and exterior."

"What about any other properties? Do they own anything else they might be working on? A winter spot or summerhouse? Something like that?"

"No. Amanda had her dad's place for a bit, but she sold it."

Susan made a note. "Does the name Hooper Landsky ring a bell?"

"No."

"Hooper's number was the other one on Amanda's phone records that came up the most. He's an architect, which is why I thought she might be working on something. Maybe something for the foundation?"

"Maybe, but I never heard the name."

"How was Amanda's marriage?" Tommy interjected. "Was it good?"

"Sure. It was a marriage. Ups and downs."

Susan stared at Gina. "Was Amanda having an affair with Hooper Landsky?"

A single tear ran down Gina's cheek. She nodded. "Amanda was having an affair. I know that, but I don't know the guy's name or what he does for a living. I didn't want to get involved. Over the last two years my husband and I have become friends with Randall just as much as Amanda, and I didn't want to keep secrets. I'm no good at it."

"But she told you she was having an affair?"

"Yes."

"Was Amanda unhappy in her marriage?"

"No. The best way I can describe Amanda is a free spirit. I don't think she ever regretted marrying Randall, and I know she loved him, but she also was a person who followed her heart. She told me she met this guy, and he knocked her off her feet, and she was seeing him. That's all I know because that's all I wanted to know. She understood."

"Any idea if Randall knew about the affair? Did he ever mention anything to you or your husband?"

Gina shook her head. "I got the impression that he was very happy with their relationship. I doubt he knew anything."

Susan stood from the couch. "I think that's all I've got for now. We appreciate you taking the time to talk to us."

Gina wiped the tears from her eyes. "You think Amanda's death was more than just an accident, don't you? I watch the shows on TV. The police don't come around asking questions about people who died in car crashes unless they're investigating something they think is suspicious. You think her lover could have something to do with what happened?"

Susan forced a smile. There was nothing that got on her nerves more than armchair detectives who thought every minute of an officer's life was *CSI* or *Criminal Minds*. "We can't comment on the details of our investigation."

"Sure, I get it. But if it is him, please catch him and lock him away. Amanda was a beautiful person. She didn't deserve to die so soon."

"We'll do our best."

Gina stood and shook hands with the two investigators. "Will I see you at the wake? Ed Franklin Funeral Home. Four to seven."

"Depends on how the day goes."

She walked them to the door and waved as they made their way down the porch steps toward the car in the driveway.

"We have a second suspect now," Tommy said, climbing into the passenger's seat. "Maybe this Hooper guy wanted Amanda to leave Randall, and she refused. He was putting pressure on her to try and cash in on her fortune, and that was a strain on their affair. Maybe after enough noes from Amanda, Hooper decided if he couldn't have her, no one could."

"Wouldn't be the first time I saw something like that," Susan replied. "Everything is on the table at this point. Everyone gets looked at twice."

22

It took the First Hudson Bank branch manager almost an hour to finally confirm that Randall was, indeed, the executor of Amanda's estate and entitled to her personal belongings as mentioned in her will. The safe-deposit box was at a branch on 46th and 6th, just a few blocks from her Manhattan office. He'd come to the bank armed with her death certificate, will, and estate paperwork, but the manager had stated that he still needed to follow proper protocol and confirm these details. Randall waited while the manager called their family attorney, Bernie Hayman, and established everything was legitimate. Throughout the time he waited in the office with his ridiculous smile and disguised placidity, all Randall could think about was what could be inside the safe-deposit box. What other secrets was Amanda hiding?

"I appreciate your patience, Dr. Brock," the manager said as he returned the paperwork. "We're all set if you'd like to follow me back to the vault to retrieve the box."

"Lead the way."

The manager used Randall's key along with the bank's master key to open box number M12. The metal box measured five inches high, seven inches wide, and twenty-four inches long, the smallest the bank offered for rent. He handed it to Randall, then led him around the corner, away from the branch floor, and into a small room that held only one chair and a shelf that was bolted to the wall.

"You can put the box down there," the manager explained, point-ing to the shelf. "Take as long as you want. The door locks, so you'll have privacy. When you're done, hit this buzzer, and I'll come to take you back."

"Thank you."

He closed the door as he left. Randall reached behind him and turned the lock on the knob. The room was snug, the size of a modest coat closet. A single pendant light hung from the ceiling. He opened Amanda's safe-deposit box and looked inside.

The box was full of papers folded in thirds like one would do to mail a letter. He slid the first stack out onto the shelf and took off a blue rubber band that was holding everything together. He unfolded the papers, skimming each one.

The first document was marked *Witness Statement: William Feder– Gary Anderson case #P37G5.*

His breath caught in his throat. Randall flattened the document out on the shelf and ran his finger down the page, reading the text, already knowing what it contained. How could Amanda possibly have this? How could she have known about William Feder?

He refolded the statement and looked at the next document. It was made up of pages and pages of xeroxed handwritten notes from his sessions with the doctors after he'd been rescued. These sessions were supposed to have been private. How did she get these?

Rage and panic began to boil within.

Randall shuffled through the notes, then pushed them away, grabbing for the next set of papers. They appeared to be a draft copy of a new will. From the date stamped on the last page, it had been completed six months ago, at the beginning of the summer. Randall read through the will. He couldn't believe it. Amanda had been retooling the distribution of her assets. In the event of her death, the foundation was to obtain eighty percent of her net worth. The house was to be sold and folded into the foundation's take. Another ten percent would be used to construct a financial-literacy wing at their local library, to be named after her father. The last ten would be used to purchase and rehab homes in the tri-state area as women's shelters for the battered and abused. She wasn't leaving him anything.

With fumbling hands, he pulled the final set of documents out of the box. He could hardly breathe now. He was angry and confused and panicked and shocked. The last set of papers was fastened with a red rubber band. Randall frantically pulled at the rubber band, ripping the pages as he did. He felt as if he might be sick. The tiny room had suddenly become suffocating.

The last set of documents was unsigned copies of divorce papers. Amanda had been planning to leave him. Like the will, the divorce papers had been created over the summer, and according to what he read, she was going to ask him to leave the house and appease him with an annual alimony payment of $200,000 for the next fifteen years.

"This can't be," Randall muttered. His voice was raspy, choking with phlegm. "This simply cannot be."

Sam's words echoed in his mind.

I know everything.

He read through the will and divorce papers again. It appeared as though they'd been edited and tweaked over the last six months, with Bernie Hayman acting as her counsel. He'd never said anything. Even after Amanda had died, even during the arrangements Randall had been making with Bernie and the estate, even that very morning when the branch manager had called, Bernie had said nothing. So did he know the entire truth or just that Amanda was going to leave him? Little prick. Bernie had known why Randall was at the bank. Why hadn't he warned him? Because Bernie wasn't Randall's attorney. Bernie Hayman had belonged to the Sturges family since the beginning. He'd served Clifford Sturges for decades and would always be loyal to Amanda. Randall was an outsider, someone who had been brought in through a marriage everyone thought was rushed and inappropriate. They didn't understand the love he and Amanda had shared, its immediacy and intensity. But now Randall questioned that love he'd thought was so strong and impenetrable. She'd found his truth before he'd discovered hers, and now she was gone. What was happening?

He took the empty box and placed it on the floor next to his feet, using the shelf to lay each page of each document side by side. He picked up the first sheet of paper and began reading slowly, carefully. He wanted to know every detail of what Amanda knew. Of what Sam knew. Of what others might know.

I know more than you can imagine. I know everything.

He would not leave the tiny room for another two hours.

23

The funeral home wasn't large enough to accommodate everyone who wanted to pay their respects. Amanda had touched so many lives. Police had been stationed in the street to direct traffic and move the crowds in and out. Mourners waited in the cold for hours. Randall was seated in the first row of chairs, facing the casket, which was surrounded by flowers. From where he sat, he could see Amanda's profile. He'd kissed and caressed that beautiful face more times than he could count. But now he could see only the secrets and the betrayal. How could she do that to him? How could she want to end what they had?

The people came, one after the other, crying, hugging, telling him how sorry they were and what a wonderful person Amanda had been. It was his house all over again, only this time the number of people coming to pay their respects was too many to count. He hugged them back and thanked them, all the while swallowing the urge to tell them how she'd been cheating on him and how she'd been planning on leaving him. He bit his tongue and played along, trying his hardest to keep it together, all the while looking for two people: Hooper Landsky and Bernie Hayman. He had something to say to each of those bastards, and for them, he wouldn't hold back.

He wasn't sure if Hooper would have the guts to show since he knew Randall was onto their affair. But Bernie came. He arrived with his wife, Audrey, arm in arm, walking slowly down the center aisle with the rest of the people in line. He was a short man, round and otherwise shapeless, bald on the top of his head with tufts of gray on the sides. He wore oval, thin-rimmed glasses on his long nose.

Randall was busy with those in line ahead of Bernie and Audrey, but he kept an eye on their progress as the couple made their way closer to the casket. He watched as they knelt down in front of Amanda and folded their hands in silent prayer. When they were done, they stood and made their way over to him. Audrey hugged him.

"If you need anything, you call us," she said, her eyes swollen from crying. "Understand?"

Bernie shook his hand, and Randall pulled him in to give him a hug.

"I'm sorry this happened," Bernie whispered.

Randall spoke through clenched teeth. "You knew. All this time, you knew what she was planning to do, and you let me find out on the day of her wake. You could've warned me. You knew I was at the bank and was about to look into her safe-deposit box. Why would you let me learn the truth alone like that? Why would you do that to me?"

Bernie pulled back and looked at him. His eyes were wide, searching. "Randall, I—"

"Shut up. I don't want to hear it. Just leave. I don't want you here."

"I didn't know what was in the box."

"Like hell."

He continued to stare at Bernie, their eyes locked. He wanted to throttle him right there in front of everyone. He wanted to tell them all what Amanda had been planning and how Bernie had been helping her. He wanted to—

"Are we good here?"

Peter was suddenly by his side, a nervous smile on his face as he gently tugged at Randall's sleeve.

"I think I need some air," Randall said.

Peter nodded. "Sounds like a good idea. Come on—I'll walk you out to the porch."

"No, I can manage." Randall took a final step closer to Bernie. "Don't be here when I get back."

He turned and walked past Amanda's casket and out the french doors that opened onto a back deck overlooking a hidden parking lot. The air was cool against his face, and it wasn't until he got outside that he realized how stifling it had been in the parlor. He walked to the edge of the patio, shaking with adrenaline and rage. His breath came quickly, illuminated in the overhead porch light, then evaporated into the darkness.

"You okay?"

He recognized Inspector Adler's voice. He didn't turn around.

"I'm fine. Needed some air."

"Who was the old guy you wanted to punch?"

"That is the estate's attorney. And I didn't want to punch him."

"Well, something was uneasy between you two."

Randall chuckled. "You read people well. Must be the job training."

"That's exactly what it is."

Randall could hear the investigator's heels clicking on the wooden deck as she came closer. "Thank you for coming," he said. "You didn't have to do that. You didn't know her."

"She's my case. It's the right thing to do."

"But the case is closed."

"Not yet."

Randall finally turned around. "No? Is there something I should know about?"

"Not necessarily."

"There'd be no other reason for you to keep her case open unless you suspected foul play. I mean, if it was an accident, it would've been labeled as such and filed away. It's still open. You're here. That tells me something's not right."

"I can't discuss it."

He wanted to tell her about Sam but knew he couldn't do that without telling her everything else.

"So what happened with you and the lawyer?" Adler asked.

"Family business."

"You seemed pretty upset."

"I was."

"You get upset like that a lot?" She inched her way closer.

"No, I don't."

"Must be something pretty big to get you angry at your wife's wake. Tough for people to compartmentalize their emotions in these types of situations. I get it. First you're sad; then you're mad."

"I'm an emotional mess," Randall snapped. "I'm not sure how you expect me to act."

"Like I said, I get it," Adler replied. "I just wanted to come out here and make sure you were okay."

"I'm fine."

A cold breeze blew across the patio, scattering fallen leaves that had been left behind since the last cleanup.

"Can you answer one thing for me?"

Randall nodded.

"Do you know a Hooper Landsky?"

She knew. She knew about the affair, and she knew about Hooper.

"No."

"Okay."

The french doors opened, and Peter stepped outside. He stopped when he saw the two of them. "Everything okay out here?"

"Yup," Adler replied. "All good."

Peter walked toward her. "Investigator Adler."

"Dr. Reems. Good to see you again."

"She's still investigating Amanda's crash," Randall explained, his voice a strained whisper. "She believes there's more to her accident than we might think. Foul play."

"Is that right?" Peter asked.

"I can't talk about an open investigation, as I've just stated to Dr. Brock." Adler looked at her watch. "You have guests inside that're waiting to see you, and I've taken up enough of your time. I'm sorry for your loss. I'll be on my way."

Randall watched her leave and didn't move until he was certain she'd made her way back down the hall and out the main exit.

"Was she upsetting you?" Peter asked.

"No. She wanted to know what my deal was with Bernie."

"She and I both. What was that?"

"Nothing. It was nothing."

"Did you tell her about Sam?"

"Not yet."

"Randall, that was the time."

"Not here. Not like this. If I tell her about Sam, I have to tell her everything. I can't do that. I'm not ready."

"You can. I'll help you."

"Not now. Not here."

Peter sighed and looked out onto the parking lot. "Okay. Let's go back inside then. People are waiting to pay their respects. Bernie's gone."

"Can I ask you something?"

"Always."

"Did you ever show my medical records to Amanda?"

"Of course not."

"Maybe you thought you were helping by keeping her in the loop?"

"Randall, no. Never. Why are you asking?"

"Amanda had this safe-deposit box. I went there this morning and got into it. It was filled with draft copies of divorce papers and a new will. She was going to leave me. Bernie knew. That's why I was so angry with him. He never said anything."

Peter stood frozen on the porch. "Oh, Randall. I had no idea."

"She had copies of my medical records too. The ones after Gary's basement and some from last year. She knew."

"How?"

"That's what I'm asking you."

"I don't know," Peter whispered. "Everything from the hospital is sealed. I can make a couple of calls, but I doubt anyone will admit to breaking HIPAA laws."

"I'm sure Amanda's money could unseal a lot of things."

"Come on. We need to get back inside."

Peter took him gently by the arm, and Randall allowed himself to be guided back into the funeral home. He felt safe when he was with Peter. He was a good friend. One of the best. But now, perhaps, things weren't what he thought they were. Perhaps Sam was right.

Everyone had secrets. And no one was the exception.

24

The morning traffic heading into Midtown was brutal. There was an accident blocking two lanes on Interstate 87, so Susan and Tommy sat in a line of cars that crawled along, mile after mile, for over an hour, her speedometer never reaching higher than twenty-five.

The twins were going to be putting on a holiday play at their preschool in a few hours, and it killed Amanda that she couldn't be there. Beatrice was going and promised her that she would record the entire event, but it wouldn't be the same. As a mother, it was up to her to get to things like that. Important events for your kids. But a homicide was the kind of case that always took precedence. There was nothing she could do. It wasn't something you could put to the side for an afternoon or a day. They had a killer to catch before the trail grew cold. So she sat in the car as pictures of them in their costumes, standing on the stage, and singing their hearts out danced in her imagination. Just the thought of it made her choke up, and she swore she wouldn't let herself miss these things as they got older. She couldn't. It wasn't right. She'd have to find a way to balance a caseload and her kids at the same time. Others could do it. She wasn't the first single-mom cop. She just didn't have a game plan quite yet.

Turning up 42nd Street was no better than I-87. Between the lights, the general congestion, and a street sweeper that eliminated an entire lane, it took them another half hour before they finally pulled into the parking garage across from the north end of Madison Square Park and got out onto the sidewalk.

Tommy pointed to a glass door. "In here."

They walked through a marble lobby and waited for an elevator that took them up to the fourteenth floor. When the doors opened, they were instantly inside a working office. There was no hallway or reception area. The elevator simply opened to a floor full of individual desks, a section of drawing tables, and a kitchen area in the back. Several of the employees looked up as they stepped out onto the floor, then went back to whatever it was they were doing.

"Fourteen, right?" Tommy asked.

Susan pointed to a sign hanging in the back. "Yeah, this is it. HL Architects."

A woman came around from the first drawing table and met them. She was tall, wearing an oversized white T-shirt that swallowed most of her frame. Her dark hair, streaked with bands of purple, was up in a single braid.

"Can I help you?"

"We're looking for Hooper Landsky," Susan said.

"He's not here right now, but I'm Jan, Hoop's second-in-command."

"Do you know when he'll be back?"

"I don't. But I can help you with whatever you might need. Are you planning a project? If you tell me a little about what you have going on, I'm sure I can get you started in the right direction."

Susan held up her shield. "Thanks, Jan, but this isn't about architectural services. Do you know where Hooper is?"

Jan's face contorted into a grimace. "Is he in trouble?"

"Do you know where he is?"

"I haven't seen or talked to Hoop since he left the night before last."

"Is that unusual?" Tommy asked. He also had his shield and ID out.

Jan shrugged. "I wouldn't say totally unusual, but normally he'd at least send me a text or something to check in. Sometimes he gets on these creative kicks and does a lot of his planning remotely. Other times he just partied too hard the night before and stays in bed. I've been here for about six years now. I know how to keep the balls in the air when he's not around. It's no biggie."

Susan put her shield back in her pocket. "Where does Hooper live?"

"Brooklyn."

"Can you call him for me? Right now? We really need to speak with him. Call his house phone and cell."

"He doesn't have a house phone. I'll try his cell."

Jan took her phone from her back pocket and dialed Hooper's number. She put it on speaker, and the three of them listened as it rang over and over.

"Hey, this is Hoop. You know what to do. I'll call you back as soon as I can."

Jan hung up. "Been like that for a day and a half."

"Does he have a girlfriend?" Susan asked. "Maybe he's with her?"

"No girlfriend that I know of, but maybe."

"Write down his home address. We'll check in on him for you."

Jan snatched a piece of paper from the table and wrote down the address. "Is this something I should be concerned about?"

"No." Susan took the paper and folded it. "We just have a few questions for him. Nothing more than that." She dug inside her bag and came away with a business card. "If you hear from him, have him give me a call."

"No problem."

They turned and waited for the elevator to arrive as Jan walked back to her workstation.

"I can feel them staring at us," Tommy whispered.

"Wouldn't you be staring if you were them? Cops coming in asking about their boss?"

"I guess."

The elevator opened, and they stepped on. Susan pressed the button for the lobby.

"So around the same time I run Amanda Brock's phone records and discover the existence of Hooper Landsky, he disappears?"

"I think that Gina lady in Randall's development knew more than she let on. Maybe she knew Hooper. Could've tipped him off after we met with her."

The elevator opened, and they spilled back into the lobby, then out onto the sidewalk. The crowds walking around the park had grown since they'd been inside.

"Looks like we have three stops today," Susan said as she looked up and down the street. "We'll head to Hooper's apartment now and see if anyone's there. I'll call ahead and have an NYPD unit with us for backup. After that I need to go visit Randall's attorney to see what all that fuss was last night. Then I want to hit Peter Reems's house as a final stop. He's a family friend of Randall and Amanda. Met him when I went to notify Dr. Brock about his wife. Saw him again last night at the wake. I want to get a better feel for this guy."

"Okay," Tommy replied, zipping his coat closed to protect himself from the bitter wind. "Let's do it."

25

The day was quickly getting away from them. Susan and Tommy had endured more traffic jams and construction reroutes into Brooklyn only to find Hooper's apartment empty. Two NYPD officers had met them there and gained access to the three-story walk-up from the superintendent. They knocked on Hooper's door and identified themselves several times, getting only silence in return. One of the officers climbed a rear fire escape to look through the windows. The place was empty. They checked the assigned parking space in the garage across from the building. It was also empty. No one seemed to know where Hooper Landsky had gone.

They now sat in Bernie Hayman's office about thirty minutes north of Manhattan, in White Plains. Bernie was a business-and-estate attorney and ran a one-man shop with no other employees except for an aging secretary who had been with him for over thirty years. There were no ornate carvings, mahogany bookcases, or oversized desks polished new with meticulousness that you might find in the larger firms, but it was nice enough, even if it was small.

"Cliff Sturges and I were best friends in college," Bernie explained as if reading Susan's mind, eager to explain how such a small firm could keep such a large client. "I was the only person he trusted with his wealth and his estate. When he died, Amanda kept me on. I'd known her since she was born. She was like family. I know the ins and outs of every plan and every penny that flows through that family and the foundation. It wouldn't make sense to go with anyone else. There'd be too much to relearn. It'd be a waste of time, and something could fall through the cracks. So here I am."

The short, pudgy man was dressed in tan khakis and a blue long-sleeve polo. He played nervously with the watch on his wrist.

"What about Randall?" Susan asked. "Would you consider him family?"

"No. Randall's a good man, but their marriage came out of nowhere. We didn't even know he existed until he moved in with Amanda."

"Did you do any investigations on him before the wedding?"

"There wasn't much out there. We did a general background check—you know, credit report and criminal records. Everything was fine."

"Did Amanda know you did the check?"

"No. She wouldn't have approved, but I needed to make sure he wasn't a wanted man or something. I'm sure you can understand, with the Sturges fortune at stake."

"Was there a prenup?" Tommy asked.

Bernie nodded. "Yes."

"And the prenup is superseded by the will if Amanda dies?"

"Yes."

Susan wrote a few notes in her pad. "Did you know Amanda was having an affair?"

Bernie looked down at the floor. "Yes. But that was none of my business. What she did in her private life was up to her. It wasn't my place to get involved."

"Had you ever met her lover?" Tommy asked. "Hooper Landsky?"

"No. Amanda never even told me his name. One day she stopped in, unannounced, and said she was thinking of leaving Randall. She explained she'd met someone, and that was it. Then she instructed me to draft a set of divorce papers and asked me to send her plans to rewrite the will. She was removing Randall from the will and giving him a small alimony stipend for the next fifteen years. Better than what was in the prenup. She didn't want to completely cut his legs out from underneath him."

"Talk about going zero to sixty," Tommy said. "One minute you're a couple, and the next she's leaving you and cutting you out of the will? Did that seem rash to you? Out of nowhere Amanda's planning to divorce Randall and adjust the will?"

Bernie shrugged. "Of course it seemed rash to me, but so did marrying him in the first place. That was Amanda. She was rash and decisive. When she made her mind up about something, she followed through. I don't know how long she'd been thinking about leaving Randall. She just asked me to draw up some drafts so she could see what things would look like. I consulted a friend of mine who does divorce work, and we mapped it out. I gave her the reworked will and the divorce documents like she asked. That's the last time we spoke about it. She never called me to have me file them or make any more changes, so I figured she'd changed her mind. Which, by the way, is also not uncommon."

Susan made more notes, then looked up at the lawyer. "I was at Amanda's wake. I saw the exchange between you and Randall. What happened? He seemed very upset."

Bernie began moving piles of paper from one end of his desk to the other. "Everything we just talked about is what happened. Randall found the draft documents in a safe-deposit box Amanda had. He was angry that I didn't tell him about it. Furious. That's why I'm here today and not at the funeral. Figured I wasn't welcome. It's no matter. I'll pay her a visit later on. Let him have his day with his wife. If he doesn't want me there, I won't interfere."

"Did you ever feel like you should've given Randall a heads-up?" Tommy asked. "Maybe an off-the-record warning or something?"

"Not my place," Bernie replied. "I'm the lawyer for Amanda Brock's estate. That's where my loyalty lies. I wasn't about to break my oath, or any laws, warning Randall that Amanda was going to leave him. Besides, she never did anything with the paperwork, so why mess with it?"

Susan looked out the dingy window toward the neighboring building. "Let me ask you something. Since the will never got changed, and Amanda is dead, how is the money allocated?"

Bernie dug through a pile of forms next to his chair and came away with a brown folder. He opened it, tracing his finger down the page as he read. "The foundation gets seventy-five percent of the estate. Randall gets the rest."

"And how much is that?"

The attorney looked up from the folder. "Randall will inherit roughly thirty million dollars."

26

Susan could hear the commotion coming from inside the house before she even rang the doorbell. Tommy took a position on the right side of the door, a habit she knew he'd developed responding to calls as a trooper. She waited for a moment, leaning in to see if she could hear what was going on, but there was nothing specific that she could make out. She rang the bell.

"You think they'll even hear that?" Tommy asked. "Sounds like they're either having one hell of a party or one hell of a fight."

She rang again, and the front door opened. A little girl, maybe a year or so older than Casey, stood before them.

"Hello," Susan said, bending down. She glanced inside and could see adults milling about, drinks in hand, plates of food, laughing, shouting, music on somewhere in the background. "We're looking for Peter. Is that your dad?"

"Uncle Peter is my uncle," the girl said matter-of-factly. "We're visiting from Maryland. I'm Zana."

"Wow, what a pretty name. Are you the only one who heard the doorbell ring, or did someone ask you to see who was here?"

"No, I heard it by myself."

"Can you get your uncle?"

"Okay." Zana stopped and thought for a moment, her brow creasing. "I think I'm supposed to ask you if you want to come in. That's good manners, right?"

"Yes it is," Susan replied. "But we didn't come for the party, so we'll wait out here. Just go get him for us, okay?"

"Okay."

The girl shut the door and left the two investigators in the cold quiet of the night. Tommy remained in his position on the porch, his hands involuntarily swinging toward the holster on his belt. Susan could remember those days, fresh off the front lines, when procedures were suddenly different but years of training wouldn't let you forget. Her hand had swung the same way for her entire first year as an investigator. Every time she was in a situation she wasn't completely comfortable with, her hand would be reaching for her holster. It was as automatic as shutting your eyes when you sneezed.

The door opened again, and this time it was Peter Reems. He was dressed in a wool sweater, the collar of a denim button-down peeking out from underneath, navy slacks, and white tennis shoes. He gripped his scotch with his right hand, his left still on the knob.

"Investigator Adler," Peter said. "We meet again."

"That's right. This is Investigator Corolla. We're sorry to interrupt your party. We'd just like to ask you a few questions about Randall and Amanda. You stated you were close with both of them, so we need to get a perspective on a few things."

"So Randall was right. You guys really do think Amanda's death is suspicious. No other reason for you to be here at this hour talking to me. Especially on such a night."

"I'm sorry?"

"We buried Amanda this morning, and tonight is the first night of Hanukkah. Needless to say, it's been a long day."

"I didn't realize. We just need a few minutes, and then we're gone."

Peter pushed the door open wider. "We can talk in my office, but I can't be away from my guests for too long."

"In and out," Susan replied. "You have my word."

135

———

The home office was exactly what Susan had in mind. Large oak desk, high-back red leather chair, dark-green carpet, red-gold-green plaid wallpaper, a bookcase full of scientific texts and published case studies, a large antique globe, awards and certifications hanging in frames on the walls, no windows. She and Tommy sat in the two smaller armchairs in front of the desk. Peter took his position in the high-back, crossing his legs and propping his elbows up on the chair's armrests.

"Ask your questions," Peter said, his voice even but stern. "I really do need to get back to my family's celebrations."

"Let's start with Randall Brock," Susan began. "What's your relationship with him?"

"He's like a brother. Randall and I went to NYU together. We were roommates our freshman year and have remained the best of friends ever since. We had a lot of things in common. Music, girls, what we wanted out of our major. Both of us were very focused on helping others. There were students in our program that were hell bent on making money and taking a different route, working for Big Pharma or major university research. Randall and I wanted to try and *cure* the patient. When he met Amanda, I knew it was a match made in heaven. I was his best man at the wedding. He was mine as well."

"You seemed very protective of him at the wake."

"Like I said, we're practically brothers. He's going through the devastation of losing a spouse, and now he learns that Amanda was cheating on him and was planning to leave him? It's too much. If I was abrupt in any way at the wake, it's because I feel the last thing he needs is the police showing up raising suspicions when he's trying to bury his wife. There's a time and a place, and the back porch of the funeral home wasn't it."

Tommy crossed his legs to match Peter. "Do you think Randall had any indication his wife was planning to leave him and cut him out of the will?"

"No."

"Did you know he's going to inherit thirty million dollars now that she's dead?"

Peter smiled and shook his head. "I see where you're going, but I can tell you with certainty that there is no chance Randall had anything nefarious to do with Amanda's death. If I thought he could be involved in any way, I'd tell you. It wouldn't make sense not to."

"Gets cheated on. A divorce. Losing all that money. That's a good list of motives right there." Tommy uncrossed his legs. "Hypothetically speaking, of course."

"My friend didn't kill his wife," Peter replied. "What about Amanda's lover? Do you know who he is? Maybe you should be talking to him."

"We're working on it."

There was a knock on the office door, and a tall boy with acne covering his face shuffled into the room. He stuffed his hands in the pockets of his khakis. "Mom needs you to help with the kugel. She told me to come find you."

"Tell her I'm coming," Peter said. The boy nodded and disappeared.

Susan stood from her chair. "I appreciate you taking a few minutes for us, and I really am sorry to barge in on your holiday."

Peter walked them to the office door. "I'm sorry you had to come and waste your time, but I really don't have anything to share with you. Randall is a good man. I know he had nothing to do with Amanda's accident."

"You keep saying that," Tommy said. "How do you know he had nothing to do with what happened to his wife?"

"Because I knew him before Amanda and after, and I can tell you that he was a changed man. Changed for the better. Amanda brought a light into his life that I'd never seen before. She made him whole. She filled his heart. He would never hurt her. You'll have to trust me on that."

Susan handed him her card. "Thank you for your time. If you think of anything or discover anything we should be made aware of, call me."

Peter took the card and opened the office door. "I can tell you one thing," he said quietly.

Susan stopped. "What's that?"

"I think someone's been bothering Randall. He mentioned it to me a couple of days ago. You might want to ask him about it."

"Who?"

"Pete! You coming?" a female voice called from the other end of the house.

"Some guy who calls himself Sam. Just mention it to him. See what he says."

"Pete!"

"I'm coming!" Peter held up his hands. "That's all I know. I have to see what my wife needs."

"We'll let ourselves out," Susan said.

Peter jogged down the hall without saying anything further. He turned the corner and was out of sight. Susan and Tommy walked down the opposite corridor toward the main foyer.

"Who the hell is Sam?" Tommy asked.

"I have no idea."

They reached the front door, and Tommy opened it. "Maybe it's Hooper."

"Only one way to find out."

27

The holiday celebration had gone off without a hitch. The twins, unfazed that their mother couldn't attend their first event, FaceTimed Susan as she and Tommy rode back from Peter's house. They told her all about the songs they'd sung and performed one of their dances for her while Beatrice held the phone. She laughed and clapped, but it killed her that she'd missed it. She wanted to apologize and hug them and promise them she'd be there next time, but she swallowed her guilt and pretended everything was okay. Beatrice had captured it all on video, and she told her it would be waiting when she got home. Susan had no idea when that might be.

Cortlandt SP was pretty much empty. The evening shift had changed over hours earlier, and everyone was out on patrol. A few troopers milled about the dispatch area making calls and writing out reports, but the general buzz of the barracks was gone.

Tommy dropped his jacket on the back of his chair and eased himself into it, elbows on his desk, head in hands. "That was a long day."

Susan sat across from him and turned on her laptop. "It's not over yet. We still have to log these interviews into the system. You take Hooper Landsky, and I'll tackle Bernie Hayman and Dr. Reems."

"Deal."

Crosby walked out of his office and sat on the edge of Susan's desk, arms folded. "Nice to see you today," he said sarcastically. "I appreciate the progress reports throughout your shift."

"Sorry. The day kinda got away from us."

"Tell me what you found."

Susan pushed her laptop to the side. Tommy sat back, watching, as she ran through the day's interviews.

"Interesting," Crosby said. "So maybe Hooper thinks Amanda is going to leave her husband, take all her money with her, and the two of them can run away. Then Hooper finds out Amanda changed her mind, and the money is no longer his. He loses the girl and the millions. That's motive to kill her right there. We've seen people killed for less."

Susan nodded. "And what you just said also gives the husband the exact same motive. Losing thirty million dollars is a serious thing. What if Randall found out Amanda was going to leave him and take her money with her? What if he discovered *why* she wanted to leave him? Maybe he found out about Hooper and the will, and he figured he had to stop it before she left him with next to nothing. No wife, no money. The life he thought he knew would be gone. So he killed her to keep everything else the way it should be. Made the homicide look like an accident so he could be a grieving husband."

"I thought you said you didn't like the husband for this."

"I don't. Not the way he's acting. I can see his hurt. It's real. If he's lying and he killed her, he's the best I've ever seen. But the motive Hooper has to kill Amanda is the same motive Randall would have. We have to keep an eye on Randall and find Hooper Landsky."

"Anything else?"

"After the lawyer, we went to see his colleague, Dr. Peter Reems. Reems is a buddy from college and is very close with Randall. He can't imagine Randall harming Amanda either, but he did mention some guy who was harassing him. Didn't have any details but said the guy's name was Sam."

"Okay, so what now?" Crosby asked.

Tommy chimed in. "We're pulling everything we can from Amanda's phone account to see what we can find there. We have a BOLO out for Hooper's car. Maroon Subaru Legacy. New York plates.

We'll be checking on associates and friends who might've seen him. We'd also like to get street-cam footage from whatever feed the NYPD can give us around Hooper's office or lot where he parks. Maybe we can get a bead on where he's heading when he leaves."

"And I'd like to run a background check on Randall Brock," Susan said. "See if anything pops out at us. The family attorney did a cursory check before the marriage, but I'd like to dive a little deeper. Maybe he's got some debts or owes money or something."

Crosby got up from the corner of the desk. "Okay. Get on it. And keep me posted."

28

He could hear the waves crashing down on the shore through the open windows in their deluxe suite. Randall got up from the bed and walked to the french doors, pulling them open and taking in the brilliant sky full of stars. A full moon was suspended over the tranquil ocean, and he could feel the salt air cool against his skin. He took a deep breath, smelling the very essence of the Amalfi Coast.

"What're you doing all the way over there?"

Randall glanced over his shoulder to find Amanda sitting up in bed. The silk sheet had fallen, and he could see her bare breasts in the moonlight. They'd been in Italy for six days, so far a different city each day. He was planning to ask her to marry him at the end of the trip. The ring was in his luggage.

"I'm just taking in the sights. It's so beautiful."

"Not as beautiful as you."

"Isn't that what I'm supposed to be saying?"

Amanda slipped out from beneath the sheets and joined him at the doorway. Her naked body pressed up against his, and they kissed slowly, deliberately. He loved her. There was no question about that. She made him feel like a complete person. He'd missed that since the Gary Anderson incident. He'd missed feeling like a human being.

She ran her fingers down his back and stopped when she hit the cluster of scars that filled the middle of his spine and spread down to the edge of his butt. Her other hand touched the scars on his stomach. "Who did this to you?" she asked.

Randall looked out at the ocean. "You know I can't talk about that."

"But you can. You can tell me anything."

"No, I can't. I'm sorry."

She leaned in and kissed up his arm, from his elbow to his shoulder. "I need to know everything about you if we're going to love each other unconditionally. We take the good and the bad. I'm ready. Whatever happened, you can tell me."

"No."

"I love you, Randall. And you love me. Tell me what happened."

Randall gently took her hands in his, pulling them away from his back and stomach. For a moment, he thought about telling her everything, but he couldn't. As soon as she learned the truth, she'd leave him, repulsed and ashamed that she'd let herself get this close to a monster. This was his chance to start over. He wasn't going to ruin it.

Amanda kissed the middle of his chest. "If you love me, you'll tell me who hurt you."

"One day," he lied. "Not yet."

He pulled her into him, their bodies warm against the chill of the night air outside. He stopped and took her head in his hands, spinning her toward the moonlight, the waves crashing outside. The light coming off the water hit her in just the right way, and suddenly he was holding Amanda's dead body. Her skin was blue. Her left eye was swollen, her nose broken. He tried to back away, but her joints had stiffened, and she wouldn't let go. No matter how hard he tried to run, she was with him. He couldn't let her go. She was part of him. She always would be.

Dead Amanda suddenly opened her eyes and looked at him. She parted her lips and let a single word slip through.

Why?

———

Randall sat up in bed, screaming as he tumbled onto the cold floor. He scrambled into the corner and curled up in a ball, searching the room for any sign of movement. The house was dark. There was no moonlight coming in the windows or waves crashing on the shore. Amanda wasn't there. It was a dream. A nightmare.

He picked himself up off the floor and took a steady breath, rubbing his eyes, discovering he'd been crying in his sleep. He stumbled out of the master bedroom to get a drink of water.

They'd been living together for about a year when they'd taken that trip to Italy. And he *had* asked her to marry him at the end of it, in Rome, right outside the Vatican. The woman he'd met by chance in a bar had turned out to be an angel who'd been sent to reconstruct his life and make him whole again. Would he disintegrate without her? Could he move on?

The clock on the nightstand read 2:37. Randall stood in the bathroom, looking at himself in the mirror. He reached behind him and rubbed the scars that littered his back like a brand. He lifted his shirt and felt his stomach. No matter how many things he changed around him, the scars would always be a reminder. There would never be an escape from his past. They would haunt him to his dying day.

In the stillness of the night, the garage door opened one floor below.

Randall turned away from the mirror, listening for the mudroom door, but there was no other sound. He ran back into his bedroom and snatched his phone from the nightstand before creeping downstairs and into the kitchen. With one finger on the emergency call button, he quietly grabbed a knife from the butcher block that was on the counter and tiptoed through the mudroom, stopping when he got to the door that led into the garage.

"Who's there?" he called out.

No one answered.

"I've called the police, and I'm armed."

Still no reply. No sound.

Randall gripped the knob and turned it, opening the door slowly and flipping on the light. The garage door was closed, which meant the noise he'd heard had been the door shutting. That also meant he'd left it open when he'd come home from the funeral. He couldn't remember. He walked down the three steps into the garage, knife poised, hand shaking slightly. No one was there. He was alone.

It had been placed on the hood of his BMW. A small metal box. At first he had no idea what it could be. He picked it up off the car and examined it, turning it over in his hand, finding the hinges and a latch to open it. He pulled off the top and peered inside. It was a set of keys. Keys to a Subaru.

Hooper drove a Subaru Legacy. Randall had seen it in some of the pictures he'd texted Amanda.

Sam had come and left the keys for him. He wasn't sure how he knew this, but he did. Unequivocally. He heard Amanda's voice in his head again.

Why?

29

Susan went downstairs, where her mother was already busy making breakfast for Casey and Tim. The twins sat in their booster seats, empty plates in front of them, a small pile of dry Cheerios to hold them at bay until the eggs were ready. Tim was paging through a book about trucks while Casey was staring out the window, watching the chickens as they walked around the yard aimlessly picking at things on the ground.

The night had gone by in a blur, and Susan had slept like the dead. She'd gotten home a little past midnight after she and Tommy had finished the reports. Beatrice had fallen asleep on the couch waiting for her, but Susan hadn't wanted to wake her. Instead, she'd shut off the television, put the extra-thick blanket over her mother, and headed upstairs. She'd taken a quick shower to wash the day off, watched the video of the twins in the holiday celebration, and gone to bed. Next thing she knew, her alarm was sounding, and a new day had begun.

"Hey, honey," Beatrice said as she fumbled with a pan. "I'm making eggs. We got a good haul this morning. You want some?"

"Sure."

"Late night last night."

"Nothing exciting. Lots of paperwork."

"Thanks for the blanket."

"Thanks for staying."

"Coffee's in the pot."

Susan poured herself a cup of coffee and looked out at the chickens. They appeared to be content, as far as she could tell, walking around the yard, pecking in the thin layer of snow that had accumulated on the grass overnight.

"Hey, guys, I saw your video last night. You were amazing. You sang so well. I'm sorry I missed it."

"Mommy," Casey said, clearly not sensing the guilt her mother was carrying about the holiday celebration. "We need a Christmas tree."

Susan turned to find her daughter staring intently back at her. There was no compromise in her little eyes.

"We'll get one, honey."

"But it's almost Christmas, and if we don't have a tree, Santa might skip our house, and if he skips our house, we won't get any presents! He's already mad that we only have the lights around the door. Santa needs to know where he's going."

"I want presents," Tim suddenly chimed in, his attention diverted from his book. "What if Santa can't find us?"

Casey was right. Susan hadn't thought about a tree or decorations since the plans with Eric had changed. She'd put up a single string of multicolored lights around the door just after Thanksgiving but hadn't done anything since.

"Mommy? A tree? Please?"

"We'll go this weekend. I promise. Should we bring Grandma?"

"Yes!" Tim shouted.

"Yes!" Casey agreed.

Susan looked over her shoulder toward her mother. "Mom?"

Beatrice was scrambling her eggs with the skill of a short-order cook. "I wouldn't miss it. Not with my two angels. Let's get that tree!"

The twins cheered, which made Susan giggle. She needed a morning like this. Sun shining outside, fresh snow lightly covering her world, her children and her mother close by, the smell of a healthy breakfast floating through the house. It was just about perfect.

Susan's cell phone rang. She walked into the foyer and snatched it from the small table where she also kept her keys and shield.

"This is Adler."

"Hey, it's Tommy."

"What's up? Where are you?"

"I'm at HQ. Got in early. Listen, we found Hooper Landsky."

She hopped over toys and tiny shoes scattered across the floor as she made her way into the living room to hear better. "That's great. Where was he?"

"I mean on the NYPD traffic footage."

"You got that already?"

"I know a few guys there from when my dad was on. Pulled a favor. We got him exiting his office building just before six o'clock three nights ago. Picked him up again entering the parking garage across the street from where we parked."

"We need to see if the garage has cams."

"Already called," Tommy replied. "No cameras on the inside. But get this. Right after Hooper walks down into the garage, we see Randall Brock pass by the entrance and turn the corner toward the rear of the place."

Susan stopped pacing. "You're joking."

"No joke. Next thing we see is Hooper's maroon Subaru Legacy leaving the garage and turning north on Madison Avenue. That's the last time we see him. No additional sightings of Randall either."

"Other cams?"

"Nothing yet. They're still looking."

"Jesus Christ."

"You think this is enough to bring Randall in?"

"It better well be. Can't get any charges filed, but we can at least have a talk with the guy. He's in the same vicinity as a missing person the day he goes missing while they're both potential suspects. We can bring him in."

"Good, then while you're doing that, I'll have a look around his property. Just a walk-around. Nothing on the inside since we have no warrant. I want to check out those woods behind his house."

"Okay, sounds good."

"I'll see you in a few."

Susan hung up the phone and walked back into the kitchen. Her mother was just dumping the eggs onto her plate. The twins were already eating.

"Was that work?" her mother asked.

Susan nodded. "Yeah. I hate to do this, but it looks like I'm going to have to get that to go. I think we might've caught a break."

30

Randall sat in the interrogation room alone. There was no clock on the wall, so he wasn't exactly sure how long he'd been in there. If he had to guess, he'd say a little more than an hour. The troopers who'd brought him in had told him Investigator Adler needed to go over a few things, but she was stuck in traffic, trying to get to the barracks. They'd sat him in the tiny windowless room, and that was the last time he'd had contact with anyone. He was, however, quite certain they were watching him through the camera that was mounted in the corner of the wall.

There was no two-way mirror like you saw in the movies. Randall tried his hardest not to look at the camera. He could imagine a group of detectives in a back room somewhere, watching him, coffees in their hands, anticipation in the air. He felt like an exhibit at a zoo. Well, let them watch. He was happy to answer any questions they had for him.

The door opened, and a young trooper stuck his head in. "Investigator Adler just got here," he said. "She should be in to see you in a few minutes."

"Thank you," Randall replied.

"You need anything? Coffee? Soda? Water? A snack?"

"I'm fine."

"You need the bathroom? Been sitting here awhile."

"No."

The trooper nodded. "Okay, hang tight. She'll be in shortly."

The door closed, and Randall fell back in his uncomfortable seat, looking up at the camera for the first time. By now Adler was getting briefed on what he'd been doing while he waited. Nothing. He hadn't been doing anything other than staring at the brown wall in front of him. She'd probably sent the young trooper in so she could adjust the volume on the recording equipment and make sure the video feed was working. He knew from experience how these things worked.

The doorknob turned, and as expected, the investigator walked in carrying a small pile of file folders and two bottled waters.

"Hello again," Randall said, purposefully tamping down the smile that would normally accompany such a greeting.

"Hello, Dr. Brock." She placed the folders on the desk and slid one of the waters over to him. "I know you said you didn't need anything, but you've been in here awhile."

"Thank you."

She sat down in the chair opposite him. Two was about the maximum number of bodies you could fit in the tight space.

"I'm sorry you've been waiting as long as you have. I was coming in from home and got caught in some traffic. Roadwork."

"Yes, they told me. Two of your troopers were waiting in my driveway when I returned from the supermarket. It's funny—I have friends and neighbors making meal after meal to show their love and sympathy for me and Amanda, but somehow no one thinks to bring milk or sugar or a bushel of bananas. I have more lasagna, cake, pie, and prime rib than I could ever eat, but when it comes to milk, eggs, salt, and cereal, I'm on my own."

"You're right. I never thought of that."

"Anyway, the men who picked me up told me you had news about Amanda?"

"Yes," the investigator replied. "And I wanted to go over a few things with you regarding your wife's accident. Details are still a bit unclear, so I'm hoping you can provide the clarity we're looking for."

"I'll certainly do my best."

She placed her elbows on the table and cleared her throat. "When we were out on the back porch at the funeral home, you asked me if there was suspicion around Amanda's death. At the time I told you I couldn't talk about an open investigation."

"I remember."

"I'm going to be honest with you now. Yes. There's suspicion around her death. We've ruled her death a homicide."

The words stopped him, and although he'd suspected as much with the way the police had been acting, the confirmation was stunning nonetheless. He rubbed eyes that were suddenly tired and heavy. He wanted to go home.

Amanda was murdered, and I know who did it. I saw the whole thing. I can help you.

Adler opened the first file. "Our autopsy results show Amanda was dead before her car ever veered off Route 202. The medical examiner found that several of the vertebrae at the base of her skull were broken, which we believe was the real cause of death. Someone hit her with a blunt object like a bat or tire iron or heavy stick. Maybe even a pipe. Something like that."

"My god."

"Can you retrace your steps that night, after you left the award ceremony?"

Randall looked at her. An anger began to boil within. The confirmation that Amanda was murdered was already too much to handle, but the fact that this woman could think he'd had anything to do with killing the love of his life made him furious. "So you think I did it."

"I didn't say that. I'm simply asking you to retrace your steps that night so we can continue to put the pieces of this puzzle together."

"How many others have you had in this room to ask such questions?"

"You're the first."

"Because I'm the prime suspect."

Adler offered a reassuring smile. "Please, Dr. Brock. Help us reconstruct that night. If you want us to find your wife's killer, we need your help."

"Okay," Randall replied. He looked up at the camera and could feel the eyes upon him. The dull, familiar ache in the back of his head began to emerge. "As I've stated several times before, I left the award ceremony early because I had some work to do at my office. You should call the school. They have cameras set up in the parking lots. You'll see my car. I was there all night."

"Yes, we're working on that."

"I called Amanda a few hours after I got to the office to make sure she got home okay, but there was no answer. I left a message at home and on her cell. The next morning you arrived and told me she'd been in a fatal car accident, and you brought me to the medical examiner's office to identify her body."

"You called her cell."

"Yes."

"She had her phone with her?"

Randall paused for a moment, his head swirling. "Yes, she always had her phone with her."

Susan made a few notes, then opened a second folder, looked up, and met his eyes. "Did you know Amanda was having an affair?"

Randall grimaced. "Only after. I found texts and emails on Amanda's phone. I saw one of the texts come in from her lover, and that prompted me to look into the phone to see who he was."

"Did you have any idea this affair might've been happening beforehand? Any strange behavior from your wife? Anything that would give you a hint that she was seeing someone?"

"Nothing," Randall replied firmly. "I never suspected a thing. As far as I was concerned, we were happily married. Needless to say, it was quite the shock to find out about her affair. Amanda never seemed unhappy or unfulfilled. I still can't understand it."

"Do you know with whom your wife was having this affair?"

"Not at the time. I came to learn his name was Hooper Landsky."

Adler pulled a photograph from the folder and slid it across the table. "Is this Hooper Landsky?"

"Yes."

"How do you know what he looks like?"

"There were photos on Amanda's phone."

"Have you ever met him in person?"

"No."

More pictures were extracted from the folder and placed side by side in front of him.

"These are pictures taken from the traffic and security cameras near Hooper's office and parking garage on Manhattan." Adler pointed to two of the photos. "Is that you, Dr. Brock?"

Randall looked at the pictures. They showed him walking in front of Hooper's garage and turning down a small alley that led around the back. He tried to sit still but could feel his body start to tremble. "Yes, that's me. I went down to his office to confront him but decided against it at the last minute. I guess when I was actually faced with the notion of walking up to him, I realized it was pointless. Amanda was dead, so why bother calling him out? What would be the point in knowing why Amanda was sleeping with him? There was nothing I could do to fix it. I think the grief pushed me there, but in the end, I just went home."

"You just stated you never met him in person."

"I didn't. I watched him from afar and never made contact."

More silence.

"Wait," Randall said, suddenly sitting up and pointing at one of the pictures. "Do you think Hooper could've hurt Amanda? Do you think he could have anything to do with her accident?"

Adler ignored the question. "Were you aware your wife was planning on filing for divorce?"

Randall slumped back down in his seat. "Yes. And I'm aware that she had drafts of her will made that cut me out of it and left me with a small alimony payment. Both of these things, along with the affair, I learned after the accident."

"After the accident."

Randall chuckled, shaking his head. He wanted to jump up out of his seat and scream, but he knew that would only give Adler the excuse she needed to paint him as someone capable of killing his wife. Instead, he took a breath and spoke slowly. The pain in his head was increasing, squeezing his skull. "I can see what you're doing. I'm not an idiot. Amanda was having an affair. Motive. Amanda was going to divorce me. Motive. Amanda was changing her will. Motive. I understand, but I can assure you I had nothing to do with what happened to her. You can check with the university. I was in my office. You can bring a polygraph in here. Whatever you need, I'm willing to comply, but do it quickly so you can catch the person responsible for her death." He gestured angrily toward the photographs with a wave of his hand. "Why isn't he sitting in here?"

Adler looked at him. "Mr. Landsky has been missing since the morning these photos were taken. He walks into a dark garage after work. You're seen around the perimeter of the garage, and Hooper hasn't been heard from since. How do you explain that?"

The room suddenly seemed eerily quiet.

You're a suspect.

Randall looked up at the camera and reached for his water. Thoughts began to come, one after the other, until he couldn't focus on a single thing. Hooper was missing. What did that mean? What was happening?

"Dr. Brock, can you explain how Hooper Landsky could go missing on the same day you're photographed near the last place he was seen?"

He gulped and shook his head. "No. I can't."

"Do you know where Mr. Landsky is?"

"I don't. I swear."

"Okay." Susan gathered the pictures and placed them back in the folder. "Last thing. You said you learned about Amanda's affair from the pictures on her phone."

"That's right."

"Dr. Brock, how did you come to possess your wife's phone?"

The question hung in the air as silence enveloped the room. Randall closed his eyes, knowing he'd been caught in a lie.

Secrets.

He cleared his throat, searching for the answer as Sam's words echoed in his mind.

Amanda was murdered, and I know who did it. I saw the whole thing. I can help you.

"I don't . . ."

"You said your wife always has her phone with her. In fact, you called her phone and left a message to ensure she got home from the party that night."

"Yes, but—"

"Now all of a sudden you have her phone and discovered proof of an affair on that phone. Funny coincidence, wouldn't you say?"

I know everything.

"I-I found her phone at the house," Randall stuttered. "I thought she had it with her, but I guess she didn't. It was still in the charger at the house. Maybe she forgot it or didn't want to bring it to the ceremony with her. I didn't know her phone was at the house because I went straight to the office."

Susan opened the first file folder again, scanning through the pages. "But we found her charger at the scene. We got her charger. No phone."

"Her phone was in my charger."

"I see."

Again, the room fell silent. Randall could feel sweat slipping down his back. "I didn't kill Amanda."

"Okay."

"Are you charging me?"

"No."

"Then I can go?"

"Yes. You can go."

He got up out of his seat and made his way numbly toward the door.

"I'm sorry," Adler said. "I lied. I do have one more question."

Randall stopped, his hand on the knob. "Yes?"

"Who's Sam?"

The name shot through him like a bolt of lightning, but Randall stayed calm by squeezing the door handle and focusing on the folders that were still on the table. "I have no idea."

"Are you sure? I ask because when we saw Dr. Reems, he told us to ask you about him."

"He must be mistaken. I don't know a Sam."

Adler smiled. "Okay. Thanks for your time."

Randall pulled the door open and stepped out into the hall. His head was pounding. He had to get outside. Peter had told the police about Sam. How could he do that? How could he betray his trust like that when Peter had been the only person he could count on? Things were beginning to spin out of his control. He felt lost, unhinged from a world he'd thought he had a handle on. How could this be?

You're a suspect.

I know everything.

31

Tommy jumped up from his desk when Susan walked back onto the floor.

"Hey, I just got back," he said. "Watched the tail end of your interview on the screen. Nice job."

"Thanks."

"You scared him good with that phone question. He walked right into it. And the question about Sam was a nice touch. He's hiding something for sure."

Susan nodded. "Looks that way." She walked toward her desk. "You find anything at his house?"

"Maybe. I obviously couldn't go inside without a warrant, so I looked through some windows. Nothing out of place. I walked the perimeter of the property and poked around in the woods behind the house. Everything is super well manicured. I guess the way the house is positioned, the sun hits the backyard for most of the day, because there was hardly any snow back there. I could see that the grass was cut evenly, hedges were trimmed, mulch had some snow in it, but there weren't even dead weeds in the beds."

"Okay, so he has a good landscaper."

"Right," Tommy replied. "But then I come across this patch of dirt, about three feet by three feet against the side of the house, just down from the deck. Freshly dug. Kind of sloppy. The dirt was still soft and dark from being turned. It caught my eye because everything else was so perfect."

"What could that be?"

"I have no idea, but I think we should check it out."

Crosby came out of his office. "Good work," he said to Susan.

"Thank you, sir."

"Couldn't hold him on what we have, but I think you shook him enough to let him know we're not screwing around. We'll keep an eye on him now and see where he goes. Hopefully something will bend in our favor. You still think he's clean?"

"I don't know what to think. Corolla here might have something."

Tommy reiterated his story to Crosby about the patch of dirt he'd found in Randall's yard. "If we could hold him for twenty-four hours, we could get a chance to look into that spot. Maybe we could even have a peek inside the house if we could get a judge to sign off."

Crosby shook his head. "We don't have anything concrete enough to hold him. And we sure as hell don't have enough to get a warrant."

"He's at the garage at the same time Hooper is, and Hooper hasn't been seen since," Tommy replied. "His wife was killed, and her accident was intentional to cover it up. Randall has her phone. I don't see how he's not our prime suspect."

"I think he is," Susan said. "But what we have is all circumstantial, and none of it will stick. Maybe she did forget her phone. Maybe he was going to confront Hooper and chickened out. Nothing we have will work with the kind of lawyers this guy can afford. That's just the way it is."

Crosby handed Susan a folder. "These are pictures from the security-camera feed from Quarim the night of Amanda Brock's accident."

She took the folder and opened it. "Anything?"

"We see him parking the car in the lot, entering the science building a little past ten thirty. His car remains in its spot for the entirety of the night. We picked up another feed from the entrance to the science building, and we can see him enter. He doesn't leave until you walk in to get him. There are no cameras inside the building, but this is pretty clean. From what we can see, Dr. Brock has his alibi."

"Damn."

"If there was another angle to hold him, I'd play it, but we're stuck."

"For now," Susan said, dropping the folder onto her desk. "We're onto something here. Just have to keep digging."

32

It was close to nine o'clock when Susan walked out of the barracks. Tommy had finished filing his paperwork from the property walk-around earlier, and she'd sent him home to get some rest. They'd been moving at a good clip since the investigation began, and she needed her partner sharp. There was no sense in him sitting around while she typed her way through the interview transcripts and uploads.

The kids would most likely be asleep by the time she got home. Another day lost. She made a promise to herself to do something fun with them once the case was over. Maybe a trip to Rockefeller Center to see the giant tree and go ice-skating. Or an afternoon at the movies. Or lunch at Chuck E. Cheese's with an endless supply of tokens for all the games. Something to reconnect them. Something to make her feel better.

It was snowing. Just flurries for now. She looked up at the lights as she made her way toward her car and marveled at how beautiful the flakes looked dancing in the glow, swirling and flipping around one another, then vanishing as they fell from the light back into the darkness. An express train heading south flew by in a rush, then was gone, and it was quiet again. Peaceful.

Perfect.

She noticed a figure standing in the shadows at the edge of the parking lot, near the roller hockey rink. He was unmoving, seemingly staring at her, but she couldn't be certain. His face was hidden beneath a large hood. He stood completely still, positioned on the opposite side of the lot from where she'd parked her car. She figured it to be a man based on his size and girth but couldn't be sure.

She casually reached under her jacket and unsnapped the holster that was fastened on her belt. The guy was probably harmless. Most likely homeless or had come from the VA down the road. He also could've been a day laborer who'd just gotten dropped off, but she was the only one outside and needed to ensure her safety. She gripped the handle of her Beretta, ready to extract it if needed but not wanting to jump to any conclusions.

"Hey!" she called, her voice booming in the quiet surroundings. "You need something?"

The figure remained.

"You need help? I'm state police. Can I help you with something?"

The figure turned and walked farther into the darkness, back through an alley that she knew would lead him to a twenty-four-hour gas station. As quickly as he'd appeared, he was gone. Like the snowflakes in the light.

She climbed into her car and started it up, flipping her wipers on to get rid of the snow that had accumulated on the windshield.

At this time of night, and with the light flurries falling, Buchanan was desolate. It only took her about ten minutes to drive across town, through Peekskill, and reach the base of Route 9, which would eventually wind her up a mountain road and into Fishkill. She took the curves carefully in case the snow had made the roads slick, but so far the pavement was just wet and too warm for any kind of buildup. She activated her Bluetooth and listened as her cell phone connected to the house.

"Hello?"

"Hey, Ma. I'm on my way. Just left."

"Okay, honey. You eat?"

Susan's stomach immediately rumbled. It wasn't until the suggestion of food was made that she realized she'd been starving. "No. You want me to stop and get something?"

"No need. I have leftover beef stew for you on the stove."

"Beef stew on a snowy night? You're the best."

"Casey and Tim just went to bed."

"Yeah, I figured."

"You want me to try and see if they're asleep yet? You can say good night."

"No, that's okay. I'll see them in the morning. I don't want you to wake them if they already dozed off."

A set of headlights emerged from a curve in the distance. Susan noticed them and flipped her rearview mirror up to cut down on the glare. They were the only cars on the road.

"Is it snowing down there?" Beatrice asked.

"Just flurries. How about at the house?"

"Same here, but I heard it might pick up overnight."

The headlights were quickly coming up behind her. Each time they disappeared behind a curve in the road, they would reemerge faster than the previous time. Susan kept an eye on them as she drove.

"I want you to sleep at my house tonight. No sense risking it if it's icy."

"I already have the bed made for me. Way ahead of you."

The headlights were coming now. Susan eased her foot off the accelerator and pulled halfway off to the shoulder, allowing the car to pass. Her tires thumped along the indentations of pavement that were designed to alert a sleepy driver that they were veering from their lane. She watched as the headlights screamed up behind her, only inches from her bumper. The interior of her car flooded with light.

"Honey, you there?"

Susan rolled down her window and motioned for the driver to go around, but the car remained behind her.

"Honey?"

"Mom, I'll see you in a few."

"Everything okay?"

"Yeah, just some jackass tailgating me. I'll see you soon."

She disconnected the call and placed both hands on the wheel, gripping it tighter as she accelerated. The headlights kept pace, speeding up as she did. The mountain road twisted and turned every few feet, the blacktop growing slicker as her altitude climbed.

What is this guy's problem?

The headlights were on her, the driver unrelenting. Susan let go of the wheel with one hand and dug into her pocket, coming away with her shield. She held it up so the driver behind her would know she was a cop. The chrome of the badge glistened in the headlights, but the car remained only inches from hers. Its horn began to blare.

What the hell?

Susan placed both hands back on the steering wheel and peered into the rearview mirror. She pressed on her brakes and used a combination of her brake lights and the other car's headlights to try and get a look at the driver. She couldn't see a face, but she could see the one distinguishing feature that brought her back to the figure in the parking lot who'd been standing in the darkness, watching her.

The driver was wearing a large hood.

Susan yanked the Taurus farther onto the shoulder and turned her head around to see if the car was following. It was too difficult with the headlights on her, but it appeared as though the car had slowed a bit.

Who is this guy?

The right front tire suddenly exploded, sending Susan lurching forward as she temporarily lost control. She skidded to a stop and could see the tire pressure warning light on the dashboard come on. The shoulder was filled with jagged rocks and small boulders protruding from the edge of the mountain. She must've swerved when she was looking behind her and hit one of the sharp edges of the rock. She pulled all the way over and placed the car in park, looking in her rearview mirror, her heart beating rapidly in her chest.

The car was stopped about fifty yards away, headlights aimed directly at her, half on the shoulder and half on the road. Susan reached for her Beretta as she slowly opened the car door and stepped out, gun down by her waist but ready if need be. She didn't know what this was, so she had to proceed cautiously. The only two people on the dark mountain road were her and the hooded figure behind the wheel of the other car.

The horn started blowing again, the noise exploding in the otherwise peaceful surroundings. Susan raised her weapon into a shooting position and waited. When the horn finally ceased, she took a breath and steadied herself.

"New York State Police!" she cried. "Turn off your headlights and your engine! Now!"

The car remained as it was.

"Turn off your lights and engine!"

She took a single step forward, and as she did, the car suddenly backed away, tires squealing, smoke rising from the burning rubber. It flew about thirty yards, then spun around in one single motion, taking off back down the mountain, its taillights giving the dark surroundings an ominous red glow. As it turned, she could see the hooded figure behind the wheel. Without the headlights blinding her, she was also able to see the make and model of the car. It was a maroon Subaru Legacy.

Hooper Landsky.

The Subaru disappeared, and Susan dove back into her car, grabbing her phone and hitting her emergency button.

"Nine-one-one, what's your emergency?"

"This is State Police Investigator Susan Adler, badge ID number four-four-two-seven, Troop K. I need a unit to track a BOLO on Route Nine South, near mile marker forty-three. Late model Subaru Legacy, maroon in color. I just spotted him but cannot pursue. I have a blown tire. I need this ASAP. Suspect is Hooper Landsky, wanted in connection with a homicide. Proceed with caution."

"Ten-four. We're dispatching backup, and I'll route roadside assistance for you."

Susan hung up and turned on the flashlight app on her phone. She walked around to the front of the Taurus and examined the flat front tire; the rim was actually bent a little. She shined the light against the base of the mountain and could see the rocks protruding at different angles and edges. She stared back in the direction in which the Subaru had fled, waiting for it to return, its headlights bearing down on her, its horn screaming. It was only at that moment that she realized she was still holding her weapon and placed it back in its holster. But she kept the snap disengaged. Just in case.

33

Randall sat in a chair facing Peter, who was behind his desk. It was early. The sun hadn't cleared the horizon yet. The campus remained deserted for the holiday break, the halls quiet, the building itself otherwise dormant. Peter sat, one leg perched atop the other, his hands folded in front of his face as if he were praying. Perhaps he was praying, Randall thought. Praying that all of their sacrifices and dedication and time spent working on one of the most critical scientific breakthroughs in decades didn't come down to the question of whether Randall could really have killed his wife. Where would they be then? The headlines and the crime itself would be too much to overcome.

It was Peter who finally broke through the uneasy silence.

"The police came to see me. The same investigator who was at Amanda's wake."

"Adler."

"Yes. And her partner."

"I know. She told me she went to see you. She also told me you mentioned Sam."

Peter nodded, looking away from his friend. "I didn't tell them anything else."

"Why did you tell them about Sam?"

"Because if this guy knows something about what happened to Amanda, he needs to be brought in and questioned. He's probably the one who hurt her."

"Are you sure that's the only reason?"

"Of course."

"You don't believe Sam exists. You think it's all in my head. Maybe you told the investigator to look into Sam hoping she'd find holes in my story."

"You're being ridiculous," Peter snapped. He spun his chair around so he was facing out the window; his back was to Randall. "I believe you about Sam. I told the police about him so they could find him."

"But we can't say anything. Not yet. You know that. If the police bring him in and he talks about William, all of this goes away. The study ends because of what I did in my past." Randall leaned forward in his seat. "We're trying to change the world with what we're uncovering here, Peter. We're trying to upend the face of psychiatry and give people a new shot at being cured. Do you really want to risk all that?"

"No. Of course not. But that's not the only issue. These setbacks scare me. What if we don't know enough about what we're doing in these studies? What if Lienhart is right? What if we're making things worse?"

"We're not."

Peter spun back around. "You've been brought in for questioning. That means the police suspect you. They think you killed Amanda, and they didn't even know this Sam guy existed."

"I didn't kill her."

"I know that. I believe you. It's the police who need convincing. We have to tell them about Sam so they can put their energy into finding out who this person is. Forget the study. Forget the work we put in. None of that matters when it comes to you and Amanda. There are consequences to our actions, good and bad. I can't risk the bad any longer. I won't."

"No," Randall replied. "We're seeing this through. You and me. I'm not going to let this study die because of what happened to Amanda. There's too much at stake. I'll handle the police and Sam, but I need you to promise me you won't mention him again."

"You're making a mistake."

"I'm not. I know exactly what I'm doing."

Peter rubbed his tired eyes. "Fine."

Randall got up and walked toward the chairs that were set up across the room. "We have Jerry today, right?"

"Yeah."

"I'll start prepping the video equipment."

———

The room was dark, shades drawn, building quiet. A floor lamp was turned on in the corner, offering enough light for the video while remaining dim enough to make the subject feel comfortable.

"Said she already got enough friends."

"What did you do then?"

"I went home and had a few beers. Watched the game. Then there's a knock at the door. I had no idea who it could be because it was late. Real late. I answer it and this guy is standing there with this smile on his face, but that smile ain't right, you know? And his eyes. I can tell he's crazy, but at the same time there's this vibe about him that makes me calm. He holds up a picture of the girl from the dentist's office. She's in her bedroom, lying in bed, under the covers."

"Who was this man, Jerry?"

"That's what I asked, but he ignores me. Tells me to come down to his car. Says he has a surprise waiting for me. So I went. We get out to his car, and he opens the trunk. Guess what's inside?"

"What?"

"Guess."

"You need to tell me. I can't guess. That's not how this works."

"The snobby bitch from the dentist's office is hog tied in the trunk. She's still in the same nightgown as in the picture. I could tell from the shoulder straps that were sticking out from the covers. She's shivering because she got nothing else on. It's cold, but this guy didn't care. He tells me he grabbed her and brought her to me as a present."

"What did this man look like?"

"Hard to tell. Kind of tall, I guess. He had this long coat he wore that made him look bigger than he was. And his eyes were, like . . . black."

"Who is this man?"

"I kept asking, but all he kept saying was he's a friend. I felt like that was the truth. I felt safe with him. Like I knew he had everything under control and I didn't have to worry about anything. I trusted him, but I ain't never seen him before in my life."

"What happened next?"

"We carried her into the woods. She's screaming and thrashing, but this guy was strong, and it didn't faze him. She was screaming at the top of her lungs, but this guy was relaxed, which made me relax. Normally I would've put a gag on her or taped her mouth shut, but if he didn't care, I didn't care. We walked about a mile until we came to a small clearing. The man dropped her onto the ground, and I got real close. I told her that this is what happens to uppity bitches who think they're better than everyone else. She was crying, but the screaming stopped. She knew what was going to happen."

"Did you have any sense of wanting to walk away or stop what you'd started?"

"No way. Plus, now I'm good because it's not my decision to stop or keep going. It's this other guy. I leaned against a tree and watched while he dumped the can of gasoline all over her. She started screaming again, begging for her life. She tried to get up and run, but he just kicked her back down. Man, I could smell the fumes. She's trying to get herself untied, but she has no leverage. I shouted out to her and said she could've lived if she'd been nice to me. Our eyes meet for a second; then the man lights a match and drops it on her."

"You could've stopped him."

"Didn't want to. Not my sin. Not this time. And *whoosh*, her entire body went up. Flames everywhere. She was screaming, trying to get away from the fire, but I could smell her flesh burning. And there was my friend, standing where I used to stand, taking it all in. We watched until she was dead, then turned and walked back out of the woods to the road. The man explained that I don't have to be the one to commit the sins anymore. He said he would come and take care of it for me. I feel like I'm free now. There's no other way to put it. He's sacrificed his soul to save mine."

Jerry looked toward the camera. "I think I might be cured."

———

Jerry was gone. Randall sat across from Peter. The shades in the office were still drawn, the building itself still asleep.

Peter closed his notebook and tossed it on the table beside him. "We can't show Lienhart this. He'll scrap the entire study. This is further regression."

"Maybe not. Maybe this is Jerry's first step toward distancing himself from the murder. Maybe the man eventually disappears and he has no more fantasy."

"Who is this other guy in Jerry's fantasy?"

"I have no idea."

Peter sighed, and for the first time, Randall thought he could see real fear in his friend's eyes. "I don't know what's going on. But it's not good."

34

As soon as she crested the small hill leading up to the house, Susan could see Randall Brock wasn't home. Two of the three garage doors were open, each bay empty but for a small, sporty convertible parked and covered in the middle one. She pulled up and parked at the edge of the flagstone path that led to the front door. When she shut off the engine, she noticed the complete silence that enveloped her and thought, for the first time, about how alone she was up there.

The night had gone by in a blur. By the time she got her tire fixed, filed her report with the responding officers, and got home, it was pushing midnight. She decided not to tell her mother about the hooded man who had essentially forced her off the road and instead explained about the tire and went to bed. The responding units spent the rest of their shifts searching for the car, but the Subaru had all but disappeared by the time anyone began looking for it.

There were no heels that clicked on the path as Susan made her way up to the door. Not this time. She was wearing boots with rubber soles, and they were quiet for a reason. But she'd forgotten a hat and gloves when she'd left the house, so she stuffed her hands in her pockets until she reached the porch.

Tommy was back at the barracks running down CCTV footage and traffic-cam data from both the NYPD and the Westchester County Police to see if he could pick up Hooper's Subaru coming out of the city or in the general vicinity of the barracks and her neighborhood the night before. Tommy had volunteered to make the calls for footage and start going over them, and she was more than happy to let him grunt his way through it. She had other things in mind.

Susan knocked on the front door. When there was no answer, she rang the doorbell and then made her way up and down the length of the porch, strolling casually in case any of the neighbors were watching. She glanced inside the two windows she knew looked in on the formal living room. The house was empty. She rang the bell one last time, then hopped back down the steps and walked around the side of the house, opposite from where her car sat in front of the garage.

Tommy had been right. The property was immaculate. Shrubs had been covered with burlap to protect them from the snow and unforgiving winds that whipped at this elevation. Gates had been tied down so they didn't swing against the horse fencing. Despite the fact that three-quarters of the property was surrounded by forest, not a single leaf was on the grass or in the flower beds. She could still see the lines the mower had made cutting the lawn. A stone firepit had been constructed next to an oversized deck that looked out in both directions, toward the woods and out over the valley and farmland below. It was breathtaking.

Susan walked to the edge of the house, right before the deck began. Just as Tommy had mentioned, there was no snow back there, and she could see the three-foot-by-three-foot patch of dirt. It was freshly dug and definitely sloppy compared to the rest of the acreage. She pressed the tip of her boot into the dirt, and it sank about a quarter of an inch. In this weather it should've been frozen.

The rest of the land held nothing of suspicion. She walked around the outer perimeter toward the woods, then came up and back, closing the distance toward the house and inspecting as much ground as she could. When she was done, she hiked back into the forest for a bit, but the leaves and snow covered everything back there, and it was impossible to see what might've been hidden underneath. Finally, she came around the end of the house where the garage was and stood in front of the two open doors. The end of the tour.

The wind whipped the back of her legs and almost pushed her over. She stumbled forward and found herself at the edge of the garage, looking in. The garage appeared to be typical. A tennis ball hung at the end of each bay to ensure no one drove into the long workbench that lined the back wall. Wire shelving was suspended from the ceiling and filled with beach chairs, umbrellas, ski equipment, camping gear, and storage boxes. On the side of the workbench, mops, brooms, scrub brushes, and other cleaning materials were hung on a pegboard. Under the board were cubbies full of boots and shoes and a single pair of pink galoshes. The garage was just as well kept as the yard and the house. Everything had its place.

Except that patch of dirt.

She walked inside the garage and was immediately swallowed by shadow. She made her way toward the workbench to examine the tools hanging on display as if she were in a hardware store, browsing before making a purchase. As she got closer, she noticed something lying on the bench, in between the table saw and straightedge ruler. It was out in the open, unhidden, next to a small metal box. The set of keys looked as if they had been tossed there and forgotten. She bent down to get a closer look and saw the Subaru logo on a single oversized ignition key. The blue sparkle key chain had *HL Architects* engraved in gold on one side.

HL.

They were Hooper Landsky's keys. Hooper's keys to his Subaru Legacy.

"Investigator Adler?"

Susan spun around to find Randall Brock standing just inside the first bay. His skin was pale in the semidarkness, his eyes almost glowing in the dying light. A tan raincoat had been draped over his shoulders, but he hadn't put his arms through the sleeves. His hands were in his pants pockets.

"D-Dr. Brock," Susan stammered. "I didn't hear you pull up."

Randall looked at her for a moment, his gaze searching for something. A weakness? An opportunity? She couldn't tell. "I had to park it on the hill. Couldn't get past with your car blocking my way."

Susan pointed. "I'm going to need you to take your hands out of your pockets. Slowly."

"Excuse me?"

"Your hands. I can't have them in your pockets while we're talking. Take them out of your pockets, and put your arms down to your sides. Please."

Randall pursed his lips and looked as if he were about to say something. Instead, he pulled his hands out of his pockets and let them fall to his sides. When he did, his coat slipped off his shoulders and landed behind him. "What's going on?" he asked. "What are you doing in my garage?"

Susan turned all the way around and pressed her back against the workbench. She reached behind her and gripped the edge of it to use as leverage if she needed it. If he made a move, she could use the bench to hoist herself for a kick or to jump out of the way. She didn't want to draw her gun just yet. No need to escalate things.

"I knocked. There was no answer."

"I was at the office. Peter and I were working."

"I thought maybe you were out back, so I went around the house. Nice property."

"Investigator Adler, can you please tell me what you're doing here? Why do I get the feeling you're frightened or tense? Why are my hands at my sides? What's going on?"

Susan took a breath to steady her voice. "Can you explain what that hole is for in the back, near the deck?"

Randall's brow furrowed; then he shook his head. "I don't know of any hole."

"It was just dug. Couldn't be more than a few days old. You bury something back there?"

"Of course not. Maybe my landscaper did. You'd have to ask him. I don't know anything about a hole, for god's sake."

Susan nodded, motioning toward the keys behind her. "Okay. Then maybe you can tell me why the keys to Hooper Landsky's Subaru Legacy are here on your workbench?"

Randall took a step forward.

"Do not advance. Stay where you are."

He stopped, looking past her toward the workbench. She could see from his expression that he saw the keys. His eyes narrowed. His neck turned red. "It isn't what you think."

"Then what is it?"

"I really can't say."

"Yeah." Susan took her phone out of her pocket and dialed the barracks. She waited for the connection to go through, her eyes locked on Randall. "This is Adler. I need an expedited search warrant on Randall Brock's property. Investigator Corolla has the information and address. I'm here now with the owner, and I'm gonna need backup. Owner will remain on the property during the search. I need that warrant yesterday. Go."

Randall took another step forward, this time his hand coming up. "You don't need a warrant," he said. "This is a misunderstanding."

Susan dropped her phone and slipped her gun out of its holster. She held it down in front of her so Randall could see it. "I told you to stay put."

"This is a mistake."

"Then explain it to me."

Randall lowered his head and closed his eyes.

"You and I are going to stay here until my backup comes," Susan explained. "When they do, we'll go inside so we don't freeze to death. You stay there, and I'll stay here. No one touches anything. No one moves. You play this nice and easy, and things will go smooth for you. Got it?"

"This is crazy. This is all crazy."

"Do you understand?"

"Yes."

"Where were you last night?"

"Here."

"You got any proof of that?"

"No."

"Too bad."

It wasn't long before the sound of police sirens could be heard in the distance, down by the farmhouse, making their way toward them.

35

Two local units from the North Salem Police Department were the first to arrive at Randall's house. They came roaring up the driveway, lights on, sirens wailing, about five minutes after Susan called it in. She and Randall had remained in the garage, both of them shivering from the cold wind that blew through. The officers approached with weapons drawn until Susan instructed both men to holster them. After things calmed, the officers escorted Randall into the house with Susan in tow. One officer guarded the front door while the other stood at the door leading to the mudroom. Susan and Randall each took a seat at the dining room table, sitting opposite one another, their hands in plain sight, their gazes locked.

A trooper from the neighboring town of Somers arrived, and it was then Randall asked for permission to call his attorney. Susan agreed, and the trooper retrieved Randall's phone from the coat that had fallen on the garage floor.

It took an hour for the warrant to arrive. During that time, Randall made the necessary calls to hire an attorney who had the skills to navigate what had become a suddenly perilous situation. He'd called Bernie Hayman, but Bernie didn't know anyone with enough power or cachet in a scenario such as the one Randall was facing—a trial lawyer specializing in search warrants and potential murder charges was too far out of his league.

Randall's next move had been a call to Wilbur Fitzgerald, the chairman of Amanda's foundation. Of course he knew someone, and the result of Wilbur's connections was Sidney Windsor from the law firm of Finn, Dystel, and Rust. Susan knew the firm. It was one of the most prestigious firms in the country and specialized in criminal law defense for high-profile clients. Mr. Windsor arrived within minutes of the warrant.

The plan was to sweep the house in a grid pattern, going room to room, careful not to destroy what might be potential evidence. Susan had a small team of four North Salem officers inside the house searching through the grid and three state police out back digging up the patch of dirt.

Tommy arrived after the search had already begun. He'd gone straight to the backyard and hadn't even announced himself until she'd texted him, asking where he was. He hadn't turned up any new hits from the surveillance cameras on Manhattan, by the barracks, or near her neighborhood. The Subaru, and Hooper Landsky, remained at large.

Susan stretched in her seat and cracked her neck. The silence in the dining room was heavy. Sidney Windsor sat to Randall's right and instructed him not to talk to any of the officers about anything. As time dragged on, the quiet became a distraction.

"You mind if I ask your client a question?" Susan asked, motioning toward Sidney. "All this silence is too much."

Sidney Windsor was the stereotypical high-profile lawyer. Tall, forties, tan even though it was the middle of winter. He wore a dark-gray suit that was tailored to perfection and Italian shoes that most likely cost more than what the officers around them took home each week. His voice-activated digital recorder had been placed on the table, its red light blinking, in case someone decided to speak.

"I don't think that would be a good idea," he replied.

"Come on. You've had that thing recording nothing for like a half hour. One question."

"No."

"I can ask it here, or I can ask it at the barracks."

"Intimidation tactics already? Charming."

"One question."

"Fine," Sidney said, adjusting his recorder. "One."

Susan looked at Randall. "Dr. Brock, can you tell me where you were last night?"

Randall cleared his throat. "I already told you. I was home."

"And this morning?"

"I told you that as well. Dr. Reems and I had a session at the Quarim campus. For our study."

"What time did you leave for your session?"

"Around seven thirty. The session was scheduled for nine, lasted for an hour; then Dr. Reems and I debriefed and filed our notes. I came home, and here we are."

"Did anyone come to see you last night?"

"No."

"Did you talk to anyone on the phone?"

"No."

Sidney knocked on the dining room table. "That's more than one question."

Susan ignored him. "Why do you have Hooper Landsky's car keys?"

"Don't answer that."

"Where is Hooper Landsky?"

"That's enough, Investigator. No more."

"Is Hooper in on this, or did you do something to him? Where is he, Randall? Tell me where he is."

Sidney slammed his hand on the table. "That's enough!"

Susan smiled, pointing at the attorney. "I want to ask your client why he's in possession of Subaru car keys the day after a maroon Subaru Legacy tried to run me off the road on my way home from work. But you can ask him instead."

"I'll do no such thing."

Randall stuttered. "I . . . I was home. Asleep. I don't know anything about a Subaru Legacy."

"Don't speak," Sidney said. "Not a word."

There was a knock on the patio door, and Susan turned. A trooper was on the deck, motioning for her to come outside. She nodded and pointed to one of the North Salem officers, who was in between the dining room and kitchen. "Watch these two," she said. "No one leaves this table."

———

It felt as though the temperature had dropped another ten degrees when Susan stepped out onto the deck. She stuffed her hands in her pockets and walked to where the officers were gathered. Tommy was wearing a bright-orange parka with the hood pulled up and tied. She had to smile when she saw him.

"That coat makes you look like an Oompa-Loompa."

"Maybe, but I'm warm. And the color has its advantages."

"Yeah?"

"When I go sledding and skiing, I never get lost in the crowd. My friends can always find me. Ski patrol, too, if things go sideways."

"That makes sense." She motioned toward the hole. "What's up?"

"I think we found our case."

Susan hopped down the steps and joined the men gathered around the hole. They'd extracted two items from the ground, and she knew exactly what they were the moment she saw them. The first was a small metal box, nondescript but for the Mercedes logo branded on the top. It was the computer memory system from Amanda's car. The other item was a long, flat piece of wood that had been broken just above the halfway point. The grip tape used at one end was red and white, the phrase *QUARIM UNIVERSITY* written over and over in the white part. It was a broken field hockey stick.

They'd found the murder weapon.

"Bag them," Susan said. "Get the car computer to our tech guys in Hawthorne, and see if they can still get anything out of it. Hopefully the dirt and cold temperatures haven't screwed anything up. I'd like to know where Amanda Brock was the night of the accident. The field hockey stick goes to Forensics today. I want them working on it as a high priority. No excuses. Go."

The men got back to work as Susan climbed the deck stairs. She made her way inside and crossed the kitchen into the dining room, pulling cuffs from a case that was fastened to the back of her belt.

"Randall Brock," she began, "I'm placing you under arrest for the murder of Amanda Brock. Stand up and place your hands behind your back."

Sidney shot out of his chair. "That is outrageous! What is the meaning of this?"

"I don't understand," Randall muttered. "What's going on?"

"We'll talk about it at the barracks," Susan replied.

"We'll talk about it now!" Sidney shouted.

Susan helped Randall out of his chair and pulled his arms around to his back, where she cuffed his wrists. "Mr. Windsor, I suggest you calm down, or you'll be riding with your client instead of following behind him. We found what was buried in the hole in the yard. I hope you're good at what you do." She led Randall toward the front door. "You're gonna need some skills on this one."

36

Randall was fingerprinted and swabbed, then moved to a new inter-rogation room. This one had white cinder block walls and three chairs instead of two. A metal table sat in the center, bolted to the floor. As in the smaller room he'd already been in, a camera was mounted in the corner. One of the troopers sat him down in the chair and left. Sidney Windsor came in a few minutes later and took a seat next to him. One chair remained.

"Do you know—" Randall began.

Sidney raised his hand. "Not a word. You say nothing unless I tell you to."

Adler entered the room after about ten minutes. She had another stack of folders in her hand and placed them down on the table. She sat in the chair, pulled it close, and pointed to the camera in the corner. "We're going to be recording this," she said. "Audio and video."

"That's fine," Sidney replied.

Adler straightened up and cleared his throat. "This is Investigator Susan Adler of the New York State Police, Troop K, file number two-two-seven-six-B. Sitting in on this interview is Dr. Randall Brock and his attorney, Sidney Windsor. Both parties understand and have agreed that this is on the record and being recorded."

Sidney nodded. Randall did the same.

Adler looked through some of her notes, then up at Randall. "Dr. Brock, I arrived at your house this afternoon to talk to you about our case involving your wife's car accident, which we have ruled a homicide.

There was no answer at the door, so I walked around the house to see if you were out back. While I was walking in your yard, I noticed a patch of dirt that was turned. Freshly dug. I only noticed it because it was in such contrast to the rest of your yard. Everything else is so well maintained. Beautiful. But this patch of dug-up dirt was sloppy. Did you dig that hole?"

Randall looked at his attorney and was given the okay to answer. The room was stifling. He could feel a headache starting to rumble somewhere in the back of his mind. "No. I didn't dig the hole."

"Do you know who did?"

"No."

"Do you have a landscaper?"

"Yes. His name is Paolo Zapa. Zapa Landscaping. He does all the houses around there."

"Did he dig the hole?"

"I have no idea."

"Did you ask or instruct him to dig the hole?"

"No."

Adler read through more notes and jotted a few lines on the back of a file. "At the conclusion of my walk around your house, I noticed that the garage doors were open. Is that normal? Do you usually leave them open?"

Randall wiped perspiration from his forehead with the back of his hand. The room was hot. "Yes, sometimes I leave them open. I don't really think about it. It's a safe neighborhood."

"I went into your garage to knock on the mudroom door, thinking maybe you didn't hear the front door. I noticed something when I walked past your workbench."

"Yes," Randall replied. His headache was coming on now. Another migraine. "The keys. You saw the Subaru keys."

Adler smiled. "I saw the Subaru keys. Said *HL Architects* on the key chain. *HL* engraved in gold. Those were Hooper Landsky's keys."

"I don't know."

"You know."

"I swear. I don't."

Adler leaned closer. "Where's Hooper, Dr. Brock? You can tell me. You're already in over your head here. Just tell me where he is, and I'll make sure the DA considers your cooperation in this matter."

"We've been over this already," Sidney snapped. "He doesn't know where this man is."

Adler ignored him. "Is Hooper working for you? With you? Or is he already dead?"

The smirk on that woman's face made Randall want to slam her head into the table. The nerve. The condescending voice. She had no right. She had no idea what he'd been through. A little smirk and a game of cat and mouse in the interview room were hardly enough to scare him. He bit the inside of his cheeks and closed his eyes against the pain that was spreading in the back of his skull. "I don't know where Hooper Landsky is. As I've stated before, you can give me a polygraph if you want. I'm telling you the truth."

"Okay." Adler pulled a file and opened it. "Dr. Brock, were you on the Quarim University campus the night of your wife's accident?"

"Yes."

"The day before?"

"Yes."

"The day before that?"

"I'd have to check my calendar, but yes, probably. Peter and I are practically living there with the case study preparation."

"So you're on campus a lot?"

"Yes."

"Do you have access to any of the sports equipment?"

Randall was having trouble hearing what she was saying. The pain in his head had moved to the center and was throbbing. His pulse thumped in his ears. "I don't know. I don't think so. Why would I?"

"Do you own bolt cutters?"

"Yes."

"Pliers? Screwdrivers?"

"Yes."

Sidney plopped both arms on the table in an exaggerated expression of exhaustion. "Investigator Adler, can we get to the point?"

Adler pulled out two photographs and placed them next to each other on the table so Randall could see.

"The hole in your yard contained what we assume to be the missing computer from your wife's Mercedes and this field hockey stick. Judging from the tape on the handle, it's safe to assume it came from Quarim University. I'll state, for the record, that the medical examiner noted that the potential murder weapon used to kill Amanda would be something like a bat or a pipe. Something that had weight at its edge and was rounded. No one thought of a field hockey stick, but here we are."

The headache consumed almost half of his skull now. Randall's vision blurred at the edges, the room seeming darker now. "I . . . I didn't dig that hole. I don't know where those things came from."

"They came from your house."

"I mean before that! I didn't take the computer out of Amanda's car. I wouldn't know how. I didn't do this."

"Then tell us all, on the record," Adler said. "Who did?"

Randall thought about Sam's warning.

I'll remind you one last time. No police.

Tears formed in his eyes. He wanted so desperately to go home.

If you tell the police about me, I'll incinerate everything you hold sacred. Your life. Your reputation. What's left of your career. Your friends and their wives and their children and their grandchildren. And then, once you've seen all the death and you know you're the one responsible, I'll kill you. Slowly.

"Dr. Brock?"

"I . . . can't," Randall muttered. "I can't tell you."

Adler stood from her seat and leaned across the center of the table. "If you know something, you need to tell us."

"I can't!"

There was a knock on the door, and a trooper poked his head in. "Crosby needs to see you."

"Now?"

"He told me to come in and get you."

Adler nodded, then looked at the two men sitting across from her. "I'll be right back," she said. "I suggest you talk things over while I'm gone. We have you, Dr. Brock. Now it's just a matter of how much you're going to cooperate and how much we're going to push."

37

Crosby was sitting behind his desk when Susan came into the office. Tommy was in one of the chairs opposite the desk.

"What's up?" Susan asked. Her breath came quickly as if she'd been running. In fact, she had been running. "You pulled me at one helluva time. I was just about to press him, and I think he was cracking. He knows what we've got, and he's shaken. I can tell."

Crosby snatched a sheet of paper from a pile in front of him. "I wouldn't have pulled you like that, but this couldn't wait. We received the results of Dr. Brock's background check, and you need to see it." He handed the paper to Susan. "This is Dr. Randall Brock. Born in Hackensack, New Jersey, in 1969. Died at Hackensack Medical Center in 1994. Was diagnosed with lung cancer while still in medical school. Never made it out of his twenties."

Susan looked at the sheet of paper. A photograph of a young man stared back at her. Tight curly hair. Small eyes. A large birthmark that stretched across his left cheek and forehead. "Are you sure this is the right person?" she asked.

Crosby nodded. "We're sure."

"Then who's in my interview room right now?"

"Our Randall Brock uses the same birthdate, social security number, and medical affiliation," Crosby explained. "The reason no one picked up on anything is the fact that our guy hasn't practiced medicine since coming back East with Amanda. There was no need for anyone to take a closer look at his credentials."

"I thought he was a professor at Quarim."

"He's not. Tommy called the school. Apparently, he's just a partner with Dr. Reems in this test study they're conducting. Reems is the one who got him his clearance for campus access."

Susan looked at the paper again. She ran through the facts about the real Randall Brock. Born in Hackensack. Went to Bergen County Christian Academy, then moved on to the University of Pennsylvania for both his undergraduate and medical-school degrees. He was diagnosed with lymphoma at the age of twenty-two and died three years later in his hometown. He was buried in Maple Grove Park Cemetery. A life stolen in more ways than one.

Crosby pulled another report from his desk and handed it over. "As to the question of who's sitting in your interview room right now, we got an immediate hit on NCIC from the prints we ran when you brought our guy in."

Susan flipped through the report. "You got a hit that fast? Who is he?"

"William Feder. *Dr.* William Feder. The same Dr. William Feder from the Gary Anderson murders in Queens."

Susan found the picture of the man she'd thought all this time was Randall Brock. She could see it now. His hair was darker than it used to be. His nose and chin were thinner. He'd had some plastic surgery. But his eyes were the same. Haunted. Desperate. "William Feder," she whispered to herself. "You've got to be kidding me."

Tommy raised his hand. "Sorry, who's William Feder, and what are the Gary Anderson murders?"

"Are you serious?" Susan asked.

"Yeah."

"It was a national story."

"I don't know what you want me to say," Tommy replied. "Never heard of it."

Susan sat down in the other chair and spread the papers out on her lap the best she could. "It happened about five years ago. William Feder was a prominent professor and researcher at Fordham University in the Bronx. One of the patients he was treating through his research was a guy named Gary Anderson. William was trying to help Gary overcome some serious childhood abuse he'd suffered at the hands of his psycho father when he was a kid. Real sick stuff. Broken bones, torture, rape. It was vicious. Anyway, over time, through all the one-on-one sessions and the treatments, Dr. Feder started to become like Gary's father figure or protector or something. Things were going well. Gary was getting the treatment he needed. All seemed good. Then one day he just snapped. Gary called Feder and told him that he was having a total breakdown and needed help. He was crying and screaming into the phone, threatening his wife and daughter, talking about killing himself and his family if Feder didn't come."

"Sounds fishy," Tommy said. "All of a sudden this guy goes nuts? Like, out of nowhere?"

Susan shrugged. "Dr. Feder eventually got him calm, but Gary wouldn't stop threatening suicide, so Feder agreed to head over to his house so they could keep talking. He never called the police. Just figured he'd handle it doctor to patient. Feder gets to the house, and he's ambushed. Knocked out cold. When he comes to, he's in Gary's basement, chained to the foundation wall, and Gary's got his wife, Rose, and his twenty-two-year-old daughter, Lily, chained up right next to him. Three prisoners in one spot. Gary had some kind of full-on psychotic break and just totally flipped out. I'll spare you the details since it's all online anyway, but our guy in that interview room basically spent the next twelve days chained in Gary's basement getting tortured and being forced to torture and rape both women. Repeatedly."

Tommy was pin straight, listening to the story. Crosby's office was silent but for Susan's voice.

"One night a neighbor was walking home late from work. Got off at the bus stop half a block away. Conditions must've been just right or the wind was blowing in the right direction or something, because the neighbor started hearing a faint screaming coming from inside the Anderson house."

"Like it was meant to be," Crosby whispered.

Susan nodded. "Exactly. Up until then, all four of them had been reported missing, and the NYPD had been by the house three separate times. But Gary had cameras hidden outside, and when he saw the units pull up, he'd make everyone stay silent. NYPD never went in after the second time through because there was nothing to find. Turns out Gary had built a wall separating the basement and his torture room, so when the patrolmen came down to investigate, they walked through and it looked empty. Never saw the door that was disguised to look like brick foundation."

"Damn," Tommy said. His eyes were wide, unblinking. "They were right there."

"Both times," Susan replied. "But on this particular night, after the neighbor called in, they came and tore the place apart. They found the hidden room, but by then Gary had killed his wife and kid, shot Feder in the stomach, then shot himself in the head. That's the official story, anyway. Dr. William Feder survived after a couple of surgeries. He quit Fordham and kind of disappeared. I guess now we know he stole a new identity and moved out to the West Coast."

Tommy thought for a moment. "You know, all that trauma could mess with a person's well-being. Maybe he didn't need motive to kill his wife. Maybe some kind of PTSD triggered something, and Dr. Brock, or whoever this guy is, just up and killed her. Maybe he flipped a switch like Gary did."

"It's possible," Susan said. She looked at Crosby. "Now that we know who our suspect is, I'd like to order his medical records from the Anderson incident. I remember he was seeking psychiatric help after everything he'd been through. I'd like to take a look at the notes from the treatment."

Crosby stood from his seat and pulled at the waist of his pants. "I'll write up a request for judicial sign-off," he replied. "I'm sure they're sealed even past the normal HIPAA regulations. I'll get them to you as soon as I can."

"Thanks."

"Okay, so now you know what we found. I think it's time you proceed with your interview."

38

Randall's lower back was starting to hurt. He slid closer toward the edge of his seat and stretched the best he could in the tight space. The room was so hot. He could feel himself sweating beneath his suit, and his migraine continued to pound in his skull. Sydney was writing on his legal pad, scribbling notes, one after the other. Neither of them spoke.

The door opened, and Adler came in carrying a new stack of papers. She placed them next to her files and sat down.

"I appreciate your patience."

"I hope it was worth it," Sydney said. He stopped writing and folded his arms across his chest. "My client has matters to attend to. We can't sit here all day."

"Your client is being questioned around the potential murder weapons found at his house in relation to his wife's death," Adler replied. "If I were him, I wouldn't be worried about other matters at this time."

Sydney sighed a laugh. "Are you going to continue?"

"Have you two had a chance to talk about where you want to go with this case? Are you going to cooperate, or are you going to force me to do things the hard way?"

"We are cooperating," Sydney said.

"I want the truth."

"You're getting it."

Adler smiled and looked at Randall. "I want the truth from Dr. Feder."

The name hung in the room. Randall knew he heard it, but at the same time he felt detached from what was happening. Images flooded his mind. Slowly at first, but then the floodgates began to open. The basement. The chains. The women. The blood.

"Who's Dr. Feder?" Sydney asked somewhere in the background.

The screams. The crying.

Adler pointed to Randall. "Sydney Windsor, I'd like you to meet your client, Dr. William Feder. Yes, *the* Dr. William Feder of the Gary Anderson case in Queens."

From his periphery, Randall could see Sydney turning in his chair and looking at him, but he wasn't in the interrogation room at the moment. He was back in Gary's basement, chained to the wall like some animal. He could smell the dampness and the mold and the stink of sweat.

"Dr. Feder," Adler continued. "I'm sure you know it's illegal to steal someone's identity, dead or alive. I can arrest you on that charge alone, so no more dancing around the truth. Talk. Now."

Sydney rubbed his forehead, his eyes darting back and forth. "Hold on. I need a moment with my client."

"No."

"What do you mean, no? I'm entitled to consult with my client, and I wish to do so."

"I said no."

Sydney slammed his hand on the table, but before he could say anything, Randall grabbed his arm. "It's okay."

"What do you mean, it's okay?" Sydney asked. "None of this is okay."

"She's right. It's time for the truth. All of it."

"Investigator Adler, I need to talk in private with my client to ensure he's not about to implicate himself in anything. I don't know what's going on here."

Randall shook his head. "No, we're fine." He looked at Adler. "So you know."

"Yes."

"Then there's really nothing left to hide." A single tear slipped down his cheek. "Yes, I stole the identity of Randall Brock. I paid good money to obtain proper identification that was already on file with the state of New Jersey. I used his social security number and birthdate to start a new life in San Francisco. Big enough city. Not a lot of scrutiny when it comes to getting a driver's license and a lease for an apartment. I was a little more concerned when I came to New York, but by then I had a five-year track record and an established life that was traceable, so as long as no one ran my prints or did an in-depth background check, I could get a new driver's license. I could get married. Amanda already had the house, and she bought the cars, so no extensive credit checks that I had to worry about. By then I was Randall Brock. William Feder was dead. He died in Gary Anderson's basement the moment he came to that house hoping to help a patient in need. What happened to William is the past."

"What happened to William is what happened to you. And it's relevant, Dr. Feder. It's motive."

It was as if Randall were floating out of his body and watching the interrogation as a spectator. His headache was pounding, gaining strength. "I won't answer to that other name, so you can stop using it. That man is dead. You'll address me as Randall Brock, or I won't answer. I'm serious."

Adler nodded. "Fine. Randall, did you kill your wife?"

"No."

"Did she find the truth about your past? Is that why she had to die?"

Randall wiped his tears and closed his eyes. "She did find out about my past. But I didn't know that until after she was dead. I found the proof she was keeping in a safe-deposit box I never knew existed. That was why she was going to leave me. She found the truth and couldn't deal with the fact that the man she married could be capable of what went on in that basement. I was forced to do things, Investigator Adler. Terrible things. I'll never forgive myself, and I don't blame Amanda for wanting to run away from me."

"Where are the papers now?"

"I burned them. I couldn't let evidence of my past exist outside in the open." Randall took a deep breath, forcing the next sentence from the pit of his stomach to the tips of his lips. "However, now that you know the truth, I can tell you this: I believe I know who might've killed Amanda."

"Who?"

"You mentioned Sam to me the last time I was at this place. I said I didn't know what you were talking about, but I lied. I don't know him, but he exists. He came to my office the day after Amanda was killed, using my little brother's name, which means he also knew about my real past. My real identity."

Sydney raised his hand. "This is too much. I need to consult my client."

Randall ignored his lawyer. "I never met this guy before. I saw him at Amanda's award ceremony the night before, but we didn't speak. Next time I saw him he was at the office. He was the one who first told me she'd been murdered. He told me before you did. He knew. He also knew about Amanda's affair and her reworking of the will and the divorce. I don't know how, but he knew everything."

"What did he want?"

I'll kill you. Slowly.

"He said he wanted to show me Amanda's truths so I could tell him mine."

"What is that supposed to mean? What truths?"

"I guess he wanted me to admit who I really was."

Adler fell back in her chair, gently tapping her pen on the table. "Did this Sam look familiar to you in any way? Maybe you met him at one of your wife's past charity events?"

"I don't think so. Just at the award ceremony. I'm pretty sure that's the first time I saw him."

"What does he look like?"

"Average size. Average build. Young. White. Dark hair."

"That's kind of broad. Can you be more specific? Anything unique about him? A scar or a birthmark? A tattoo? The color of his eyes."

"His jacket," Randall said. "He always wears a long black coat that has a giant hood attached. The edge of the hood is lined with fur. Covers his entire face, like he's trying to hide. He's always wearing that coat with the hood up. But I've seen him without the hood. I know what he looks like."

"Yeah, average size and average build."

Randall nodded.

"A man with a large hood? You're sure?"

"Yes."

Adler shook her head and sighed, tossing her pen onto the table and folding her arms across her chest. "You know this all sounds like it's straight out of a movie, right? Pretty tough to swallow."

"What?"

"I mean, if a stranger came into my life out of nowhere and knew all these things about me and my dead wife, the very *first* thing I would've done was go to the police. No, scratch that. The first thing I would've done was suspect him of my wife's murder, and then I'd go to the police. You're a smart guy. Educated. A professor. Why would you only be telling us about this guy now?"

"Because I was trying to hide the truth about who I am. I knew that if I told you about Sam, I'd have to tell you everything. But now you already know, so there's no reason to keep it a secret any longer."

The pain in Randall's head was overwhelming. He squinted to narrow his vision. When he spoke, the words sounded hollow, like he was in a tunnel or a cave. "He threatened me. Told me he'd hurt me and those around me if I went to the police."

"Of course he did."

"Watch the attitude," Sydney barked. "We're cooperating here."

"Your client is feeding me a bunch of crap to save his own skin. Come on, Mr. Windsor. You're too good an attorney and get paid way too much to be expected to believe this."

"It's the truth," Randall whispered, the pain completely overtaking him now. He could smell the dampness of Gary's basement. The roughness of the foundation wall. "It's the goddamn truth."

"Then I suggest you make bail, and the next time you see this Sam, try and get a print. Take a picture. Maybe a video of your encounter on your phone. Come back to me with proof of a hooded, all-knowing, dangerous stranger, and I'll drop the charges. Deal?"

Sydney's face turned red. "This sarcasm is unprofessional. We're talking about a serious matter here."

Adler looked at him. "Let's recap. Aside from these new revelations we discovered today about your client's real identity, I have your client on video at Hooper Landsky's parking garage the day Mr. Landsky disappeared, and Hooper's keys in your client's garage. The probable murder weapon and his wife's car computer were buried in his yard. He's also in possession of his wife's cell phone, which we're now holding as evidence. How would he have her phone if she drove from the Bear Mountain Inn off the Goat Trail?"

"Sam gave me the phone," Randall muttered.

"The affair," Adler continued, ignoring Randall as she spoke to Sidney, "the divorce, and the money are all motives. And now we have a new motive, given his real identity. But suddenly he has this story about a mysterious hooded visitor the day after he knows I saw such a person when I was run off the road by a maroon Subaru Legacy?" She turned and looked at Randall. "You sure you want to go with that? You had the keys, after all."

"I didn't know you were run off the road," Randall said, his voice barely audible. "I'm telling you the truth."

"This is my client's official statement," Sidney barked.

"It's a bunch of garbage," Adler shouted. "And I'm taking him down."

The last thing Randall remembered was the sound of the interrogation-room door opening and a voice in the background as a trooper pulled his arms behind him and cuffs were tightened around his wrists.

"Dr. Feder, my name is Mark Peters. I'm a deputy district attorney for Westchester County . . ."

Randall started to scream. He couldn't help it. And somewhere in the background, behind the pain and the panic and the noise and the screaming, he heard his lawyer objecting to the charges.

Then came blackness.

39

Susan and Tommy spent the rest of the afternoon filing their arrest report and processing the evidence they'd found on the Brocks' property. It would take Forensics a few days to get back to them with anything from the field hockey stick, and the tech team needed some time to analyze the car's computer.

The Cortlandt barracks was too small to house a jail cell, so they transported Randall to the Hawthorne headquarters. Neither she nor Tommy escorted Randall for processing, but they got word when everything was done, and Susan was sent his booking photo via email for her file. He'd be placed before a judge in the morning and would likely make bail by lunch. That's just how these things worked for those who had money and influence.

When Susan got home, Casey and Tim came running down the hall as usual, arms outstretched, straddling the edge between balance and calamity as only children could do.

"Mommy!"

"Hi, Mommy!"

She dropped her bag and knelt down just as the twins made impact with hugs that almost knocked her off her feet. This was always the highlight of her homecoming. No matter how bad a day she was having or how crappy the world made her feel, coming home to those sweet little arms wrapping around her always made her feel better.

"Mommy, Grandma got the decorations out of the attic, and we decorated the whole house!" Tim cried, jumping and spinning.

Casey twisted her mother's hair in her small hands, nodding. "We still need a tree, though. We need to decorate a tree."

Susan stood up. "We'll get a tree tomorrow. I promise. We'll bring it home and decorate it, and we'll put on Christmas songs and bake cookies, okay?"

"Yes!" Casey replied, hopping up with her hands raised.

"Yes!" Tim cried, mimicking his sister.

Susan stepped to the side, realizing she'd been blocking Tommy from coming all the way in the house. "Did you guys say hello to Tommy?"

"Hi, Tommy!"

"Hi, Tommy! We decorated. Come see!"

Tim grabbed Tommy by the hand and dragged him into the living room to show him the lights and the garland and the small Christmas village they'd set up on a side table. He was most proud of the snowflakes they'd made by folding construction paper and cutting shapes with their safety scissors. Casey then took over and brought Tommy to the train set they'd built to go around the tree as well as the stockings they'd hung over the fireplace. Tommy took it all in stride, oohing and aahing as he went. He was a champ, even though Susan could tell he wasn't used to being around kids. She left him and slipped into the kitchen, where her mother was loading the dishwasher.

"Mom, you can leave that. I'll do it. You've done enough today. You certainly didn't have to go into the attic for those decorations."

Her mother didn't turn around. "Can't have Christmas without Christmas decorations," she said. "And with this case you got going on, I had to make sure my babies had a house full of spirit."

"Thank you."

"You're welcome, sweetie." Beatrice faced her daughter and shook her head. "You look tired."

"I am. But mostly I'm feeling guilty about missing all this holiday stuff with the kids. I should be here with them to go to their pageants and hang the decorations. I'm their mother. I should be the one sharing these memories with them instead of being stuck at work."

Beatrice walked across the kitchen and hugged her. "You'll get there," she said. "The twins will be getting involved in more things as they get older. You'll figure it out, and I'll help you. What I do with them takes nothing away from what an amazing mother you are. When Eric left, you kept this family together. No blame. No feeling sorry for yourself. You never let Casey and Tim feel anything but love for their father. I admire that, and I love you, sweetie. But more importantly, your kids love you. We'll figure it out on the fly. That's what we do best."

Susan smiled and let herself fall into her mother's embrace. "Thanks, Mom. I needed to hear that."

Tommy came into the kitchen dragging the twins, one on each leg. "Great job with the decorations, Mrs. Adler."

Beatrice let go of Susan and closed the dishwasher. "Thank you, dear. We had meatloaf tonight, if you two are hungry."

"I'll get it," Susan said. "We're going to work on the case for a little while. You go rest. You spent the day climbing into the attic and decorating. You need to relax. You're spending the night, right?"

"Yes. It's a little late to go back home now."

"Good. Then I need you with your feet up watching TV ASAP. That's an order."

Beatrice saluted her daughter. "Yes, ma'am."

"How're my chickens?"

"All accounted for." Beatrice got the dishwasher running and folded the towel she'd been holding across the edge of the sink. "Before I get ready for bed, I'm going to get these beauties in their pajamas."

Susan walked over to Tommy and peeled the twins off his legs. "You heard the boss. PJ time." She watched her mother chase them upstairs and heard the patter of footsteps running about from room to room.

"They crack me up," Tommy said when they were alone.

"You're good with them," Susan replied. "I appreciate it."

He took his usual spot against the counter by the stove. "That was something today."

"It sure was."

"I can't believe we found all that in his yard. I mean, you'd think he'd toss that stuff in the river or bury everything deep in the mountains or something. He buried it right on his own property."

"Could've been a brilliant move." Susan hopped up on the counter next to Tommy and sat. "If the grass grew back, no one would ever suspect he'd have evidence like that in his yard. They'd think exactly what you just said. That the evidence was discarded far away. Instead, he kept it close. Maybe as a reminder or maybe because he was trying the old hide-in-plain-sight thing. Probably would've pulled it off if you weren't walking back there."

"And all that Gary Anderson and William Feder stuff. What was that?"

Susan shrugged. "Survival, I guess. He couldn't live being the man that came out of that basement, so he took on a new identity in order to get on with his life. But it also gives him an additional motive for killing Amanda. He admitted she found out about his secret. I'm guessing he flipped and killed her. Crime of passion."

"Maybe she confronted him after her ceremony."

"And then he had to make it look like an accident."

She hopped down from the counter and opened the refrigerator. "You buying this Sam thing?" she asked.

"Not really. I said it was the husband from the get-go. I'm sticking with that. What about you?"

"Not likely, but we still have to check it out. If Sydney brings it up at the hearing or trial, the first thing the judge will ask is if we've investigated that possibility. We need to be ready, which means we need to investigate. I tried not to let it show, but when Randall mentioned this guy always wears a hood, it caught me off guard." She grabbed two beers and handed one to Tommy, then went back for the tray of meatloaf.

"The car that drove me off the road last night? Driver was wearing a hood. A big one. Just like how Randall described it. I saw him outside the car in the barracks parking lot first. Same guy. Had to be."

Tommy took his beer and twisted it open. "So either that was Randall driving Hooper's car, or maybe Sam is real."

"Or maybe Sam and Hooper Landsky are working together. Maybe this is all about blackmail. They want money."

"Okay, where do we start?"

Susan walked into the hall to get her bag. "We start with the profile Randall gave us of Sam and go from there. This case has legs. We can't let it run away from us."

40

Randall let the hot water singe his skin as he stood motionless in the shower, unable to do anything but replay his life over the last twenty-four hours. He'd sat in that small cell, scared and alone, having been arrested for a crime he didn't commit, with evidence that overwhelmingly pointed to him. He wasn't sure if he'd ever be able to convince anyone—the police, his friends, the university, a jury—that he had nothing to do with Amanda's death. The police had discovered too much.

The cell had been stifling. He spent his time pacing in tight circles and sitting on the steel bed, which instantly hurt his lower back. It wasn't long before fear turned to confusion. He tried to recall the exact steps he'd taken to get himself in the situation and couldn't quite connect the dots. He'd never asked for any of what had happened to him. He'd never wanted Gary Anderson. He'd never asked to have his life destroyed. He'd tried to be the best man he could in his new life, yet death still managed to find him.

At some point during the night, Randall had heard the sound of chains on bars in another cell and had been instantly transported back to Gary's basement. He could hear Gary's wife, Rose, crying, and his daughter, Lily, pleading for her life. He could smell the dampness again, the mold, the perspiration, the blood, the piss.

When Sidney Windsor had returned in the morning to go through the procedure for when they were placed before the judge, he'd found Randall curled up on his metal bed, crying and drooling and mumbling incoherently, reliving his subterranean life with the Andersons, the world around him having dimmed to nothing more than a dull gray. It had taken Sidney half an hour to coax Randall back to reality, and with the help of two Xanax and a decent enough breakfast, he'd been able to stand in front of a judge, nod, answer yes-or-no questions, and remain still until bail was set at two million dollars. He was a free man by noon.

The water was scalding, but Randall didn't mind. His skin reddened as the steam overtook the rest of the bathroom. He needed to burn off the filth of the cell along with the memories that came with it. He needed to feel clean again, like himself. Human. Somewhere in the distance, he heard banging. It took him a minute to figure out what it was.

Pound!

Pound!

Pound!

The door. Someone was at the door.

Randall was content to let them knock until they wore themselves down and left. He closed his eyes and winced as the water burned him. It felt glorious.

Glass shattered in the foyer downstairs.

He opened his eyes and quickly turned off the water, grabbing a towel that was hanging outside the shower door. He wrapped the towel around his waist and made his way from the bathroom through his bedroom and out into the hallway.

Footsteps crunched the broken glass below.

"Randall!"

Randall climbed halfway down the stairs. Sam was waiting for him at the bottom landing. Glass shards were scattered across the foyer. He had broken the side window next to the door and unlocked the dead bolt from there.

"Go away," Randall shouted, his voice trembling. "I told the police everything. They know who I am. They know the truth. You can't threaten me or blackmail me anymore. I have nothing left. You're done."

Sam placed a boot on the first step. "You're wrong. They know *a* truth. They don't know *your* truths."

"Get out of my house!" Randall cried. "Leave, or I'm going to call the police!"

"Yes, call the police," Sam growled. "You told them about your real identity. And about me. So call them. We can talk about so much more."

"I need you to—"

"I don't care what you need!" Sam's voice exploded like thunder in a hurricane. "Did you think I cared about your identity? This is so much bigger than that. This is about the truth. The real truth. Your real truths. And we're not done. I warned you not to go to the police. I told you I would destroy your life and the lives of everyone you hold close if you went to the police. Was I not clear about that? This is between you and me. This is our journey."

Randall backed up a few more stairs. "I'm not talking to you anymore!"

"I showed you her secrets. Her truths. I showed you the person she really was. She found out who you were and was going to leave you with nothing. I stopped it. I saved you!"

"How? How did you save me?"

"You know how." Sam began matching steps with Randall, climbing up after him.

"You killed Amanda."

"Not me. Us."

"What are you talking about?"

"We killed Amanda. Together."

"No." Randall shook his head, backing up the stairs. "I had nothing to do with what happened to Amanda. You're nuts! I wasn't even there!"

"Your brother. Rose and Lily Anderson. And now Amanda."

"Shut up."

"You know what it's like to take lives."

"Shut up!"

"You know what it's like to feel a person take their final breath. How they look at you just when they realize that dying is imminent. No more panic or fear. Just resignation. There's a certain calm that comes over them. You've seen it. We both have."

"Stop talking!"

"You killed them all."

With unadulterated panic overtaking him, Randall ran back down the stairs and threw himself at Sam, knocking them both down the first few steps. When they landed, Sam planted his elbow in Randall's ribs to stop the momentum. He regained his balance and, in a flash of movement, punched Randall in his right temple, sending him rolling down the rest of the stairs and onto the floor. He was over Randall in seconds, punching him a second time, knocking a tooth loose.

"Tell me your truths."

"You . . . killed . . . Amanda."

"Tell me! I want to hear your truths!"

"You . . . killed . . . my . . . wife."

Sam got off of Randall and walked toward the door. Randall remained on the floor. He could taste his own blood and spat it out. He got to his knees and wiped his mouth as tiny shards of glass fell from his wet body. "Why don't you just kill me," he panted. "That's what's eventually going to happen, right? You toy with me, and then you kill me? Just do it now. I'm ready."

"I'm not going to kill you. I just want to hear your truths."

"What truths? What are you talking about?"

"You know."

"I don't know!"

"Then you're not ready. And we're not done."

Sam disappeared into the house for a moment, and Randall closed his eyes, wanting this all to be a dream. He could hear him in the kitchen. Pots and pans clanging. Drawers and cabinets opening and slamming shut. He scrambled to his feet and made his way toward the front door, reaching for the knob, desperate to escape. But Sam was suddenly on him again, pulling him away by his hair.

"Look at me."

"No."

Another punch to the side of his head. "Look at me."

Randall opened his eyes into slits.

Sam was holding a photograph in his hand, and Randall recognized it instantly. It was the picture Peter had on his desk in his office, taken by a professional photographer on the beaches of Grand Cayman. The entire Reems family was dressed in white shirts and blue shorts. Sam must've stolen it.

"I know every move you make. I know every thought. I know every plan. I hear every conversation. You can't escape your truth. I warned you that if you went to the police, I would destroy the people you love."

"No, please! I'm sorry! Please!"

"Do I have to kill Peter's entire family for you to know I'm serious?"

"No!"

"His wife. His three precious children. The dog."

"No. Please."

"And if I kill them, I'll deliver the cops a case that's airtight and points only to you."

"Don't hurt them. I'm sorry."

"What are your truths, Dr. Brock?"

Randall began to cry. "I don't know."

"You do."

Sam stuffed the picture into his pocket and pinned Randall against the floor, kneeling on his chest. He grabbed Randall's left hand and forced it down onto the floor. "What are your truths?"

"Leave me alone!"

Sam grabbed a stainless steel tenderizing mallet from his back pocket and slammed Randall's hand with it. Randall screamed out in both fear and pain. Tiny bones snapped upon impact. The mallet came down again, its jagged surface cutting the skin around his knuckles and fingers.

"Stop! Please!"

"Everything's changed now," Sam said, panting. He climbed off of Randall and tossed the mallet onto the floor. "Your actions have consequences, and your inaction only makes things worse. I want your truths. About your little brother. About Rose and Lily Anderson. And about Amanda. I won't rest until I get what I want."

Randall cradled his hand against his chest, tears streaming down his cheeks. Just before he passed out, he heard Sam leave through the front door. He tried to stay conscious but was suddenly so tired. He needed to close his eyes. Just for a second. He needed to rest.

41

"This has to end," Peter said as he got up from the couch. "Who is this guy, Randall?"

Randall looked up at him. They were alone in Peter's living room. The house was quiet. "I'm telling you, I don't know. One day he shows up, and the next thing I know I'm being arrested for Amanda's murder and my life is in chaos. Now he's threatening you and your family. Please, Peter. Just take Becky and the kids and go away for a bit. It's the holidays. Go on vacation."

"You know I can't do that. Not with all the work I have to get done."

"Look at me." Randall held up his left hand. Three of his fingers were in splints, and he was wrapped in a bandage from knuckles to forearm. "This guy isn't playing around. He has your picture from the campus office and knows your family."

Peter began pacing. "So the police know about Gary Anderson and Lily and Rose. They know about William Feder, and you told them about Sam. They'll need to fill in the parts that're missing, which means they're probably already working on subpoenas for your medical records. This is all falling apart. Your life. My life. The study. Everything."

"We need to find Sam."

"But who is he?"

"I don't know!"

"And he confessed to killing Amanda?"

"Not in so many words. He said we did it. Together."

Peter knelt down next to Randall, grabbing him by the shoulders. "You have to consider the possibility that Sam is like Jerry or Stephen or Jason."

"No. Impossible."

"How can you say that? Look at the things he's done! And the police will come to the same conclusion."

"It can't be."

Peter got up and began pacing again, running his hand through his hair over and over. "What does Sam want?" he asked. "Think for a second. What does he really want?"

"He wants me to relive what happened with my brother. And with Rose and Lily. He says they're my truths, and he wants to hear me talk about them, but I can't. I won't. It's too painful."

"Okay, why does he want you to admit these truths?"

"I have no idea."

"Maybe this Sam was a relative of Rose or Lily? Could even be a distant relative of yours who learned about what happened. The fact that he needs you to 'confess your truths' to him leads me to believe he's emotionally invested in what happened to someone you hurt."

"Maybe."

"And you're not giving him what he wants, so he's turning violent. He's escalating."

"Yes, he certainly is."

Peter stared at him. "You have to go back to the police and tell them what happened."

"I'm afraid to. Somehow he knows my every move. If I go back to the police, he'll come after you. For all I know, he might be planning to do that already. Please, Peter. Tell me you'll take the family away for a week or so. Maybe the police can find him by then."

"I'll see what I can do," Peter replied. "But you need to go to the police."

"I can't," Randall said. "He'll know, and he'll start hunting the people I love."

42

The town began to convert the auxiliary soccer field into the Christmas tree lot about a week before Thanksgiving, and it became fully operational on December 1. Each tree purchased at the field included a donation to the local volunteer fire department, so the lot was popular among the residents, and the mood was always festive.

Susan walked through the maze of spruces and pines, gazing at the string of lights that hung from the poles at each corner of the field. Snow was falling, the tiny flakes whirling and spinning in the cold breeze, making the moment all the more perfect.

Coming this late in the season meant that the majority of trees would already be taken. Susan, Beatrice, and the twins were among a smattering of people milling about, all of them last-minute shoppers with only days to go before Christmas.

"Mommy, how about this one?" Tim asked, pointing to a ten-foot pine that looked dead toward the bottom and top heavy at its peak.

"Honey, that wouldn't fit in our house," Susan said. "I'm not sure that would even fit through the door."

"But I want a big tree," Tim whined. "It has to be giant so Santa won't forget us."

"Santa won't forget us. You wrote him your letters, right?"

"Yeah."

"And you told him you'll be at your own house instead of with your dad, right?"

"Yeah."

"Okay, so we're good. We don't need a giant tree. Santa knows what he's doing."

"Does he?" Beatrice asked.

Susan turned to her. "Yes, he does. It's all under control."

"Anything I can do to help?"

The kids ran on to the next row of trees.

"Nope, I got it. Eric already got most of what was on their list since they were supposed to be with him, so I'm going to take a run over to his place and pick everything up. Anything he wasn't able to get is already sitting under my desk at work. All under control."

"Well, good for you. You continue to amaze me with your inner strength and determination to make this all work."

"Was that sarcasm?"

"Of course not," her mother replied, smiling. She winked, and the two women laughed.

Casey stood next to a tree that looked full throughout and appeared to be about six feet tall. "How about this one?"

Susan walked up to it, shook a few of the branches, and could see that very few needles fell off. "Yes, this could work. What do you think, Tim?"

Tim sized up the pine, walked around it twice, then stuck his nose in the needles, taking a long sniff. "I like it," he finally said. "And I think it's big enough for Santa to see."

"We can put lights on it, too, so Santa *has* to see it!" Casey exclaimed, jumping up and down.

"So should we get it? Grandma, what do you think?"

Beatrice hugged the twins. "I think it's perfect."

Susan snapped the ticket from the branch and checked the price, reminding herself that part of the proceeds went to the fire department. "Okay, I think we got ourselves a tree."

The twins jumped and clapped. Her mother took a few pictures with her phone. The snow continued to fall. It was the perfect moment. Picturesque. Norman Rockwell. Americana.

But then she saw him.

Standing in the last row of trees, just under one of the corner poles. The spotlight atop the pole cast him in shadows. She could see the silhouette of the hood covering his head, the tiny furs along its edge blowing in the breeze. He was unmoving, staring only at them. It was the man Randall had described. It was the man who'd been standing in the parking lot at the barracks and sitting behind the wheel of Hooper's car.

Sam.

Without thinking, Susan stepped in front of her family, her back to the man. She reached inside her coat and unsnapped her holster. "Mom, can you bring this ticket up to the guy and let him know we'll take this one?"

Beatrice took the ticket. "Sure. Are you going to wait here?"

"Yes. Take the kids with you."

"Are you all right?"

"Yes. Just take the kids."

"Okay."

When Susan turned back around, Sam had retreated a few steps. He was now on the outer perimeter of the lot, about thirty yards from a patch of forest that surrounded the field, swallowed by the darkness outside the spotlights. Once the kids were gone, she gently pulled her weapon from its holster and held it down in front of her. She took a step, then another, then without warning broke into a sprint.

Sam peeled away and dashed toward the woods. She followed, running as fast as she could, hopping over the orange mesh fencing that had been erected to mark the perimeter of the lot. He disappeared past the tree line, and as she broke from the lights and into the shadows, she stopped, realizing that her eyes had not adjusted to the dark and she was vulnerable.

She got down on one knee, her focus on the woods in front of her, her Beretta aimed straight ahead. Her breathing was deep and heavy. She tried to calm herself.

There were too many tracks in the snow to determine which direction Sam had run. Kids used the path to cut through to the high school campus and a popular deli. Susan waited until she could see and then ran toward the woods, stopping only when she was past the first line of trees. The woods were quiet, pitch black. There was no moon to guide her, and she was reluctant to make herself a target by turning on the flashlight on her phone. She took a careful step, scanning the area for any sign of movement. Her boots crunched in the snow, sounding like a cannon in the serenity of her surroundings. She stopped, wincing at the sound, knowing she'd given away her position.

Adrenaline was coursing through her. She leaned against a thick elm and squatted down again, straining to see her target through the blackness.

Where are you?

Susan steadied her breathing and turned from side to side, listening for anything that would tell her which way Sam had run. There had been maybe twenty or thirty seconds between the time she'd had to wait for her eyes to adjust to the dark to when she'd broken through the first line of trees. Depending on how fast Sam had been running, he could've put a fair amount of distance between them, but she was certain she would've been able to hear his feet crunching in the snow as he ran. But there was nothing. No sound. No movement.

He's here. Close. With you.

She stood up a bit and looked over a set of bushes, still listening for movement, her weapon aimed out in front of her.

Come on. Where is he?

She looked behind her. Nothing.

He's gotta be close.

From left to right.

Close.

Nothing.

Here.

Movement, to her left.

Susan spun around as soon as she heard it, but as she turned, something hit her in the chest, sending her to the ground and knocking the wind out of her. She struggled to take a breath and tried to get up. Her fumbling hands wrapped around the Beretta as the woods suddenly filled with the sound of footsteps thumping in the snow, running away from her. She poked her head up the best she could and caught a glimpse of the hooded figure disappearing deeper into the woods and out of sight.

She got to her knees and wiped the snow from her face. Her breath finally returned, ragged and short. When she knew she was alone again, she dug inside her bag and retrieved a small tape measure she always kept with her. She walked to the nearest set of footprints and bent down, stretching the tape across the length of the left print. It was just under twelve inches, making the shoe size about a twelve or a thirteen, give or take. She took several pictures with her phone, then did the same thing with the right print. The woods were quiet again.

Sam had been watching her this entire time.

He'd been watching them all.

43

The Christmas tree lot had become part of the crime scene. Town officers and a handful of state police personnel had descended on the soccer field after Susan had called it in. K-9 units had been sent into the woods to try and track Sam's scent. Portable spotlights had been erected so the uniforms could see what they were doing as they canvassed the area. Susan had sent her mother and the twins home in the back of a state police unit with instructions to the troopers to stay with them until she arrived back at the house. It killed her that she had to let them go without her, but she was a witness and the primary investigator on the case. There was nothing she could do.

Crosby emerged from the woods and stood with Susan just outside the tree line. "K-9s are having trouble picking up a scent."

She watched as the others worked. "I want to get in there."

"Not gonna happen. This isn't our jurisdiction, and secondly, you're the victim. You need to stay removed from the scene."

"You didn't have to come all the way up here."

"Like hell I didn't. One of my people call for help, I'm gonna be there. Day or night. You know how it is."

"Yeah, I know how it is."

"How's your chest?"

"I'm fine."

"EMTs look at it?"

"Yeah, just a bruise. Knocked the wind out of me, but I'm good."

"You better not be bullshitting me."

She turned when she heard footsteps approaching and watched as Tommy traipsed through the tree lot toward the edge of the woods. He was dressed in an oversized parka and ski pants.

"What're you doing here?" Susan asked.

"What do you mean?" Tommy replied. "My partner called in a 10-33. Where do you expect me to be?"

"But don't you live like an hour in the opposite direction?" Susan took a step back. "And why are you all wet?"

"I was night tubing at Hunter Mountain."

"Night tubing?"

"Don't look at me like that. You should try it. The kids would love it. Anyway, I came straight from there. What happened?"

Susan pointed to the lot behind them. "I was getting a tree with my mom and the twins, and all of a sudden I see this guy watching us. Big hood, fur along the edge. Matches the Sam description Brock gave us, and he also looked like the guy who was at the barracks tailgating me the other night in the Subaru. I draw my weapon and pursue, and he runs into the woods. I lost him in the dark, and while I was waiting on him to make a move, he hit me with a tree branch and ran off. Called for backup. Here we are."

"Why is he targeting you?" Tommy asked, looking into the thicket of trees. "First he runs you off the road. Now this."

"Maybe we're getting close, and he's trying to scare me. Maybe 'Sam' is Randall, and he's trying to convince me he's innocent and there really is another guy out there."

"Maybe." Tommy motioned toward Crosby. "Anyone check on Dr. Brock since he left the barracks?"

"I have a unit rolling," Crosby replied.

A K-9 officer came out of the woods and walked up to Susan. "We tracked him for a little bit but lost the scent near the creek in the back there. Maybe he jumped in or walked through it or fell, but the scent goes cold there. I'm guessing he went southeast, though. You know where that might dump out?"

"Somewhere near the high school."

The officer nodded and called for a unit to take a drive through the high school grounds.

Crosby took Susan by the shoulder and walked her back toward the tree lot. "I want you to go home and be with your family," he said. "If we find anything, I'll call you. Your house will have a unit out front twenty-four seven until this is put to bed."

"Brock's house too," Susan said. "We need to either protect Randall or keep tabs on him until we figure out who Sam is. At this point, I'm thinking it's gotta be Hooper Landsky in disguise, or he and Randall are working together. Something like that."

"It's under control. Go home. I'll see you tomorrow."

"We gotta catch this guy, boss. I can't have a unit outside my house forever."

"We'll get him. It's just a matter of time. He'll slip up, and we'll be there. I promise."

44

Instead of going straight home, Susan walked into the barracks and up to the front desk. She was tired, and her body ached.

"What're you doing here?" the dispatcher asked, looking up from the 911 computer monitor. He was a young kid, fresh out of the academy. She couldn't remember his name. "I heard Crosby ordered you home."

"Yeah, well." She made her way down the narrow corridor toward the investigator's unit. "Anybody here?"

"Nope. Everyone's out on calls or looking for your hooded man."

The kid said something else, but Susan didn't hear him. The investigator's unit was completely empty. It didn't usually get this still until two or three in the morning. She checked her watch and saw that it was only ten. Troop K appeared to be running on all cylinders tonight.

She sat in her chair and pulled a stack of files that she hadn't had the time to go through in the last few days. It was busywork, but she couldn't go home yet. Her adrenaline was still too high, and she knew she'd never get to sleep. She also knew she wouldn't be able to endure her mother's questions. Better to use the pent-up energy and quiet to catch up on things. Once they had a better handle on the investigation, she could handle Beatrice's interrogation. But she knew if she went home now, it would only be white noise, which would most likely end in an argument.

The troopers assigned to guard Randall's house had reported in that they had arrived and Randall was home. She called her mother and told her about the unit that would be out front. As suspected, Beatrice was scared and told her so. Susan assured her that they were safe and she'd be home as soon as she could. The one thing she couldn't admit to her mother was that she was scared too.

The top file contained the supervisor acceptance form for Tommy's transfer as well as Tommy's personnel information. There was a Post-it on top of it from Crosby. It was already a few days old: *Review and sign ASAP!*

She opened the HR file and scanned the transfer document, snatching a pen from an old mug that was on her desk. She should have gotten the sign-off back to HR no more than twenty-four hours after Tommy had come on board. That obviously hadn't happened. Time always had a way of getting lost when she was on a case.

Tommy's file wasn't that thick because he hadn't been around the department for that long. Susan flipped through it, skimming as she went, most of the information familiar from what Tommy had told her. He'd been assigned to Wolcott, New York, out of the academy and had worked there for six years. His father, Martin Corolla, was a retired NYPD homicide detective. Mother worked part time at Macy's. Tommy had grown up in Port Jefferson, as he'd said, but the family had moved just before he'd started high school. Susan stopped when she saw the neighborhood the Corollas had moved to.

Queens. Saint Albans section.

Tommy had graduated from Queens Academy High School. The rest of the file was full of past job-performance evaluations, accolades, and awards Tommy had received since joining the state police. His biggest commendation had come after the largest drug bust in Wayne County's history. He'd been part of the team that stopped the trafficking of some serious drugs. Tommy was a good officer. But that was not the part of his story that interested her.

She grabbed her laptop and logged into the NYPD database of old case files that were shared with the state police. She typed in Gary Anderson's name.

The file was seventy-six pages long, and she scrolled through each page, looking to confirm what she thought she already knew. The confirmation came in the *General Information / Background* section. The Andersons had lived at 119 196th Street. Susan pulled up a map of Queens on another screen and traced her finger. The Corollas had lived only a few blocks away on the other side of Linden Boulevard, on 116th Avenue. Lily Anderson had gone to the same high school as Tommy and graduated three years after Tommy, which meant she was a freshman when he was a senior. They could've known each other.

Tommy's the same height and build as Sam.

He showed up right after Amanda's accident.

Susan continued scrolling through the Anderson case file until she got to the page listing the investigating officers. She read the name of the lead detective on the case.

Martin Corolla.

Tommy knew you were going out with the kids to get a tree.

He was wet when he arrived on scene. The K-9 officer said they lost the scent at the base of a creek in the woods.

No. Impossible. Susan shook her head, refusing to believe what her mind was whispering to her. Even in the short period of time she'd known Tommy, she couldn't picture him killing anyone. Why wouldn't Tommy have said anything about the Anderson case when it came up earlier? Why would he pretend not to know anything about what had happened?

Tommy knew.

45

It took most of the next morning for Susan to track down Tommy's father. He was no longer at the address listed in Tommy's file, so she called a few friends at the NYPD, who, in turn, called a few of their friends and got her word that Martin Corolla had moved back to Long Island and was living in Stony Brook, near the university. She was on the road by midafternoon.

She'd been ignoring Tommy's calls, letting them roll to her voice mail. She needed to get things clear in her head before she decided if she was going to call him out on what she discovered in his file. She'd sent an email letting both Tommy and Crosby know that she was following up on a lead and wouldn't be heading into the barracks that day. Tommy had emailed back, requesting her location so he could meet her there, but again, she ignored him.

It was already late afternoon when she pulled up to Martin Corolla's house. It was a petite split-level ranch, yellow with white trim, a big picture window next to a red door. It sat on a tree-lined street that looked as if it had been manufactured in the early seventies. The sidewalks were cracked where the roots of the large elms poked through, but the road had been recently paved, and it was quiet. Several cars were parked at the curb along the block and a few more in the driveways of the other split-level ranches, but for the most part, everyone seemed to be at work.

She climbed slate steps to a brick pathway, rang the bell, and waited.

Martin Corolla appeared behind a storm door wearing a sleeveless T-shirt despite the fact that it was December. His hair was mostly gone, so he'd shaved it down to a tight silver crew cut. Aside from his age, he looked remarkably like his son. Same jawbone. Same eyes. If Tommy took a close enough look at his father, he'd know exactly what he'd be in another twenty-five years.

Martin pushed the storm door open. "Yeah?"

"Detective Corolla? Martin Corolla?"

"Depends. What do you want?"

Susan held up her badge and ID. "I'm Investigator Susan Adler. State police."

"Okay."

"I was hoping I could have a few minutes of your time. I'm working with your son, and we're on a case involving Dr. William Feder. I understand you knew him from the Gary Anderson investigation, and I'd like your perspective on that case and Dr. Feder in general. Off the record, of course."

Martin winced at the sound of Anderson's name. "Where's Tommy?" he asked.

"Back at the barracks following up on some other leads. Didn't make sense for both of us to come out."

"Makes sense to see his parents."

"That's what days off are for."

Martin laughed and pushed the door open farther. "All business. I like that. Yeah, okay. Come on in."

Susan stepped inside the house and looked around. White walls, family pictures hanging crooked on the way up to the second floor, a collection of Hummels in a glass display case, cheap furniture, clean.

"My wife's visiting her sister in Orlando," Martin said as he walked up several steps into the living room. "She'll be sorry she missed you. She's so happy Tommy's back in the area. She always said he was too far away upstate."

"I bet." She pointed to the large gold ring on his finger, the black onyx gem surrounding a small diamond. "West Point?"

"Class of seventy-two. How'd you know?"

"My uncle was a cadet. Same ring."

They walked into a small living room that held a blue couch, a matching love seat, and a red La-Z-Boy chair. Martin sat in the chair, and Susan sat on the love seat. The television was on in the background.

"So how's he doing?" Martin asked. "Settling in okay? Adjusting? This was a big promotion for him."

"Fine," Susan replied. "He's doing fine. Fits right in with the rest of the team."

"That's my boy." Martin kicked up the footrest that was attached to the chair. "Tommy hasn't mentioned anything about Feder or Anderson. What's the case?"

"I really can't say."

"Come on," Martin coaxed with a wink. "You said we're off the record. Give me some professional courtesy. Just between us girls."

Susan hesitated for a moment, then nodded. She needed him on her side, so why not disclose a little to get him talking? "Dr. Feder changed his identity to Randall Brock. His wife was involved in a fatal car accident, and we have reason to believe the crash was intentional."

"Changed his name, huh? I guess I can't blame him. You guys looking at murder or manslaughter?"

"We're leaning toward murder. Obviously we want all the information on Dr. Feder that we can get, and I know you were involved with the Gary Anderson incident, so I wanted to pick your brain a little. See what you thought of him."

"He's a nutjob."

"Is that your opinion as an investigator?"

"That's my opinion as a human being. How long you been working this case?"

"A few days."

"Well, I was with William Feder for a lot longer than a few days. Try almost an entire year. Took us a while to wrap our case, and I had to keep coming back to him for more statements and details on things. Trust me—he's not right in the head. Not after what he went through. If you like him for the murder, you're probably right."

"I just want to hear about the Anderson case from your perspective," Susan said. "I remember some of the details when it happened, but I was hoping to get a more nuanced angle on what we're looking at."

Martin shrugged. "Sure, okay. Don't really think about it much these days. For me it's fishing and hunting. Retirement the way it should be." He stared up at the ceiling and was quiet for a moment. "I can tell you two things with one hundred percent certainty. The first is that I moved back here from Queens because I couldn't be near that house anymore. Once I saw what happened in there, it was like the place cast a dark cloud over the entire neighborhood. I couldn't keep driving past it without thinking about everything that went down."

"What's the second thing?"

Martin looked at her. "The Anderson case was the most brutal thing I'd ever seen in my career. Ever."

"Tell me."

Martin let out a deep sigh that cut through the temporary silence. "To this day no one really knows what made Gary snap. There're some stupid theories that make no sense. Cults and possession and all kinds of crazy crap. I think it was people trying to wrap their heads around how a father and husband and neighbor could go from being normal one day to a complete psycho the next. There was no rationale around it, so how could it not be supernatural or a cult, you know?

"Gary was a mechanic out at LaGuardia. I forget which airline. Was doing that job since he got back from the first Iraq War in ninety-two. Paid his taxes, paid his bills. Lived simple. He was known in the neighborhood to be a drinker, and units were called out to his house every now and again on domestics. He'd drink and get to slapping around his wife, Rose, but she'd never press charges, so there wasn't much we could do. The last time he was arrested, the judge ordered mandatory counseling, and that's when Dr. Feder came into the picture. I don't remember how long his sessions lasted for. Couple years, maybe? But if you ask me, I think Feder was the one who lit the fuse in Gary's brain. I think it was all that therapy, all that dredging up of the past that brought out the beast. That's my theory anyway. Makes more sense than cults and possession."

Susan looked out the picture window and watched as two boys rode down the street, one on a skateboard and the other on a bike. They were laughing and talking about something she couldn't hear. Those kids had no idea how brutal and unforgiving life could be.

"So Gary tricks Dr. Feder into coming to his house to save him from suicide," she said. "And when he gets there, he becomes one of Gary's victims."

"Yeah, kind of," Martin replied. "I know that's how the report reads, but it's a bit more involved than that."

"How?"

"Feder was kept prisoner in the basement with Rose and the Andersons' daughter, Lily, but Gary didn't treat Feder like you might think. It was weird. Gary used him so he didn't have to do all the sick shit himself. It was like Gary got off on watching his wife and kid get brutalized instead of having to participate in the act himself. The first few times, Feder refused to do what Gary wanted. He tried using his psychobabble to talk Gary down, but Gary slashed his back up with a razor over and over until he complied. At one point Gary was going for one of his eyes. Feder eventually agreed to do what Gary said. Over the course of twelve days, Rose and Lily were caught in this cycle of torture. They were raped repeatedly and had things done to them that I can't even say out loud. Both women were beat within inches of their lives, and in the end, well, just read the file. It'll tell you how it ended. I don't want to talk about it."

Susan could see Martin replaying the images in his mind. The torture. The pleading. The tears. The pain. "I did read the file," she said quietly.

"Then you know."

"Yeah, I know." She waited a few beats before continuing, hoping her next lie would sound convincing. "I also saw in the file that Lily and Tommy were close."

Martin nodded. "Lily was a good girl. Kind and gentle. Always thinking of someone other than herself. Tommy loved her very much. We all did."

Bingo.

"How long had they been dating?"

"I don't know. A few years, on and off. It was hard because he was older. They dated throughout his senior year; then they broke up when he was away at college. Then they reconnected when he was graduating. They started dating again, but by that time she was on her way to college, and he was about to head into the academy. He never said anything, but I figure they called it quits for good when he got assigned upstate. Her life was in Queens, and they both knew she wasn't going to move all the way up there. So they were done, and life moved on. Next thing I know, I'm calling my boy with this horrific news. He came down for the funerals but went right back upstate. I don't think he could face the fact that he hadn't been here to protect her." He looked up at Susan. "Must be strange for him to be working this case with Feder involved. Has Tommy mentioned any of this?"

"No. And don't worry, I won't say anything. I just wanted your perspective on the Anderson case to see how the experience could've affected Dr. Feder. Clearly he suffered the kind of trauma that could change a person."

Susan got up from her seat, thanked Martin for his time, and made her way to the door. Martin followed behind.

"Can I ask you one thing?" he said. "A favor for a favor."

"Of course."

"Tell Tom to call his mom and dad more often. A visit wouldn't hurt him either."

"I will. And thank you again for seeing me."

As she walked to the car, Susan thought about the relationship between Tommy and Lily Anderson that he'd never disclosed. Martin said they'd been in love. That they'd been together for years. Then she was dead. Brutally murdered. And the one person to survive that horrific incident was now having his life torn apart, piece by piece. She reminded herself of what Tommy had told her in the kitchen when they'd first gotten the case.

There are no such things as coincidences.

46

With dusk approaching, Susan turned onto Linden Boulevard. She hadn't been planning on coming into Queens, but when she saw the exit off the Long Island Expressway after leaving Martin Corolla's house, she realized she was close to the Andersons' residence and should take a look. She knew the twins were waiting for her to decorate the tree, so she'd have to make it quick, but she didn't want to give up the opportunity to check out the old crime scene while she was in the area.

She took a left on 196th Street and came upon the tree-lined, working-class, suburban neighborhood of Saint Albans. Tract houses crowded both sides of the road, separated by only the width of a single-lane driveway. She took her foot off the accelerator for a moment, looking at the houses, as she coasted through. She continued down 196th Street, passing 118th Road. As she crossed 119th Road, Susan saw a mailman on foot, his oversized bag causing him to tilt as he walked, hurrying before it got too dark.

The Anderson house was a slightly dilapidated two-story tract home, light blue in color with navy-blue trim and shutters. A narrow driveway hugged the left side of the house and ended at a detached one-car garage in the back. Dead leaves filled the front yard. The flower beds were nothing but dark stalks of corpse flowers that once were. The concrete path leading to the concrete front porch was cracked, with dead weeds poking through. One of the windows on the top floor had been broken and covered with a piece of plastic that had since torn, allowing the elements inside. The house was dead, unoccupied, left to rot in its own sin. Given what had happened, it was no surprise that no one wanted to live there.

Susan parked at the curb and climbed out of the car. She walked up the driveway and peeked behind the house. More weeds in an overgrown yard. An old charcoal barbecue lay on its side, rusted and disintegrating. She approached the back door and could see that it opened into the kitchen. She tried the knob and found it turned free in her hand. The entire locking mechanism had been broken.

The kitchen was frozen in time. The small stainless steel sink, the white Formica countertops, the blue plastic dish drainer still full of the last set of dishes Rose Anderson had ever washed. An overwhelming odor of sewage came over Susan as soon as she walked in. A Formica table and four mismatched chairs remained in the center of the room.

The carpet in the living room was littered with debris. A tiny dining room off the kitchen held boxes full of papers and bills and old magazines. It appeared the room had been used for storage and nothing more. Black mold climbed up the walls like sickly fingers reaching toward the ceiling. Susan turned back into the kitchen and opened a door next to the refrigerator that she figured led to the basement. She was right.

The steps creaked as she made her way down, the dampness and mold hitting her at the same time. She took her phone from her pocket and turned on the flashlight, sweeping the beam from side to side as she stepped onto the concrete floor.

The basement walls were cracking. Long, thin lines spiderwebbed all the way down. The boiler and hot-water heater were in the far corner. A pipe over the oil tank had burst and flooded half of the basement until it had turned to ice.

Susan walked to the opposite end of the dark room, trying to imagine what it had been like for Rose and Lily to be trapped down there or for Randall to be forced to do the things he'd done. She felt a twinge of sympathy for the man. He'd been through so much. But she also knew it was that very sort of trauma that could cause someone to step over the edge of sanity and never come back. She thought about Amanda's body lying in the medical examiner's office and knew it wasn't a far leap to imagine Randall had been responsible. There was a loneliness to this place, a kind of desolation where hope simply could not breathe. She could feel the desperation and futility in the air. To be part of what had happened down there was unthinkable. The pain. The fear. The torture. The madness.

A noise.

Susan heard some kind of scraping coming from the far end of the room. She walked toward the sound, making her way around shelving that had been fastened to one of the walls, figuring a mouse was running around but cautious that it could be a raccoon or something bigger. She pulled her weapon from its holster in case she had to take a rabid animal down and swept her light in front of her as she walked.

She could see the section of the basement where Gary Anderson had built his false wall. Pieces of the beams and metal studs remained bolted to the concrete foundation. Part of the steel track that had slid the wall in place was still attached to the floor. The police had removed everything else after the raid. She stepped over the track and shined her light inside what had once been a torture room.

The walls still had holes where the manacles had once been fastened. In the corner was a large iron vent that shot out of the floor and curled up into the ceiling, which eventually led through the rest of the house and through the roof. On one end, a shiny chrome chain was clasped around the vent pipe. The other end was attached to the wrists of a man who was cowering in the corner, his eyes wide with terror, his mouth covered with some kind of cloth that was fastened to his head with packing tape. Dried blood covered his face from a head wound she couldn't see. His hair was dirty and matted. He was wearing a black-and-red flannel shirt and boxer shorts. No coat or blanket. Nothing else to keep him warm. He shivered as he kicked himself farther into the corner, muffled cries coming from his throat. The sound she'd heard was the heels of the man's shoes scraping the ground.

Hooper Landsky.

Susan rushed toward him and bent down, turning off the light so she could work her phone. She placed a hand on his shoulder as they were swallowed by the darkness.

"Hang in there, Mr. Landsky," she said. "Help is on the way." She dialed 911 and alerted the operator that she needed medical assistance as well as backup and a crime scene team. She hung up and slipped her phone back in her pocket. "I can't remove your gag right now. There might be evidence on it. Just hang tight. I got you."

Tires crunched on gravel outside of the house. Susan listened and could hear an engine idling. She got up and made her way toward the stairs, her pulse racing. Backup couldn't have arrived that quickly.

Hooper began screaming through his gag.

She turned and held a finger to her lips. "I'm not leaving you, but I have to check on who that is."

She crept up the basement stairs and slipped into the kitchen. If whoever had done that to Hooper had come back, better to confront him up here than down in that dark basement. But the house was still. She could hear her breathing, but nothing else made a sound.

If the car was still outside, the noise of its engine was muffled by the home's insulation. Susan tiptoed across the kitchen, weapon aimed in front of her. She eased the back door open and placed one foot on the outside stoop, crouching just a bit to try and get a look at the driveway in both directions.

An engine roared to life from the direction of the garage. Susan made it outside in time to see the maroon Subaru Legacy speeding down the driveway toward the street. Without thinking, she leaped onto the hood as it passed, gun still in hand, screaming as the car careened into a small retaining wall in the front yard, then righted itself.

"Police! Stop the car!"

She tried to get a look at the driver, but everything was happening too quickly. Her fingers fumbled for something on the hood to hang on to, but as the Subaru hit the curb and bounced onto the road, Susan flew off and crashed onto the sidewalk, slamming violently into a stone retaining wall in front of the house next door. In the distance, she could hear the car speeding away, then registered the pain in the back of her head where she'd hit it on the wall. The pain quickly spread across her right shoulder and collarbone. All she could do was sit up and keep the gun on her lap until backup arrived. If the Subaru returned, she'd be ready. Until then, she wasn't moving from the scene.

47

Randall heard the mudroom door open, and he paused the documentary he was watching on the television. "That you?"

Amanda appeared in the hall, the shadows hiding her face. She dropped her pocketbook on the kitchen table and kicked off the sneakers she'd been wearing.

"How was the meeting?" Randall asked, getting up from the couch. "You get all the donors in line?"

"The meeting was fine."

He could see her face in the light when she opened the refrigerator. She was crying. Tears glistened on her cheeks. Her eyes were swollen. The lipstick she'd been wearing was gone.

"Honey, what's wrong?" Randall asked, crossing through the family room. "Why are you crying?"

"I don't want to talk about it."

He walked into the kitchen and stood on one side of the island, watching as she pulled a bottle of merlot from the chiller under the sink. "I think we should," he said softly. "I'm here. Whatever's bothering you, tell me."

Amanda poured herself a large glass of wine and took a gulp, shaking her head and wiping her mouth with the back of her hand. "I don't even know what to say."

"But honey—"

"Just leave me alone, okay? Let me figure this all out, and we can talk. But not now. Not yet."

He walked around the island and placed his hands on her shoulders. "Are you sure?"

She pulled away. "Don't touch me."

"Amanda—"

She pushed past him and ran down the hall, stopping when she reached the bottom landing. "You love me, right?"

"Of course."

"I thought I knew you."

"Amanda," Randall said as he walked down the hall toward her. "Please, tell me what's going on."

She shook her head and disappeared up the stairs.

———

When Randall opened his eyes, he was in bed. It was already dark out. He looked at the clock on his nightstand and saw it was just after six. When had he gotten home? How long had he been sleeping?

"It's time."

Sam was standing in the doorway, his coat buttoned up to his chin, his hood covering his face. The only thing Randall could see peeking out from beneath the hood was Sam's mouth and chin. He was smiling. His teeth looked like razors.

"Please," Randall said, pulling his covers up to his neck. "I can't take this anymore. I can't do this."

"I want your truths. I want you to confess to being the man you are and not the man everyone else thinks you are. You're no victim, Dr. Brock. Maybe you've convinced yourself that you are, but I know. I know because I always know. Everything. It's time for you to face your truths. I'll help you see. I'll show you who you really are."

Sam stepped forward and produced a straight blade he'd been hiding behind his back. "Does this look familiar?"

The mere sight of the blade froze Randall in place.

"Gary told you to do things. He told you to do things to Rose and Lily, and when you refused, he cut you with a blade just like this one. Isn't that right?"

Randall absently lifted his T-shirt and rubbed the tiny scars that littered his back. He could hear the whimpering, the crying, the shouting echoing in the basement. He could remember the way the blade slid across his skin, so sharp he didn't feel it at first. Only the warm blood as it trickled from the wound.

"Get up," Sam commanded.

Randall kicked the covers off and rose.

"Let's go."

"Where?"

"Away from here. You do everything I say, or I cut you like Gary cut you. Only deeper. Do you understand?"

Randall nodded.

"We're going out the back door and through the woods to avoid the police out front. You're going to be quiet. If you call for help, I'll cut you."

"I have to get dressed."

"No, you don't."

"I'll freeze out there."

"Then you better walk fast."

Randall crossed the room, and Sam grabbed him by the back of the neck. All the lights in the house were out. They made their descent to the first floor and walked through the kitchen, then out onto the back deck. As soon as the wind hit his bare legs and arms, he began to shiver.

"I have no shoes," Randall whispered. "My feet will get frostbite. I'll slow us down. I at least need to get something on my feet."

Sam slashed the razor across Randall's arm without speaking, then grabbed him by the hair before he could cry out, snapping him back so they were face to face. "Walk. Quietly."

Randall tried to clasp his hand across the wound on his forearm, but the cast on his hand got in the way. Tears slipped down his cheeks as he stepped off the deck and into his yard, closer toward the dark woods that stretched beyond his property. He had no idea where he was going.

He had no idea how this was going to end.

48

The first set of NYPD cruisers arrived within minutes of Susan's 911 call. Four officers swept the house to ensure no one else was inside; then two came down into the basement while the remaining two stood outside the front and back doors.

One of the responding officers had a small pocketknife, and they were able to remove the tape and gag from around Hooper's mouth and bag them so Forensics could take a look. They had to wait for the tactical team, however, to come with something to cut through the chain.

Hooper was alive but delirious. He hadn't eaten or drunk anything since he'd been abducted from inside his parking garage in the city, and dehydration was beginning to get the better of him. Another officer retrieved a bottle of water from his squad car, and they let Hooper sip it until the EMTs arrived.

The ambulance came at about the same time as a small tactical team pulled up with bolt cutters. The EMTs got Susan on a stretcher and loaded her into the back of the ambulance, then went into the house to retrieve Hooper, check his vitals, and call in a prognosis. He was loaded into a second ambulance that arrived within minutes of the first.

Her phone rang, and she fished it out of her pocket. It was Crosby. "Yes, sir."

"Jesus, Susan. Are you okay?"

"Looks like I dislocated my shoulder. They set it on scene. Bumped my head too. They're going to have a look at me at the hospital, but I'm fine."

"You found Landsky?"

"He was being kept in the basement of the Anderson house. Just like William Feder."

"What gave you the hunch to go to Queens?"

She didn't want to tell him about Tommy and her suspicions. Not yet. Not until she had a chance to get the story from the kid. He deserved the benefit of the doubt. She wasn't going to ruin a budding career without learning the facts.

"Just a hunch, I guess. Thought I'd take a quick ride to get a feel for what Randall went through, and I end up finding our guy."

"Did Landsky tell you anything?"

"He was pretty out of it, and I was getting treated, so we'll have to interview him when he's stable. One of the uniforms told me he said someone knocked him out in the garage. When he woke up, he was chained in the basement. I had them show him a picture of Randall from my phone, but he was too woozy to know one way or the other. We're both heading to Mount Sinai. In the meantime, I suggest we bring Randall back in and have a chat."

"Randall Brock is gone."

Susan sat up on her stretcher, the phone pressed to her ear. "What?"

"When I got the call that you found Landsky, I had the troopers who were sitting outside his house go knock on his door. He wasn't there. We gained entry, and the place was empty."

"You gotta be kidding me."

"Doesn't look like he took much of anything, so I'm thinking he somehow got word that you found Landsky and fled. Didn't even take his wallet."

"How would he get word?" Susan asked.

"No idea," Crosby replied. "I have a BOLO out on him. He didn't take his car."

"Yeah, well, if he's the guy who hit me, he's driving Hooper's maroon Subaru Legacy. Update the BOLO to include that car."

"Already done."

"You hear from Tommy today?"

"No. He's out running down some leads. You need him there?"

"No, I'm good." Susan could see a lieutenant from the NYPD standing just outside the ambulance bay, waiting to talk to her. "I gotta go give a report before they take me to the ER. I'll be back up as soon as I can. Just get everyone looking for Randall Brock. North Salem. Somers. Brewster. Everyone."

"We're on it," Crosby replied. "And I'll be down there in an hour. You're not hanging in that hospital alone. I'm leaving now."

Susan hung up and motioned for the lieutenant to step into the ambulance. It had crossed her mind that perhaps Hooper and Randall had been working together, but maybe she had things spun around and backward.

You hear from Tommy today?

No. He's out running down some leads.

49

Susan sat on one of the beds in the emergency room, her knees pulled up to her chest, a curtain separating her and the patient on the other side, who'd come in with the flu. They'd put her shoulder in a sling for the time being, but the doctor on duty said she shouldn't be anything more than sore for the next two days, and she could return to work once the soreness subsided. As for her head, it was cut, but no signs of a concussion. They were just waiting on the results of two other tests before they would sign her release.

Over the last few hours, troopers, fellow investigators, NYPD officers, and a few detectives had begun milling about the waiting room, lending support by simply being present. That's what cops did when one of their own was hurt in the line of duty. Just showing up was always enough. But the mass of bodies with radios crackling and conversations growing louder was a distraction to the staff of doctors and nurses, who had other patients to tend to, so she knew they'd be asked to leave soon. Hopefully, she could leave with them.

Crosby slipped through the curtain and walked to her side. Susan tried to sit up but couldn't get the right leverage with her arm in the sling.

"How you doing?" he asked.

"I'm fine."

"You don't look fine. You look banged up."

"I look high." Susan pointed to the IV sticking out of her arm. "Whatever they have me on is some serious stuff. Can't hardly feel a thing."

"I stopped by your house to talk with your mom. She's pretty shook. I told her you'd be home later and that I'd drive you. I offered to bring her here, but the kids were already asleep, and she didn't want them to see you like this."

"Good call on her part."

Crosby nodded and sat in a chair positioned next to the bed.

"Any word on Brock?" she asked.

"Nope. No sign of him. You really think he could've been behind the wheel? He doesn't seem like the kind of guy to go looking to hurt a cop."

"I don't know."

"Maybe you finding Hooper Landsky pissed him off."

"Maybe." Susan thought for a moment. "Hard to put the puzzle together with my brain swimming like this."

Crosby got up out of his seat. "I'll be waiting to take you home. I'm going to send Tommy in. He wanted to see you. Just got here."

"Where's he been?"

"Said he was up at the Quarim campus. Didn't hear what happened until he called into the barracks."

"Tell him the doc said no more visitors or that I was sleeping. I don't want to see him."

"Why?"

"I just don't. No more visitors."

"You two okay?"

"Yeah," Susan lied. "I just can't handle all the questions right now."

Crosby nodded. "All right. I'll come get you when the doctor gives the all clear. We still have the unit at your house. Like I said, he stays there until this is over."

244

"Thanks, boss."

She watched Crosby slip back under the curtain and disappear. She tried to move her shoulder, then winced as the pain slipped through the numbness for just a second. She pushed her magic red button and waited for it to do its thing.

50

Beatrice's Versa was parked on Ringgold Street in Peekskill, across the road and half a block down from the house Tommy was renting three blocks up from the Hudson. The sun was just beginning to lighten the sky, and there wasn't a cloud to be found. Tommy's black Accord was parked in the one-car driveway, but there were lights on inside the house, which meant he was awake and getting ready for work.

By the time Susan had walked out of the ER, there'd been only a handful of officers still lingering in the lobby. Crosby had driven her home. She'd gotten in around three in the morning, her adrenaline still pumping from finding Hooper and her run-in with the Subaru. There was no use resting with only a few hours left before she'd have to get up again. Crosby had ordered her to take a few days and recover, but she'd had other plans. She'd checked on the twins and peeked in on her mother, who was snoring on the couch, before slipping into the shower. As she'd watered the tree they'd put up, she'd noticed the protective unit out front. Seeing it made her feel more vulnerable than protected.

She was gone before anyone had a chance to wake up and took her mother's car to try and disguise herself. She left a note letting Beatrice know where she was and that she had her phone if anyone needed her. The sky-blue Nissan Versa was quite the departure from the Taurus she'd grown used to. This was like driving a four-door go-kart.

The front door opened, and Tommy emerged a few minutes before seven o'clock. Susan straightened up in her seat when she saw him, ignoring the throbbing in her shoulder. She knew she couldn't take the

Percocet they'd given her and drive, so she'd have to fight through the pain until she got home. Even with her arm in the sling, the pain was worse than she'd been expecting. It was going to be a long day.

Tommy hopped down the steps and turned in the opposite direction from where his car was parked. She watched him walk down the street and round the corner onto Hudson Avenue. From where she was parked, she could see him heading away from the river. But if he turned down another street, she'd lose him and would have to drive over in that direction.

He walked two blocks, then popped into a corner deli. After a few minutes, he came out with two paper bags full of groceries, then disappeared inside his house again. Susan relaxed. Just a quick deli run. No biggie.

There was a part of her that felt foolish for tailing a colleague, but the coincidences in the case were too many to ignore. She just wanted to see what a typical day in Tommy's life looked like, and with her supposedly sidelined for the time being, this was his opportunity to make a move if he was, indeed, involved in Amanda's murder.

Tommy had called her two more times while she was at the ER. She'd let them both roll to voice mail, not sure what she was going to say or how she was going to broach things, and figuring ignoring him was the best plan for now.

He came out of his house about an hour after his trip to the deli. Again, he hopped down his stairs, but this time he turned toward his car and climbed in. The engine came to life, and steam billowed from the exhaust. Susan put the Versa in gear and waited as he reversed out of the driveway and began to drive farther down Ringgold. When he took a right on Frost Avenue, she sped up and arrived at the corner just in time to see him make a left onto Washington Street. She kept a close enough distance to track him but stayed far enough back to blend in with the traffic that had picked up for rush hour.

He merged onto Welcher Avenue, made a left on Post Road, then pulled onto the ramp for Route 9. Susan was four cars behind when he eventually merged onto the Taconic State Parkway, then onto Interstate 287 East. Her stomach began to rumble when they picked up the Hutchinson River Parkway South, and she realized she hadn't eaten anything since the night before. The adrenaline was finally wearing off, and she found herself both hungry and tired, the pain in her shoulder a constant thudding.

Tommy drove over the Whitestone Bridge and got onto the Long Island Expressway. At that point Susan had a pretty good idea about where he was going. Interesting that only a day after she'd visited Martin Corolla, Tommy was heading to see his father. Another piece that either didn't quite fit or fit too easily.

She parked a block before Martin's house. From where she sat, she could see father greet son with a hug and usher him inside. She pulled her phone out and dialed the barracks.

"New York State Police, Troop K. Trooper Barton speaking."

"Bart, it's Susan. I need to talk to Corolla."

"Hey, Susan. How you feeling?"

"I'm good. I'll be back in a few days."

"Good to hear it. Tommy's out, though. You try his cell?"

"Yeah," she lied. "Went to voice mail. Thought he might be at his desk."

"Nope. Checked in at roll call, then went on patrol. If I hear from him, I'll have him call you."

She hung up and leaned back in her seat, watching the house, heavy eyes scanning the perimeter of the property for Randall Brock, a maroon Subaru Legacy, or anything else that might look suspicious. She opened her mother's glove compartment and found a half-eaten pack of M&M's. It would have to do.

51

She was back from Long Island and lying on the couch, flipping through channels as shadows cast by the setting sun danced across the living room walls. Beatrice was playing in the backyard with the twins, trying to take their minds off the fact that Mommy had come home with a pretty significant boo-boo. They'd decorated the tree, and Beatrice had made Christmas cookies, hoping to distract the twins and keep them occupied. Tim seemed okay with his mother in a sling, but Casey's questions came one after the other. Susan did her best to answer, but it was hard to explain everything to someone so young. She could tell, as Beatrice looked on, that her little girl was worried and anxious and furious and scared, but she also knew Beatrice would never admit just how worried or anxious or furious or scared she was. So after everything else was done, her mother got Tim and Casey dressed in their winter gear and took them out to the swings while Susan remained relegated to the couch, half watching the television and, despite the painkillers that tried to lull her to sleep, thinking about what details of the case she could be missing.

The doorbell rang.

She sat up and looked out the window. Someone standing at the door, but their identity was hidden by the way the foyer wall jutted out and blocked the porch. She checked to ensure the police unit was still parked at the end of the driveway. It was. That could only mean whoever had come calling was safe as far as the trooper protecting her was concerned. She climbed off the couch and fought dizziness on her way to the door.

Tommy stood on the porch, his hands in his pockets, an expression of uneasiness about him. The sun was setting on the horizon in the distance.

"Hey, Tommy."

"Hey."

"What's up?"

He took his hands out of his pockets and offered them up in surrender. "How about my fellow investigator got attacked and wounded in the line of duty on a case we're both working, but she won't call me or see me, won't pick up the phone when *I* call, and is doing her best to avoid me? What the hell, Susan? We're supposed to be in this together."

Susan shook her head. The drugs were making her woozy, and she didn't want to have this discussion while impaired. "I'm sorry," she said. "I can't talk right now."

"Yeah, well, I'm here, so we're talking."

"Come back tomorrow."

"Why were you following me this morning?"

She felt the muscles in her neck tighten. He'd seen her. "I don't know what you're talking about."

Tommy turned and pointed to her mother's car. "Light-blue Versa. I'm not an idiot, Susan. I know when I'm being tailed. Why were you following me?"

Susan started to close the door, but Tommy stuck his arm inside at the last minute.

"You think I'm dirty?"

"Let go of the door, Tommy."

"Answer me."

"Why would I think that?"

"Because you went to see my father. And he told you everything."

She stopped struggling and allowed the door to swing back open. She looked at her partner through a lens of blurred vision, unsure of what to say.

"Why didn't you tell me you went to see him?"

"I didn't get a chance. I went to Gary Anderson's house after your father's, and then everything went down."

"What made you go to him in the first place?"

"You know what."

Tommy nodded and looked toward the ground. "I couldn't say anything about knowing our suspect and dating Lily and all the Gary Anderson stuff. I wanted to, but I had to play it close to the vest and be professional. You and I both know that if Crosby found out I had an inside track on this family, he'd take me off the case, and I couldn't have that. Not on my first case. I was just trying to come onto the troop smooth. I had no idea Randall Brock was really William Feder until we got those prints back. You would've done the same thing."

"No, I wouldn't have."

"Yeah, right."

Susan leaned against the edge of the door. She felt weak on her feet. "Just tell me the truth," she said. "No more bullshit. You asked Crosby to let you partner with me as soon as the call came in about the Brock case. You knew who he really was, and you wanted a firsthand look at the man who was forced to torture and beat your girlfriend. You wanted to look him in the eye and see what made him tick. You wanted to see if you could tell if he'd enjoyed it."

Tommy shook his head. "How would I know Randall was William? Hell, I didn't even know there was an investigation until I met you at the scene, and when I met you at the scene, we hadn't ID'd the driver yet. Think about it. But I will admit one thing. Once we found out who Randall was, I wanted nothing more than to get a firsthand look into that bastard's eyes to see if I could find guilt or pleasure or something in there that would tell me if he liked what he did to Lily and Rose. So on that point, yeah, you're right."

"Gary made him do what he did."

Tommy snorted. "I was up in Oswego when all that went down, but I started doing research on my own. I called my dad a few times to find out what happened, but he just kept trying to protect me from the truth. He was my father, and he didn't want me knowing what my girlfriend went through. I ended up placing a few calls to the others who were on scene or part of the investigation unit. Professional courtesy. They let me in on the facts that weren't being disclosed to the public. Some of the things they left out of the official file."

"What'd you find?"

"I found out *Dr.* Feder was the one who butchered Rose and Lily. The police told the media that it was Gary who killed them, but it was Feder." Tommy's eyes began to tear. "Rose was found with her head detached. Lily had been set on fire. Burned her alive, right there in the basement. Dumped gasoline all over her and lit a match. The NYPD said Feder had been tortured himself, forced into committing the acts. That Gary kept cutting him up with a blade. Beating him. The whole nine. But it was Feder who killed Gary's family, and they just let him walk free. Said he'd suffered enough. I always wondered if there was a part of him that enjoyed what he was doing."

He wiped the tears away with the back of his hand. "I always wanted a chance to find that out, but then he disappeared. When we ID'd him, I thought it was a dream. He'd fallen right into my lap. Just like that. It was unreal. So no, I didn't say anything. I couldn't. But I still needed to look into his eyes and see, for myself, if there was pleasure in the acts he'd committed. Including what he did to Amanda."

"But you never did."

"What?"

"Look into his eyes. You've never met him. Even when we were interviewing him. Every time he's around, you're not."

Tommy was silent.

"You were the one who found the hole that was dug in Randall's yard."

"Yeah."

"You said you wanted to go up there and look around the woods."

"That's right."

"How did you know there were woods surrounding his property? You'd never been up there before."

A breeze blew fallen leaves end over end down the street and across the porch. Tommy looked at her. "Ever hear of Google Maps? I surveyed the property to see what it looked like. That's what gave me the idea in the first place. You can check my workstation if you want."

Susan stared at him. "Are you part of this?" she asked, her words slurring just a bit. "Are you Sam?"

Tommy's eyes widened. "Susan . . . what the . . . of course not. How could I be?"

"You said it yourself. In our line of work there are no such things as coincidences. Amanda Brock gets killed, and you show up. Sam jumps in the creek behind the field at the Christmas tree lot to throw off the scent, and you arrive on scene wet. You've never actually talked to or met Randall Brock, despite you telling me how desperately you've wanted to since you learned his real identity. You found the hole in his yard that hid the evidence to Amanda's murder. I was alone at Gary Anderson's house last night when I found Hooper. You weren't there."

"You wouldn't return my calls! I didn't know where you were!"

"You know the route I take to my house from the barracks. The night I was run off the road and blew a tire. How would Randall know that would be the road I was taking?"

Tommy laughed. "Susan, the drugs they have you on are messing with your head. Seriously. You said this guy in the hood was already in the parking lot at the barracks when you came out that night. He just followed behind you. He didn't know in advance where you were going. And I wasn't there. I'd left hours earlier. I didn't even know Brock was Feder then."

"You have motive. Revenge for Dr. Feder killing your girlfriend. You've been trying to pin this on him since day one. You said, 'It's always the husband.' Remember that?"

"I can't listen to any more of this garbage."

"Are you Sam?"

"Of course not! You and I both know Randall killed Amanda, and we both know this Sam guy is a made-up story. He killed his wife, and he's trying to get away with it. Makes me wonder if playing the victim a few years ago helped him get away with what he did to Rose and Lily."

Susan waved her hands at the trooper who was parked at the bottom of the driveway, signaling that she needed him. "I don't believe you," she said.

"I didn't know who Randall was until the prints came back," Tommy insisted. "Maybe I would've recognized him if you took me to Amanda's wake. And I have a ticket from the goddamned tube sledding if you want to see it! This is crazy!"

The trooper rushed toward the house. "What's going on?" he asked.

Susan wouldn't take her eyes off Tommy. "I'd like Investigator Corolla to leave my property, and I don't want him back anytime soon."

"You got it."

"Susan, please," Tommy said as he began to back away from the door. "Think about what you're saying."

"I don't want to hear it," she said. Her head was spinning, and she needed to lie down. "I suggest you get back to the barracks and disclose all of this to Crosby. Don't make me tell him. Do the honorable thing here. The sooner we get everything on the table, the faster we can figure out how to get past it."

Tommy was about to say something else but stopped. He nodded and turned to walk with the trooper toward his car, which was parked across the street. Susan watched them leave, then closed the door, fell against the wall in the foyer, and began to cry quietly so her mother and the twins wouldn't hear if they came back in.

Everything was careening out of her control.

What was happening?

52

Randall knew exactly where he was. The walls were the same rough cinder block. The floor was still hard and cold. The smell of standing water, rotten with decay and rust, was enough to make him want to vomit. But most of all it was the aroma of blood and death that flooded his senses. He would never forget that smell for as long as he lived. He was in Gary Anderson's basement. Of that he had no doubt.

The room was so dark Randall couldn't see his hand in front of his face. He tried to stand up, but a chain on his right wrist pulled him back down. He listened for the sound of Lily or Rose crying, but there was only the drone of silence. His head ached, and he tried to remember how he'd gotten there. The last thing he could remember was . . .

"Hello! Is anyone there? I need help! Please, I can't stay here! Help me!"

A rustling came from the other side of the basement.

Randall's stomach tightened as he backed himself up against the wall. His heels slipped on the ground, and he suddenly realized how cold it was in the basement. He was still in his T-shirt and underwear. His body was shaking. He began tugging on the chain.

"Please! Help me! Somebody, help me!"

Footsteps crossed the room. Visions of Gary and his punishments flashed through his mind. The razor. The hot poker. The whip. The hammer. His mind began to cave in on itself as he sobbed and cried out for help. It was too much. It was all too much.

How did you get here?

"I need help! Please!"

The footsteps stopped. Randall continued tugging on his chain, panic overtaking him as he pulled and screamed.

Who is that?

"Leave me alone!"

"Stop screaming or I'll hurt you."

Sam.

Randall was crying uncontrollably. "I can't be here. I have to get out of here! I can't be in this place!"

Sam shook his head and stepped closer. "No. This is *exactly* where you need to be."

Randall couldn't stop tugging on the chain that was attached to the wall. The familiar sound of the metal jingling and clanging rang through the dark basement. He was trapped. Just like last time. Helpless. A victim.

"It's time to face your truths."

"I can't! Please. You have to let me go. I won't say anything. I won't tell anyone about any of this. Just get me out of this place! I can't be here. I can't be here!"

"Tell me the name of Gary's wife."

"I need to go. This place . . ."

"Tell me the name of Gary's wife."

"I can't. I don't—"

Sam suddenly grabbed him in the darkness, and Randall felt something slide across his forearm. It took a moment for the pain to bubble up to his senses. He could feel the warm blood trickling from his wound. Sam had slashed him with the razor again. Just like Gary used to do.

"Tell me the name of Gary's wife."

Randall was crying harder now. "Why won't you leave me alone?"

Another slash. "Tell me the name of Gary's wife."

"Rose!" Randall panted as he fell to one knee, holding his arm as best he could with the cast. "Her name was Rose."

"And his daughter?"

"Please, I can—"

Another slash. More blood.

"Lily! Her name was Lily!"

Randall knew Sam was next to him, but he couldn't see anything. Sam's breath chilled the back of his neck. Gary used to get close like this. His mind was spinning faster and faster, collapsing from the stress. A migraine burst from the base of his skull and spread like colored dye through water.

How did you get here?

"What did you do to Rose?" Sam asked, his voice suddenly distant.

You're going to die.

"I can't do this!"

Slash.

"I need to hear your truth, Dr. Feder. What did you do to her?"

"Please! Stop!"

Slash.

"Tell me."

How did you get here?

"No!"

Sam grabbed him by the hair and pulled his head back. Randall's eyes remained shut, his face moist with tears. He felt the blade touch the inside of his thigh and work its way up toward his groin. "Tell me."

"I can't!"

"You can!"

"I can't face it."

The blade dug deeper. "Tell me!"

"I killed her!" Randall screamed. "I killed her."

The blade stopped.

"How did you kill her?"

"Please don't make me say it."

Another slash. "How did you kill her?"

"I . . . I cut off her head. Gary made me slit her throat and wouldn't let me stop until I cut off her head."

Randall was crying uncontrollably now. His body shook as he recalled the murder. The screams. Gary laughing madly in the background of it all.

"Your first truth. Very good."

Sam let go of him, and Randall recoiled into the corner. He was bleeding from wounds on his arms and inner thigh, but it was too dark to see how deep he'd been cut. His head throbbed, and he was panicking, floating between consciousness and dream.

You're going to die here.

How did you get into the basement?

How did you get here?

You're going to die here.

You're going to die!

"What did you do to Lily?"

"I can't. *Please.*"

Sam bent down and wrapped his hand around Randall's throat. "Tell me your next truth," he said calmly, the tip of the blade touching the corner of his eyelid.

Randall instinctively grabbed at Sam's hand, which was tightening around his neck. He couldn't breathe.

"Tell me."

"I . . . I . . ."

Sam let go. "What did you do to Lily?"

You're going to die.

How did you get here?

"I set her on fire," Randall replied through tears that suddenly began to turn to laughter. He was laughing but couldn't understand why. "You're getting me to confess to everything. Yes, I set her on fire. Gary made me burn her alive."

Sam stood over Randall, his breathing ragged. "A real man would've protected those women. Your weakness sealed their fate. You're a weak man, Dr. Feder."

"I am," Randall replied, still laughing. "I'm weak. So very weak."

"You're pathetic."

"I'm sorry."

"Are you?"

"Yes!"

It was hard for Randall to concentrate on what was happening. He was growing light headed and was certain he was going to pass out. His body was shutting down. His laughter turned back to crying. Blood seeped from his wounds onto his hands, down his legs, and onto the floor. He couldn't see anything, but the smell remained. It was part of him. The dank, musty smell of sweat and hatred and blood.

Sam gently cupped his hand around the back of Randall's head. "It's time for your next truth."

"No more. Please. I can't relive this."

"Did you like torturing and killing Lily and Rose?"

"No. Never. I hated it. I hate myself for doing it. Even now."

"But you didn't do it. Not all of it."

"What do you mean?"

You're going to die.

How did you get here?

"Over time, you had help. And you didn't kill Rose or Lily." Sam leaned in closer so Randall could see his silhouette in the darkness, the blade barely glistening in a light Randall couldn't find. "Tell me who helped you."

53

Morning roll call was complete. The troopers filed out of the barracks and into the parking lot to begin their shift. Tommy sat at his desk, listening to the activity die down until he was the only person on the investigators' floor. The encounter with Susan played back in his mind, consuming his every thought.

The trooper assigned to Susan's house had escorted him to his car and stood at the curb until he'd pulled away. Susan had been under the impression that he was going to drive to the barracks and disclose his relationship with the Andersons to Crosby right then and there, but instead, he'd driven to a bar on the banks of the Hudson, a few blocks up from his house. Half a bottle of tequila later, he'd walked home and crashed out on his sofa before rising early to take care of a few things.

He sat up and stretched. His head ached from a slight hangover, but it wasn't anything he couldn't handle. Crosby was out at a burglary scene in Putnam Valley. When he got back, he'd tell him everything about his father working the Anderson case, as well as his relationship with the family and with Lily in particular. At that point, if the boss wanted to kick him off Amanda Brock's homicide, so be it. But one fact that he wouldn't be able to escape from would be the gossip surrounding his romantic relationship with Lily Anderson and the fact that Susan thought he could be involved in Amanda Brock's murder. It was just a matter of time before the whispers would start and turn into something bigger than they needed to be. He knew he'd have to tread carefully and answer whatever questions were thrown at him. He was the new guy with no friends, and he hadn't earned anyone's trust yet. Susan was the veteran. She was respected, smart, and a good cop. She'd earned the veneration of the men and women at the barracks. If word got out that she thought he was dirty, Tommy would never be able to get out from underneath that.

The message light was blinking on his phone, indicating he had voice mails waiting. He picked up the receiver and dialed to retrieve them.

"Yeah, this message is for Investigator Corolla. This is Manny Stevens from Elmsford HQ. Wanted to let you know we were able to get the computer from your vic's Mercedes working again. I emailed the navigation report to you, but I thought I'd drop you a line to give you a heads-up. GPS shows the Mercedes drove from North Salem to Bear Mountain, and then to Quarim University, and then back onto the Goat Trail, where the accident occurred. If you have any other questions, call me. My number is in the info I sent."

The message ended, and Tommy sat frozen for a moment.

"Corolla!" a voice boomed from the dispatcher's office. "You here?"

"Right here," Tommy shouted back. "What's up?"

"Adler got a package for the case you guys are working on. You want it?"

"Yeah."

Tommy got up and walked out into the hall, where a courier was waiting. He signed for the oversized envelope and brought it back to his desk. Their subpoena was taped to the envelope showing case and file number. It came from Wayfair Psychiatric Hospital in Poughkeepsie. Inside were William Feder's medical records.

Tommy ripped open the envelope and pulled out a thick file full of notes, transcripts, photographs, and copies of prescriptions. He skimmed each page as he went, trying to get the full picture of what he was looking at without wasting his time reading every single thing. He stopped when he got to the patient admission form.

Patient: William Feder
Doctor: Peter Reems, MD/Psychiatrist

He turned to the next page and read carefully. When he was done, he picked up his phone and dialed Susan.

"This is Adler."

"Susan, it's Tommy. Don't hang up. This is important."

There was a pause for a moment. "What."

"First of all, we got the GPS back from Amanda's car computer. She wasn't heading straight home after the award ceremony that night. She went to Quarim University, where Randall was working. That's what we were missing. *She* went to *him*."

Silence on the other end.

"We also just got Randall's medical records. Or William's. You know what I mean. They contain his records from Wayfair, and there's an ongoing shadow file from his personal sessions away from the hospital. Randall and Peter Reems aren't partners in their case study. Randall is Peter's *patient*. The treatment files are from Peter, and the case study is Peter's alone. Randall is the *subject* in the study."

Susan took a breath on the other end. "Wait. I thought Dr. Reems had a bunch of patients he was working with. You're saying Randall was one of them."

Tommy clenched the paper. "According to this, Randall Brock was *all* of them."

54

Randall raised his head up off the floor and rubbed his eyes, which burned with dried tears. He didn't remember falling asleep, nor did he recall Sam leaving, but when he checked his arms, rubbing his fingers across them in the dark, he knew it wasn't a dream. He could feel the blood that had hardened on his skin, and the reality of his situation sank in.

"Hello," he called out. No one answered.

Time didn't exist in the basement. The darkness was too thick for him to see anything, let alone know what day it was or how long he'd actually been down there. The screams and tormented pleas echoed in his mind as the quiet gave way to memories he wished he didn't have.

"You didn't kill them."

Randall jumped when he heard Sam's voice from the other side of the room, instinctively pulling on the chain that was around his wrist.

"You didn't kill Rose or Lily, but you know who did. I want you to tell me."

"I swear I don't know what you're talking about," Randall said.

"You do." Sam's voice was calm, steady. "Think about it. You know this truth. Who killed Rose and Lily?"

Randall strained to see Sam in the darkness. "I . . . don't . . . know."

"Think!"

"I killed them."

"No, you didn't. And you know you didn't. I want your final truth."

Randall heard the match strike before he saw the flame. It was a small dot of light at the other end of the basement. Behind it was the ghostly glow of Sam's face. He dropped the match, and a larger fire erupted on the floor, as if they were outside camping.

"Tell me," Sam said. "Who killed them?"

Tears began to form again. "I promise you, I don't know what you're talking about."

"Do you remember this?" Sam held up a fireplace poker. "Do you remember what Gary did to you with this?"

"Please—"

"Do you remember what he did?"

Randall rubbed the back of his knee and could feel his rough skin, scarred and singed from the burns. "Yes."

Sam stuck the tip of the poker into the fire. "Good. Now, understand, I'm going to burn you with this poker just like Gary did if you don't tell me your final truth. Do you remember how he burned you? How much it hurt?" He stood from the fire and walked across the room. "Who . . . killed . . . Rose . . . and . . . Lily?"

Randall was crying again, tugging on the chains again, his head beginning to ache in the back of his skull again. "I don't know! I don't know! I don't know!"

"Who came to rescue you from the torture and the torment? Who stepped in for you when you couldn't take it anymore?"

"Please, I—"

"Who came to kill Rose? Who came to set poor Lily on fire? Tell me."

"I—"

"Tell me!"

Randall remained on the floor, head down, crying helplessly. "Stephen Sullivan killed Rose. He came and killed her. He liked it. He wanted to do it, so I let him. I let him when I should have saved her."

"And who killed Lily? Who set her on fire?"

"Jerry Osbourne. Jerry set her on fire. I couldn't do it, and he said he would. He said he would help me, and I was so grateful. I let him. It was the only way."

Sam leaned in closer. "And your little brother? Sam. Who pushed him into the stream and held his face under the water until he stopped struggling? Who came up with the idea to let the current take him downstream, and who came up with the story that he slipped on the rocks?"

"I did," Randall sobbed. He was outside his body now, watching two men in a dank basement, one chained to a wall, the other standing over him, their voices echoing off the brick foundation. He couldn't think. He couldn't breathe. He couldn't form a conscious thought. There was just pain and confusion and terror and truth. "I killed my brother."

Sam shook his head. "That's not your truth."

"It is. I killed Sam. I held him under the water and drowned him so I could have my parents back. It was only supposed to be the three of us. He wasn't ever supposed to be born. It was only supposed to be my mom and dad and me."

"No," Sam replied, pulling Randall closer and staring deep into his eyes. They were nose to nose, and Randall could see him now. He could see Sam smile a thin, horrific smile. "You didn't kill your little brother. I did. I came and did it for you so we could have Mom and Dad back. And I did the same to Amanda. She was going to ruin us and everything you've worked so hard for. We couldn't allow that to happen. I came because you called me. I came because I *am* you."

Randall said nothing. He stared at the man in front of him, knowing he was right but unwilling to believe what he was hearing.

"We have more to do," Sam whispered. "You've done well and admitted your truths. Now you know who you are. Who I am. And we have to save ourselves. This isn't over. Peter knows the truth, and he's become dangerous. He'll turn you in to the police, and we'll spend the rest of our lives in prison. We can't let that happen. We have to take care of Peter."

"No. I can't."

"*We* can. It's the only way."

Randall wiped the tears from his eyes and slowly shook his head. He couldn't say the words aloud, but he knew Sam was right. There were tracks that needed covering. This was about survival. Sam's words swam through his mind like a dream he couldn't wake up from.

I came because you called me. I came because I am you.

55

Susan followed Tommy and Peter Reems down the hall and into Peter's home office. She still wasn't sure what to believe but needed Tommy in her corner for the moment. There were too many loose ends to try and get through, and she didn't want to jump to any conclusions. Better to keep the kid close and on her side. She'd adjust if she had to. But for now, they were better off working as a team.

As soon as Peter sat behind his desk, Tommy slammed Randall's folder down. "A couple of details you forgot to share with us," he said. "Randall Brock is William Feder. And he's not your partner. He's your patient."

Susan watched from the back of the room as Peter pulled the folder toward him and skimmed the first page, his index finger sliding down the paper as he read. "Randall told me you discovered his identity. I was wondering how long it would take for you to come knocking. How did you get this?"

"Subpoena." Susan leaned against the closed door. "We got his identity from running his prints when we arrested him. You knew all along, and you kept it from us. Misled us by saying you two were working together. You said Randall was your colleague."

"We are working together." Peter pointed to the file. "As doctor and patient. And he is my colleague. *Dr.* Feder is just as much a doctor of psychiatry as I am."

"Dr. Feder doesn't even exist anymore." Tommy lurched over the desk. "You knew what we were investigating. You knew we labeled

Amanda's accident a homicide. Why wouldn't you come forward and tell us the truth about who Randall was and that you were treating him? That he *needed* treatment?"

"Because I knew you'd pin Amanda's accident on him without conducting a proper investigation, and I'm not convinced Randall's guilty of anything."

Tommy's voice was growing louder. "How can you say that? Your own diagnosis tells us that not only is Dr. Brock capable of murder but he has the capacity to take on a different personality while committing the act. All of a sudden he starts talking about a mysterious visitor named Sam? There's no way you thought he was completely clean. No way."

Peter shot up from his chair. "Do not question my treatment. Yes, Randall suffers from dissociative identity disorder brought on by the trauma in Gary Anderson's basement. But I can't imagine him being capable of hurting Amanda. You don't know him like I do. He loved her. Whether what happened to her was an accident or murder, I knew it couldn't be Randall. Those personalities are unique and exclusive to what happened with Gary Anderson. They have nothing to do with any other aspect of his life."

Susan pushed herself off the door and walked across the office. She placed her hand against Tommy's chest and gently moved him back. "Tell us about your study with Randall. What are you doing, exactly?"

"I've been conducting a new treatment to rid Randall of his personalities and the memories of the violent acts he had to commit in that basement. He builds scenarios around these personalities and talks through the murders until they become less and less the focal point of a memory or urge he's unaware he's having."

"You talk to Randall during these sessions, or do you talk to the personalities?"

"I trigger the personalities. I make Randall talk about what happened with Gary, and when he can't take the memories any longer, his transition takes place. It's brought on by a massive headache. A migraine. And then he's triggered."

"Go on."

Peter's chest was still rising and falling, but his voice was calmer. He looked at Susan, ignoring Tommy. "As Stephen, his fantasy is to slit his girlfriend's throat. That's how Randall killed Rose. As Jerry, his fantasy is taking a dental receptionist to the woods and setting her on fire. That's how Randall killed Lily. Jason Harris's fantasy involves killing his abusive father, which is really Randall wanting to kill Gary, the man who lorded over him and made him do these horrible things. Our progress has been extraordinary, and Randall has been very receptive to the treatment. Each telling of the fantasy involves less violence." He paused for a moment, his eyes darting back and forth, his mind churning. "That's why I don't think he would ever hurt Amanda. He doesn't turn violent for the sake of violence. Amanda wasn't part of what happened in the Anderson basement. Him killing her doesn't fit."

Tommy shook his head. "But you still didn't tell us. You didn't want to put an end to your new kind of treatment. You thought you were making progress and didn't want the inconvenience of a murder to sidetrack you."

"That's not the case. I couldn't break patient-doctor privilege. Besides, I owe it to Randall to get him better. I'm the reason all of that happened to him."

"How do you figure?" Susan asked.

Peter was quiet for a moment. "I was the one who passed Gary Anderson to Randall," he said finally. "My patient capacity was full, and he had room to add. I gave him Gary. I handed my friend a maniac who altered his life forever. I owe it to him to get him better, and I didn't need the police targeting him as a murder suspect."

"You had a duty to warn, and you chose to keep quiet," Tommy said.

Susan moved next to Tommy. "I think my partner's right. You never told us any of this because then you'd have to admit that your subject not only developed another personality on top of the three he already had and killed his wife while undergoing your experimental treatment, but you helped conceal his identity in the first place. You knew Randall was William Feder, and if you told us that, you knew you'd lose your funding, and your reputation would be flushed right down the toilet. Now Randall's missing, and if I didn't happen to come across Hooper Landsky locked in Gary Anderson's basement, we might be talking about another victim here."

Peter looked at both of the investigators. "Randall's missing?"

Susan nodded. She sat in one of the chairs facing the desk and took out her notepad. "We found the murder weapon and the computer from Amanda's Mercedes buried in Randall's backyard, so I don't want to hear your opinion on his innocence anymore. What I do want is for you to tell us everything you know. And let me emphasize *everything*. Go."

Peter looked horrified. "I admit we've had some recent hiccups in his treatment, some backsliding. I had no idea you had evidence. I . . . oh god, he really killed Amanda, didn't he?"

"Now's your chance to come clean. Talk."

Peter began to play with the buttons on his shirt cuffs. "When Randall . . . William . . . was a young boy, his little brother died. It was widely reported as an accidental drowning in a stream behind the Feder farm upstate. But when I started treating him after his imprisonment by Gary Anderson, I found an old patient file that had been sealed because he was a minor. In it, there are notes covering Randall's therapy. He was suffering from what we would today call PTSD. The death of his brother affected him a great deal. More than you'd normally see, especially based on his age and the fact that he and his brother weren't that close. At one point, the notes brush upon the possibility that Randall himself might have drowned his brother. My theory was that Randall had been so troubled by his brother's death, perhaps because he *had* been responsible for it, that he created an imaginary friend to compensate for the absence of his brother. Maybe even to take some of the guilt away from Randall himself. Eventually, that imaginary friend grew into a second personality, and that personality disappeared as Randall got older. In his mind, his brother's death became nothing more than a tragic accident." Peter looked at them. "Randall's brother's name was Sam."

Jesus, Susan thought as Tommy sat down in the chair next to her. *It's worse than I thought.*

"Things changed after Gary Anderson," Peter continued. "The things Gary made Randall do were too horrific to contemplate, let alone actually carry out, so Randall shut down. His mind completely closed itself off to the reality of his situation, and two new personalities emerged. One was Stephen Sullivan, and one was Jerry Osbourne. I have no idea where the names or intricacies of each personality came from, but they took over for Randall whenever he was forced to do something to those women. Stephen took care of Rose Anderson, and Jerry stepped in whenever Lily was involved."

Susan looked over at Tommy, who was staring at the doctor, his hands clenched in balled fists. "How could personalities just pop up like that?" she asked. "One minute there's nothing, and the next he's got two completely different people taking over his mind?"

"Don't forget, Randall's mind was already predisposed to this condition. He suffered from it when he was a child, calling his personality an imaginary friend, and then suppressed it without really knowing what it was. He simply grew up, and the need to be someone else, to have that crutch, dissipated. But when Gary Anderson forced him to torture those women years later, that predisposition rose again, and new personalities were born. As Stephen or Jerry, he could shut down his consciousness and let them do what needed to be done. When he was Randall again, he'd have vague memories of some things, but for the most part, the details were gone, and the guilt was manageable. It was his mind's way of coping."

"So how does this new Sam personality fit?" Tommy asked.

Peter sighed. "I don't know. All I can think is that Randall somehow stumbled upon Amanda's affair and her plans to leave him. Maybe he panicked, and in that panic, a new personality rose. This personality would be much stronger than the others. Much more self-assured, otherwise he wouldn't be named after Randall's little brother. This version of Sam could have helped Randall kill Amanda and take her lover hostage. Perhaps this could even be the original personality being born again. The name harkens back to the death of his brother." Peter paused for a moment. "I mentioned the hiccup in his treatment. Just recently his other personalities have talked about a stranger helping them in their fantasies. This could've been Sam, and I missed it. I didn't know what all of it meant until now."

"That's everything?" Susan asked.

Peter nodded. "I swear."

Susan stood and put her notepad in her bag. "If you hear from Randall, you call me right away. Don't try and talk him down or treat him or hide him or anything. Just call me."

As she made her way toward the door, Tommy got up and leaned over Peter's desk. "I hope you have a good lawyer," he said. "You better start making some calls."

———

Susan waited until they were outside.

"We need to find Randall," she said. "This is growing out of our control."

"Tell me what to do."

"Go back to HQ. Extend the BOLO to include the five boroughs, Rockland, Dutchess, Putnam, and Orange Counties. Get Crosby up to speed on what we know and how Dr. Reems was keeping information from us."

"Done."

"Did you talk to him about your prior relationship with the Andersons and this case?"

"Not yet."

"Good. Don't. We'll address it when the case is over. I need all the manpower I can get at this point, and I can't afford him sitting you down now." Susan walked over to her car and opened the door. "I'm going to head back up to North Salem. Poke around Randall's house. See if I can find something that might tell us where he is, because right now, no one has a clue, and I feel like we're running out of time."

56

When Randall opened his eyes again, he was still in Gary Anderson's basement, but things were different now. The room was bright. The sun was shining through two small storm windows on the opposite side of the room, near the boiler and water heater. He could see everything clearly, the blackness gone. The basement door was wide open at the top of the stairs. More sunlight streamed in from the kitchen above. He looked down at his wrist and saw that he was no longer chained to the wall. In fact, there was no chain anywhere to be found, nor was there a firepit or the poker Sam had threatened to burn him with. Only two things remained to prove that Randall hadn't been dreaming and that Sam had been with him in the basement, in one way or another. The first was the cuts on his arms and leg, rough and ragged. Some of them had been deep. Dried blood stained his clothes and skin. Tiny droplets dotted the cement floor where he'd been sitting. The second was the knife lying next to him. It was from his kitchen back home, not a razor as he'd first suspected. A faint voice whispered in his ear.

Your truths are yours. Keep them safe.

A last truth to come to terms with. He could see it now as clearly as he could see the walls and foundation beams and scattered items in the basement. It had been a partnership all along, a bond that was as solid as the cement he sat upon. Sam had come and helped him take care of what needed taking care of. He'd given Randall his life back and ultimately showed him his sins of the past so he could finally come to terms with who he was and how that was never going to change. Randall would always have his *friends* to rely on. That's who he was, and neither Peter nor Amanda nor the doctors he'd seen after being freed from Gary's basement would ever be able to take that away. He was one with Sam, and Sam was one with him. A perfect match. The final piece to his complex and sometimes confusing puzzle. But now it all made sense. It all fit. There was no reason to fight it any longer. Acceptance was the greatest gift Sam had given him. Randall now knew who he was completely, and a wave of relief washed over him.

Your truths are yours. Keep them safe.

He picked up the knife and made his way across the basement to the stairs. His body was sore, and his head still ached, but he felt better than he had in a long time. He'd thought he knew what happiness was, but this was a different kind of joy. This was the joy of being free from one's doubts and fears. This was an awakening, a true acknowledgment. Amanda was dead, and he was thankful Sam had taken care of it for him. He didn't want to remember any of it. It was better this way.

As Randall reached the top of the stairs, he looked around the decrepit kitchen. Only days ago, the mere sight of this place would have sent him into a frenzy of panic and terror. Now, with the clarity of knowing who he was, he had no real emotion. It was a room in a house. Nothing more. Sam's voice kept whispering to him, pushing him forward.

Your truths are yours. Keep them safe.

Hooper's maroon Subaru was parked in the garage. Randall reached into his pocket and came away with keys he hadn't known he had. He opened the driver's-side door, climbed in, dropped the knife next to him, and started the engine. Somehow the smell and sound of the car were familiar to him, but he had no real memory of driving it or parking it in the garage. That had also been Sam, making sure everything was as it should have been.

As Randall pulled down the driveway and onto the road, Sam's voice was soothing in his mind, pushing him forward, giving him the strength he needed.

Your truths are yours. Keep them safe.

Giving him acceptance and freedom and understanding.

And rage.

57

Susan walked through the front door and dropped her bag. She glanced into the living room to find the twins watching television.

"Hey, guys."

"Hi, Mommy."

"Hi."

They were like zombies staring at the screen, completely engrossed in whatever it was they were watching. Beatrice was in the kitchen, cleaning the counters and wiping them dry.

"Mom, stop. You're not my maid. I'll do that."

Her mother shook her head. "How are you going to clean and do laundry and dress the twins and all the other stuff you need to do with one arm?" she snapped. "You're not a superhero. I think that sling proves that."

"Whoa," Susan replied. "What's with the hostility?"

"Nothing."

"No, really. Talk to me."

"I'm fine."

"Mom."

Beatrice finally turned around. Her eyes were glassy with tears. "I'm scared, Susan. It's as simple as that. I'm scared. One of your criminals or suspects or whatever you call him was watching us at the tree lot, and now we're in danger. I'm scared."

"Everything's fine. I know this is new to you, but we're fine."

"Are we? Is that why we have a police car parked out front all day protecting us? Or is he waiting for your stalker to come back and try to finish the job?"

"It's not like that."

"Well, it's something. It's dangerous enough that we need a police presence all day and night. And look at you. This guy attacked you, and you're lucky all he did was dislocate your shoulder. He could've killed you. Dammit, Susan, you have children who expect their mother to come home each night." She started to cry. "And you have a mother who expects the same."

Susan scurried across the kitchen and hugged her mother tight. "I'm sorry," she whispered. "I want to be here for you and the twins. I will be. I know this is scary for you, but you have to believe me when I tell you we have everything under control. The unit out front is a courtesy. No one thinks we're in true danger. It's more a cover-your-ass thing for my boss. We're fine. And as soon as we catch this guy, I'm going to make sure I spend more time home with all of you. Maybe I'll take some vacation days and hang out. Just to make sure we hit the right reset button. I know I've been away a lot. I'm sorry about that, and I'm going to change things. For all of us."

Beatrice nodded and wiped her tears. "Okay. I'm trusting you here. If you say we're okay, then I'll believe you." She rolled up the rag and tossed it in the sink. "I think I'm going to go watch some TV with the kids. You need anything?"

"No. You're spending the night?"

"Yes, I think so."

"Good."

Susan watched as her mother crossed the kitchen and made her way into the living room. Just as she was opening the pantry to grab a snack, her cell phone rang in her back pocket.

"This is Adler."

"Hey, it's Tommy. Got some news."

"Go."

"We got more security footage from the university and can confirm that Amanda did visit the campus before she drove off the Goat Trail. We can see her Mercedes entering and parking in a different lot. We were so focused on watching Randall's car we never bothered to search for anything else."

"Good. So we have video evidence that confirms what the Mercedes's computer is telling us."

"There's more."

"What?"

"We just got a call from the barracks out of Wappinger's. Poughkeepsie PD and fire department was dispatched to a fire on the Quarim campus a few minutes ago. It's the building housing the psychiatry wing."

Susan slammed the pantry shut and raced toward the front door. "I'm heading there now."

"Me too."

"And Tommy, in the future, you wanna lead with that kind of info." She hung up and snatched her bag, holding it down at her side while looking in on her mother and the twins.

"I gotta go," she said. "I know I just walked in, and I know I promised I'd make time, but something's happened, and I need to be on scene."

Beatrice smiled through a new set of tears. "You see these beautiful children?"

"Yes."

"Then please, be careful. For all of us."

Susan nodded and left the house. There was nothing more to say.

58

Emergency lights filled the darkening sky as Susan pulled through the gates of the university. She parked next to Tommy's Accord and took a moment to assess the scene. Three engines, two ambulances, and a handful of local Poughkeepsie police cars were parked haphazardly in front of a half-charred brick building. Three of the police units had set up to act as a barrier between the public and the first responders.

It appeared as though the blaze had been contained. Clusters of firefighters milled about the property and parking lot, packing up gear and rolling up hoses. The science building was stained black with soot. Its roof, where a team of firemen had poked holes through the shingles for ventilation, was badly damaged, as was the west side of the structure. Glass had been punched out of every window, and the doors had been ripped off their hinges. The adjacent buildings looked to be in good condition, and the one set of offices connected to the science building only had a few windows missing. Everything else looked intact.

Tommy jogged toward Susan as she climbed out of her sedan. "Hey, can you grab my recorder out of the glove box in my car?"

Susan nodded and opened the Accord's passenger door. She leaned in, opened the glove box, and rifled through a pile of papers, maps, and a garage door opener until she found the small recording device. She took it and walked toward the officers standing guard, her shield draped around her neck.

"She's with me," Tommy shouted.

The two officers nodded and let her pass.

"Hey, you okay?" Tommy asked, stopping when he saw her. "You look a little pale."

"Shoulder's barking." She handed him the recorder. "Haven't taken my pain meds all day."

"You wanna sit this one out? I can catch you up."

"Just tell me what happened. What'd you find?"

They started walking toward the building. Susan could smell the scent of charred wood and metal wafting through the air.

"We have arson and a homicide."

"Randall?"

Tommy shook his head. "Looks like it's Peter Reems. The inspector found the accelerant in his office, so we're figuring that's where the fire started. Gasoline. Campus security called Peter's house, and his wife said he was heading up here to do some work. Once they got the blaze under control, they were able to get inside and found the body. It's too damaged for a normal ID, but the inspector confirmed that there is a slash wound across the neck. Cut deep enough to get the tendons and jugular, so it's likely he was dead prior to the fire. We'll need dental records to ID and an autopsy for cause, but everything indicates that it's Dr. Reems."

Susan stared at the building and found the window on the first floor that was part of Peter Reems's office. There was still smoke snaking out from inside as two firefighters pulled down what remained of an interior wall with an axe and a Halligan bar.

"We also have security footage of a maroon Subaru Legacy entering the main gates about twenty minutes before the fire was reported," Tommy continued. "We followed the car on the video and got a good look at the plate this time. It's Hooper's Subaru. Randall was driving. Wasn't even trying to hide himself this time."

Susan gently closed her eyes, listening to everything around her. The crackle of the radios, the shouts of instructions, the buzzing of the gas-powered tools the firefighters used to cut through the office. These were all sounds she was familiar with, but this time they seemed alien. "Why would Randall kill his friend? Peter was trying to help him."

"Maybe Randall's past help," Tommy replied. "Maybe he finally realized that, and the only thing he can do at this point is keep his secret. I don't know. Could be tying up loose ends, maybe? Maybe he's killing everyone who knew about his dissociative disorder, and then he'll try to escape?"

Susan opened her eyes and nodded. "So then what if Randall didn't kill Amanda for the money or because she was going to leave him? What if he killed her because she'd learned about his dissociative identity disorder? Think about it. Living a normal life was all he ever wanted. At one point he was a renowned doctor of psychiatry. He was a professor at a prestigious school. People knew him in academic circles. But he lost all of that the moment he agreed to go to Gary Anderson's house. So he moves to the West Coast, adopts another identity, and is living like a regular guy. No violence. He meets Amanda and they eventually get married. Still no violence. He's living the life he wants to live. But then Amanda discovers the truth, and his life isn't normal anymore. So Sam is born to set things right again."

"We're reaching," Tommy said. "But there could be something there."

"Who else knows about his disorder?"

"I'm not sure. We'd have to see his recent records, and I'm guessing most of that information just went up in flames."

Susan began to walk back toward her car. "Let's get back to the barracks and take another look at the records we have."

Tommy reached out and grabbed her arm to stop her. "Hold on," he said. "We know about his disorder. We know."

"But he doesn't know we know. You just got the medical records, and we went straight to Peter's house to get the full story."

"What if Peter told Randall we knew before Randall killed him? What if Randall . . . got it out of him somehow?"

Susan pulled her phone from her pocket. Her shoulder was a constant throbbing. She wanted nothing more than to take a shower, pop a Percocet, and go to bed. She needed to recharge, but there was so much more to do. "I'll call my house and make sure everyone is okay, and then I'll contact the unit in front to give him a heads-up. I'll meet you at the barracks."

Tommy let go of her arm. "No. I'm not leaving until I know everyone's okay."

Susan dialed and waited, staring at the man she'd thought could have been involved in all of this. She now realized how foolish that was. She owed him an explanation and an apology.

"Hi, honey."

When Susan heard her mother's voice, a wave of relief she hadn't known was building washed over her. Everyone was fine.

59

Even though Beatrice had told Susan that everyone was okay, she was certain she could still hear worry in her mother's voice, and she was anxious to get home. Unfortunately, it was three more hours before she and Tommy finished overseeing the evidence collection at the university and notifying Peter's family. That had been particularly brutal. She'd watched Peter's son try to absorb the news, and all she could think was that she hoped her kids would never have to go through anything like that. She tried not to think about it.

As she pulled onto her street, the clock on the dashboard read a little past eleven. Most of the lights were still on at the house, which was unusual at this time of night. She'd told her mother not to wait up for her. She peered over the steering wheel, and her breath caught in her throat.

The front door of the house was ajar.

She shut off the car's headlights and parked at the curb, silently opening her door and pulling her weapon from her holster. She wanted to scream for her mother and the twins to make sure they were okay, but she swallowed it instead. Every maternal nerve in her body pushed her to run into the house, but the cop in her knew that was foolish. She had to stay calm. Control was the key. There was a reason the lights were on and the door was open. Good or bad, she would find out why. But she'd do it carefully. She had to.

The trooper who'd been watching the house was still parked at the end of the driveway. A sense of relief washed over her when she saw him sitting behind the wheel. She waved at him as she approached. But when he didn't acknowledge her, that sense of relief quickly became a knot in her stomach.

The glass on the driver's-side door was partially fogged up, and she couldn't see inside. She opened the driver's door.

The young trooper, no more than twenty-seven years old, was staring out the windshield, his throat cut. Blood darkened the front of his gray uniform, and spray from his jugular covered the dashboard and steering wheel.

Just like Peter Reems. Just like Rose.

Susan felt her stomach lurch. She straightened and caught a glimpse of a figure standing in the house's open doorway. Randall looked at her and waved, knife in hand. The hue of the red and green Christmas lights strung around the door gave him the evil glow of something supernatural.

He smiled at her—the most chilling smile she'd ever seen in her life. Then he shut the door, locking himself inside with her family.

Locking her out.

60

No! Please!

Frantically, she reached into the patrol car and snatched the radio from its cradle. She thought about her mother and the twins inside and wondered how long Randall had been in there. What had he done? That smile. It was haunting.

"All units, this is Investigator Susan Adler. We have a 10-33 at my home. Address is three twenty-three Briar Court, Fishkill. One officer is down. I'm in need of assistance ASAP. Suspect is Randall Brock, and he's in my house with my mother and my two kids. Possible hostage situation. Hurry!"

She threw the radio back inside the car and ran toward the house, slipping on the icy bricks that lined the path to the front door. She tugged on the knob and noticed the keyhole had been filled with some kind of glue or silicone. There was no way she could get her house key in there. She ran and checked the living room windows. Locked. Of course they were locked. It was the middle of winter. She ran around back, her feet thumping in the snow, until she reached the patio doors. They were locked as well. Silicone in the keyholes. She looked through the glass but couldn't see anything. There was no movement inside. No sound.

Come on!

She ran back to the front door and aimed her weapon, firing two shots that exploded in the quiet night. The shots splintered the wood around the knob and dead bolt. She kicked the door in, immediately dropping to a shooting position, taking cover behind the doorframe outside.

The house was still. Susan took a careful step inside, her left arm raised, her right still in the sling. She could see her mother lying face-down, half in the hall and half in the kitchen. Blood pooled around her midsection. She scurried over to her and rolled her onto her back. Beatrice was alive, but her heartbeat was weak. Her eyes were open, try-ing to focus. A thin line of blood seeped from the corner of her mouth.

"I tried to stop him. I tried to push him back out. He got me."

Susan examined the knife wound. "I can't tell if it's bad or not. He got you in the side." She grabbed a dish towel from the counter. "Try and put pressure on it. Stay down and don't move. Do you know where the twins are?"

"No."

"Did you see where he went?"

Beatrice began to cry. "No."

"Okay. Stay here. Try and stay calm."

"I love you."

Susan backed away, slipping her arm out of the sling and swallow-ing the pain that shot through her as she extended her arm and placed her second hand on the Beretta to steady it. Her adrenaline was trying to push the hurt away. She was focused, tuned in.

"Randall, come out with your hands up. I'm armed and will fire. Backup is on the way. It's over. Come out now."

There was no reply. She swept through each room on the bottom floor. The living room was empty, as were the dining room, bathroom, and closet. The house was too quiet. She walked into the kitchen as her mother faded in and out of consciousness. She flipped on the patio light and could see her footprints around the door as well as a set of larger prints stamped in the snow leading from the chicken coop up to the patio doors. He'd been watching them. He'd known she wasn't home.

She walked into the foyer and turned toward the stairs.

"Hey, you guys up there? Casey? Tim? It's Mom."

"Mommy," Tim whined, quietly. It wasn't quite a whisper, but it scared the hell out of her. She could sense a tremble in his voice like he'd been crying. Again, the instinct to rush up the stairs tried to overtake her, and she fought it with every ounce of strength she could.

"I'm coming, buddy."

She placed a foot on the first step.

Please, God. Let them be okay. Please!

"Stay where you are."

His voice froze her. Susan pointed the gun toward the stairs and watched as Randall emerged from the darkened second floor. He walked toward her with Casey in one arm and Tim in the other, stopping only when he reached the top landing. That same unnerving smile was on his face. His knife was in his right hand, but that hand was being used to hold Casey against his chest, so his weapon was actually pinned behind her. He pressed Tim close with his bandaged left hand. Both kids had tears in their eyes. They were scared. Tim was trembling.

"Mommy," Tim said again.

"I'm here, baby."

"I want to get down," Casey whimpered, looking first at Randall and then at her mother.

The gun was so heavy in her hand. Her shoulder was burning. Susan held it as steady as she could. "Randall, put the knife down. It's over."

"Randall's not here."

"Put the knife down. We can talk after I know the kids are safe."

"No."

"Randall—"

"Randall's not here!"

The twins began to cry again as Randall's booming voice, filled with rage and contempt, echoed through the house.

Susan remained calm, thoughts burning through her mind, one after the other. Where was that backup? "Sam?"

He nodded.

"Sam, let my children go."

"I can't do that."

"What do you want?"

Randall took one step down and paused. "I suggest you back up into the living room, or I'll toss these two beautiful babies right down these stairs. You and I both know the fall will crack their skulls or break their necks. This tread is steep. They'll be dead before they stop rolling."

Susan did her best to stay focused, ignoring the screaming pain in her shoulder. She could feel the joint bulging as if it was about to pop again.

"Get in the living room."

She matched steps with Randall, backing into the living room as he made his descent down the stairs. The gun trembled in her grip. She wasn't sure how much longer she could hold it.

"Why are you doing this?" she asked.

Randall turned when he got to the landing and shuffled into the hallway. He faced her, twins tucked in front of him with only his eyes and nose showing between their tiny bodies. "I'm reclaiming my life. I'm taking back my identity."

"What does that even mean?"

"I know who I am now. I know what I am. I can live with my friends, but only after I keep my truth. And I can't keep my truth until I silence everyone who knows my truth." He looked at her, his gaze focused, intense. "My truths are mine. No one else's. I have to keep them safe."

"Put the kids down. They have nothing to do with this. They don't know who you are or what your truth is. Let them go."

"I can't do that," he said. "If I put them down, you'll shoot me. I think I'm going to hold on to them instead. I'll hold them until you put that gun in your mouth and pull the trigger. Once you're dead, I promise I'll let them go. But you need to make the first move. For the sake of your beautiful, wonderful, vulnerable children."

Susan dropped to one knee and leaned her elbow on her thigh for support. Her shoulder was about to dislocate again. Her hand shook violently. "I'm not going to kill myself for you."

"You're not killing yourself. I'm killing you, but you're helping me. It's the only way I'll let your children go. I need to know you're dead. I can't have my truths out there. Those truths are mine."

"I have to—"

"Stop talking and put the gun in your mouth!" Randall cried. "After you pull the trigger, I'll put them down, and I'll leave." He glanced toward the kitchen. "The old woman is already dead. There's just you now."

Susan thought about Randall's medical file and some of the notes Peter had written about triggers. "Tell me how you killed your wife."

"You know how."

"I want to hear the details from you."

Randall thought for a moment, his eyes darting back and forth. His brow creased as he glanced toward the floor. "I can't remember," he muttered to himself.

"Tell me how you got Hooper Landsky to Gary's basement."

He shook his head and closed his eyes. He was squeezing the twins closer, gnashing his teeth and grunting. "I . . . can't remember."

The gun was wavering from side to side.

"Tell me about Peter. Was he dead before you burned him?"

"Yes."

"You burned him like you burned Lily."

"No! He was already dead. I wouldn't do that ever again."

"Can you still hear Lily's screams as she burned alive in front of you? Can you smell her skin and hair?"

"Shut up!"

"Can you hear Gary laughing while his daughter died?"

"Stop it!"

"Can you feel Rose's blood all over your hands and arms?"

"Stop!"

"Can you hear Lily screaming as you killed her mother?"

The kids began to cry.

"Put that fucking gun in your mouth, or I swear I'll kill your kids! I'll do it!"

Susan paused, the gun almost slipping from her grasp. The pain in her shoulder was making her light headed, and she feared she might pass out. "How, exactly, are you going to kill my kids?" she asked.

Randall looked at her, head cocked to the side. "I'll cut their throats like I did to the trooper in your driveway. Like I did to Rose and Peter."

"Yeah, but as soon as you do that, I'll kill you. I thought the point of all of this was for you to keep your truth and get away."

"If you don't put that gun in your mouth, I'll kill them slow."

"Okay," Susan replied. She had to keep blinking to keep her target in focus. "That could work. I mean, if you started cutting them, I would probably do what you said."

"Then do it!"

"But in order to slit their throats or cut them, you're going to need that knife. And in order to get that knife, you're going to have to put my daughter down. You're holding her with the hand you'll need, and that knife is useless with it pinned against her and pointing toward the floor. As soon as you drop her, I'm going to open fire and end this. So tell me again: How are you going to kill my kids? Can't use the knife. Can't strangle them. You need a free hand for that too. And you don't even have two working hands at the moment. That bandage is going to get in the way. Can't even bend your fingers with the splint. Now you're on the bottom floor, so you can't throw them down the stairs. What's your next move, Randall?"

"I told you," Randall growled through clenched teeth. "Randall's not here."

"Yes, he is. I'm staring right at him."

Pots and pans crashed in the kitchen, and Randall instinctively turned toward the noise. As soon as he did, Susan slid forward to get closer to her target, steadied the Beretta on her thigh, and fired. The shot exploded in the quiet house, smoke immediately filling the bottom floor. The bullet hit Randall just above his knee. He screamed, which made the twins scream.

"Put the kids down and drop the knife!"

"I'll kill them!" Randall cried, the pain coursing through every pronunciation of his words.

Susan fired a second shot into his other leg. Randall screamed again and fell to his knees. He let go of Casey and immediately brought the knife up to Tim, exposing the entire right side of his upper body.

Time slowed down for Susan in that instant. She fired three more shots, hitting Randall once in the chest, once in the neck, and a final time in the head, just below the right eye. His body rocked back, and he fell against the stairs. Tim landed on the floor, crying and confused, hollering for his mother. Susan scurried on her hands and knees, grabbing her children and dragging them into the living room.

"Mommy!" Casey cried.

"I'm scared!" Tim sobbed.

Susan hugged them to her chest, the pain in her shoulder unrelenting. "I know. I know," she whispered, kissing them and pulling them in to her. "It's over. I promise. It's over now."

Sirens were approaching in the distance. She got to her feet and carried the twins into the kitchen. Beatrice had managed to crawl toward the island and pull a towel full of pots and pans she'd set out to dry onto the floor to act as a distraction. She was now lying in a pool of blood, pale and weak.

Susan knelt beside her. "Mom."

Beatrice nodded once, then closed her eyes.

"Hang in there. Help is coming. I can hear them." She looked behind her and saw Randall's lifeless body lying in the hall. "It's over. All of it. It's over."

61

Susan sat on the couch in her living room, watching her friends and colleagues, people she'd known for years, people she'd had drinks with, gone to dinner with, celebrated birthdays and anniversaries and holidays and weddings with, process her house as a crime scene. It was like a dream. Like she was removed from this new reality. They worked around her, refusing to make eye contact to avoid starting a conversation that could end up on record. They nodded their hellos, then got right to work, taking pictures, extracting carpet and soil samples, taking measurements, and dusting for prints to retrace Randall's steps once he'd gotten inside her home. She'd seen it all a thousand times, but she'd never been on the other side. She'd never been the one the team didn't talk to. The witness. The victim.

The twins were upstairs playing with Miranda, one of the neighborhood teens who sometimes babysat when Beatrice wasn't available, and a social worker the department had sent to monitor the kids' emotional and psychological states. Susan hadn't seen Casey or Tim since the first few units had responded and taken them away to be examined by the EMTs. She desperately wanted to see them. She needed to hold them and kiss them and smell their hair. She needed to hear herself tell them that everything was going to be all right. She needed to hear them respond with the blind trust only a child could have in their mother. She needed to feel their love and offer them her love in return.

The first set of EMTs had rushed her mother to Mid-Hudson Regional Hospital. The on-scene assessment showed Beatrice had sustained defensive wounds to her hands and forearms as she'd tried to push Randall back out the door. But he'd overtaken her, stabbing her in her side, possibly nicking her liver and piercing a lung. She'd lost a lot of blood and had been only semiconscious when backup had arrived. Susan hadn't heard any updates since she'd been taken away.

Footsteps came into the living room. She looked up to see Tommy walking toward her.

"Hey," she said.

"Hey."

"Sit."

Tommy eased himself onto the couch and watched the chaos alongside his partner. "You okay?"

"I think so. My mom's in pretty bad shape, though."

"The kids?"

"Upstairs."

Tommy exhaled the breath he was holding.

"I don't think you're supposed to be talking to me," Susan said. "Protocol."

"Screw protocol," he said. "I need to make sure you're okay. I should've been here with you. We should've figured he'd be making a move on you. He was already stalking you. How could we not see that?"

"We did see it. That's why we had the unit out front and I called before we headed back to the barracks. There was no way we could've known this would happen."

"We should've done the work here. We didn't have to go back to the barracks."

Susan looked down at her hands folded on her lap, still trembling. "Stop second-guessing yourself, Tommy. It is what it is."

"But the trooper. And your mother."

"I know."

She watched the men and women walking through the house. "Look, I want to apologize for accusing you of being part of all this.

And tailing you. And trying to get the drop from your dad. Everything was just so jumbled up. It was hard to see what was the truth and what was a lie. When I saw your file and after I talked with your dad, I thought you had to be Sam. Too many pieces fit too perfectly."

"You don't have to apologize," Tommy replied. "I was stupid for not saying anything as soon as we found out who Randall really was. I should've come clean about me and Lily as soon as those prints came back. I never would've imagined all this could happen. And for the record, if I found out about my connection to Randall the way you did, I would've thought the same thing. You don't know me. I get that. I'm sorry."

Susan forced a smile. "If I don't get to apologize, you don't get to apologize. Deal?"

"Deal."

Crosby walked through the front door and came into the living room. He stood over the two of them. "You give your statement yet?"

"Not entirely."

"Then why is Corolla talking to you?"

She looked at Tommy. "I told you."

"Yeah, protocol. Got it." Tommy stood from the couch and walked out front to talk to some of the other officers. When he was gone, Crosby sat next to Susan and gently put his arm around her to pull her close.

"How you holding up?"

"Okay, I guess."

"Dutchess ME has Randall's body. We're just about done here. Units found Hooper Landsky's Subaru parked a few blocks away. We're processing it."

"How is Hooper doing?"

"He'll be released soon. Gave his statement, but there wasn't much to give. He was knocked out on his way to his car after work. Woke up chained to a wall. Couldn't tell how long he was there, but he wasn't given any food or water. Then you found him. Didn't see who did any of it."

Susan looked at the blood that had pooled in the hallway and run into the living room, staining the edge of the carpet.

"How's your shoulder?" Crosby asked.

"They stabilized it as best they could. Hurts like hell."

"And the kids?"

"They're upstairs. I haven't had a chance to be with them, so I'm not sure how much of this they comprehend. They were pretty scared during the whole thing."

"Any news on your mom?"

"No. To be honest, I feel like I should be there instead of sitting in the living room where no one can talk to me. I'm helpless here. I *feel* helpless here. I need to get to that hospital. My mom needs me."

"Then you better go. Finish your statement, get the kids, and go see your mom. Tell her we're thinking of her."

"I will."

"You call me if you need anything. Anything. That's an order."

"Yes, sir."

Susan got up from the couch and began to make her way upstairs to see Casey and Tim. As she placed her foot on the first step, she stopped. "Couple things still bother me," she said.

Crosby turned toward her. "What's that?"

"When I asked him about killing Amanda and kidnapping Hooper, he got confused. Like he wasn't sure what I was talking about. He knew generally about both but couldn't give me details. When I asked him about killing Lily and Rose and Dr. Reems, he was right there. And Sam wasn't even the personality that took over when he was hurting Lily and Rose."

"Maybe his mind was all jumbled. Didn't know what was what."

"Maybe."

"What was the other thing?"

"He came to the house as Sam, but there was no coat. No hood. Same with the video we saw of him getting out of his car at Quarim when he was going after Dr. Reems. Whenever Randall talked about Sam, he always mentioned the coat and the hood. And in all my encounters with him, a large hood covered his face. But now, nothing. To hear Randall talk, that outfit *was* Sam. It's what differentiated the two personalities."

"Maybe he didn't need the coat and hood anymore because, in his mind, Randall was dead."

"I guess. Has anyone found the coat?"

"Not yet," Crosby replied. "We got a team at his house and at the university, and like I said, we're processing the Subaru. We'll get it. But it's over now. You did good, Susan. You always do."

62

Rain tapped the hospital windows in a rhythmic fashion. It had been raining and sleeting most of the day, making holiday travel an absolute mess.

"Mommy, can we go get some juice from the lady?"

Susan looked up from her magazine and saw Casey standing in front of her, tugging on the bottom of the green velvet dress she wanted to wear for Christmas Eve dinner. It was December 24, and they were spending it in Beatrice's hospital room, as a family, as it should be. Tim was sitting in one of the plastic chairs playing a video game. He'd been quiet since the incident at the house but liked it when everyone was around. It made him feel safe. Beatrice was sitting up, trying to stay awake, but dozing with the help of the oxycodone the nurse had given her the last time she'd been in to check on things. She'd been given a private room as a courtesy, and Susan spent almost every waking minute at her mother's side. The surgery to repair what turned out to be a pierced liver, nicked intestine, and collapsed lung was a success. Now there was the recovery, which would be somewhat slow and aggravating. But Susan was moving Beatrice into her house permanently, and she would help in any way she could.

"Mommy, I'm thirsty," Casey whined. Her cheeks were red from the hot air blasting out of the wall heater. "Can we get juice? Please? I said please, so you have to say yes."

"That's not how it works."

"Please, *anyway*?"

"Go get my purse."

Casey skipped to the corner of the room and grabbed Susan's pocketbook, which was next to the stack of magazines they'd brought from the hotel. Susan closed her magazine and rubbed her shoulder. She was out of the sling now, but mobility and pain were still issues. Casey didn't talk about Randall or about what had happened, and seemed to be her old self, which was encouraging. The child psychologist had warned that she could relapse as long as a year from now, so Susan knew they weren't out of the woods just yet. But each day was a blessing when Casey acted like Casey.

"Wow!"

Tim looked up from his game, and his face lit up. "Cool!"

Susan turned in her seat. Tommy was standing in the doorway holding a three-foot artificial Christmas tree in one hand and two black garbage bags in the other.

"Hey, guys." He winked at Susan as he stepped into the room. "I heard you were spending Christmas Eve here with your grandma, and I didn't think you could do that without the proper Christmas decorations to hang. And you need a tree, right? You wanna help me put things up?"

Both twins dropped what they were doing and scurried over to Tommy, pulling him farther into the room and grabbing the bags to see what was inside. Casey wasn't thirsty anymore. Tim didn't care about the high score on his video game. It was Christmastime. Finally.

Susan got up from her seat and joined them in the corner. Casey was snatching cheap wall decorations and silver garlands from one bag while Tim was in the other, rummaging through decorations to put on the tree. Smiles that had been hit or miss for the past few days returned instantly, broad and beautiful.

"What's all this?" Susan asked.

Tommy shrugged and placed the tree in the corner. "Like I said, you can't have Christmas Eve without it looking like Christmas. This place is drab."

"Yes, it is."

He leaned in to whisper. "I got their presents in the car. Wrapped. Pink for Casey and blue for Tim. I hope that's not too gender specific."

"It's perfect."

"When I called Eric about what happened, he told me where the spare key was. I got the gifts from his house and found the ones you were stashing at the barracks. And maybe a few of us chipped in for some extra stuff too."

"You didn't have to do this," Susan said.

"Yes I did," Tommy replied. "You're up to your neck in all this fallout from Randall, so I wanted to make sure the kids were taken care of. We all did."

"Well, tell everyone I said thank you. This is above and beyond."

"Have you talked to Eric?"

"Yeah. Flight comes in tomorrow morning. He's meeting us here."

Susan looked on as the kids ripped through the packages and began hanging bulbs and tiny figurines on the tree. They were laughing and scurrying about in a haphazard way, from decorating the tree to hanging things on the wall. They looked happy. And for the moment, Susan believed they could all get past this. She believed in a new future.

"They find the coat or the hood yet?"

"Not yet. We'll find them."

"We better."

Tommy clapped his hands to get the kids' attention. "Hey, I got some presents in the car for you guys. You want me to go get them?"

"Yes!" the twins shouted in unison.

"Okay, I'll be right back. Keep hanging your stuff."

Susan grabbed him by the jacket and leaned in to whisper. "Not all the presents. Santa, remember?"

"Right."

She watched him leave and began unloading decorations from the bags. As she worked, she glanced back toward the door and saw the wet and muddy footprints Tommy had left. She stared at them, thinking. Knowing.

There are no such things as coincidences.

She walked over to where her bag was hanging and dug inside, eventually pulling out the tape measure. This would have to be quick. She bent down and grabbed her phone from her back pocket, watching to make sure Tommy was still out of sight.

63

The storm had eventually passed, and visiting hours were over. Tommy shut the door to his car, switched on the engine, and turned up the heat. It was almost eight o'clock on Christmas Eve, which meant it was probably late enough for people to already be in their homes, celebrating with drinks and desserts and tucking their kids in bed as the anticipation of Santa grew to a fever pitch. He hoped the roads would be clear enough to make the trip to Stony Brook an uneventful one. He didn't want to spend all night in traffic.

Despite his stiff upper lip and calm exterior, this case had taken a toll on him. Of that, there was no doubt. He knew it would be hard going in, but he hadn't expected the kaleidoscope of emotion he'd been faced with along the way. Doubt, fear, anger, love, confusion, sadness.

Hate.

He'd been forced to come clean about his relationship with Lily when Susan read through his personnel file and visited his father, but the truth was he and Lily were so much more than what his father had described. Lily had been, unquestionably, the love of his life. She'd been the reason he got up in the morning, determined to start a career from which they could then build their life together. They had planned to get married after she got her master's in education, and she'd been more than willing to move upstate to be with him for the beginning of their forever. What had begun as a chance meeting in the school cafeteria when she was a lost little freshman and he was a confident, self-assured senior had blossomed into a relationship that grew beyond high school crushes and adolescent infatuation. Their love had been the real thing—forever, unrelenting.

And William Feder had taken it all.

———

Tommy picked up his phone and placed a call as he turned onto the Taconic Parkway.

"Yeah, it's me," he said. "I'm on my way. Be there around ten, depending on traffic." He paused and took a breath. "She's still asking about the coat and the hood. We need to end this."

He hung up after listening for a bit more, then settled in for the long drive ahead.

After Lily's death, Tommy scoured newspaper reports about what Gary forced William Feder to do to her. What made everything worse was that Tommy *knew* Gary. He knew he was a drunk and a general loser, but he'd never thought he was insane. There was neighborhood gossip about Gary slapping Rose around every once in a while, but whenever Tommy confronted Lily about it, she always swore those rumors were just that and assured him there was nothing to worry about. His biggest mistake had been believing her. He'd left Lily and Rose alone with no protection. They'd been tortured and murdered because of him. The guilt had been crushing.

When he came home for the funerals, he implored his father to talk to him about the details of the case that weren't in the press. At first his father resisted. He was devastated, too, knowing his son had lost a partner he'd never had a chance to start a life with. It took some time, but eventually Martin shared classified details, here and there. It was Martin who told Tommy that William had been the one who actually killed Rose and Lily. Gary forced him to do it, but their blood was on William Feder's hands alone.

Tommy merged onto Interstate 684. Traffic was heavy but flowing. He turned on the radio.

The revelation of William's guilt had morphed into an addiction that had no cure. Tommy found himself hunting every piece of detail he could about William Feder, the supposed third hostage. He called in favors the way favors could be called in, cop to cop, and got his hands on William's sealed file from when he was in therapy as a kid. He learned about his little brother, Sam, and the drowning and how the doctor deemed it suspicious, although no further action was taken because nothing could be proven. He got ahold of William's medical records and learned about the dissociative identity disorder William had suffered with as a child, how it resurfaced during his time in Gary's basement. And how it could be triggered.

Then one day, William Feder was gone. He simply disappeared, leaving no trace. Tommy scoured the internet for any piece of information that could tell him where the doctor had fled to, but there was nothing. Calls to other departments across the country and favors from a few FBI agents he'd befriended also went nowhere. William had vanished and taken his secrets with him.

But then, five years later, Tommy's father called. He'd seen William in the paper. A small article about Amanda Brock getting married in a Central Park ceremony. William was going by the name Randall Brock now, and he'd had some plastic surgery done, but Martin Corolla was a good detective. No matter how different someone might look aesthetically, it was the eyes that never changed. And the haunted look behind Randall Brock's eyes was all Martin needed to know. William Feder had returned.

Tommy felt a new sense of purpose when his father showed him the picture from the paper. A plan began to emerge. He would rid himself of the guilt that was crushing him, avenge Lily's death, and show Randall Brock what it felt like to lose things. He'd start with Randall's new wife, move on to his sanity, and end by taking either his freedom or his life. He had to show the world that Randall Brock was William Feder and that William was a man absolutely capable of the things he did to Rose and Lily. The public had treated William like a victim, but he was an accessory. He was a killer. Tommy's vengeance couldn't come in the form of a bullet in the back of the head or a rope around Randall's neck. That would be too quick. Too merciful. He had to show the world the man Randall really was. This was the only way. Everyone needed to look behind the curtain.

At first, Tommy didn't think he'd have the nerve to kill someone, but he used all of the hate and anguish he'd been feeling and molded it into a single ball of fury that was like a tumor needing to be excised. He learned of Amanda Brock's affair after tailing her while on leave from the barracks upstate. That was a welcome surprise. He'd been planning to use that to gain Randall's trust, but then he found her safe-deposit box key while searching the house and bribed a teller to let him look inside. The fact that Amanda was planning to leave Randall and cut him out of the will was simply icing on the cake. The motive was right there, folded in thirds, tucked away for safekeeping.

He was there at Amanda's award dinner and watched Randall leave early. He waited until just before the ceremony ended, then called the inn hosting the event and asked to speak with Amanda. When she got on the phone, he identified himself as a police officer and asked her to come up to the Quarim campus, explaining that her husband had been stopped for a DUI. She came right away, and as he walked her toward the psychiatry building, he hit her in the back of the head with a field hockey stick he'd taken from the university's team equipment shed. He swung hard, knowing exactly where to make contact at the base of her skull. She was dead before her body hit the ground.

He put her in the trunk of her Mercedes and drove the car back to an old abandoned garage on Route 9 in Garrison, where he removed the car's computer, placed her in the front seat, and drove the car onto the Goat Trail. Once he was there, he aimed the car toward the fencing he'd cut, got out, placed a small boulder on the gas petal, and put the car in drive. Game over.

Now, as Tommy made his way along Interstate 684, he encountered more holiday traffic than he'd expected. The highway was even more congested than the Taconic, and he had to slow down. He arched his back and stretched, thinking about everything he'd gone through, wondering if there was anything he was forgetting.

His original plan had been to visit Randall as Sam and exploit Randall's sadness, driving him toward an inevitable relapse. He used his little brother's name both to trigger a memory that Randall was never really able to suppress and to let him know Tommy knew about his past. The thought of the truth coming out to others was enough of a leash to make Randall obey Tommy's every command. The rest had been easy enough. He let himself into Randall's garage with a remote he'd taken from Amanda's car and simply appeared to Randall, making himself seem otherworldly or supernatural. And it worked. He began to see the cracks in Randall's psyche.

One thing he hadn't counted on was Susan tagging the case as a homicide so quickly, but as an investigator, Tommy was able to play both sides. He continuously pushed Susan toward the possibility of Randall being the killer, while at the same time ensuring that Randall never saw him as anyone other than Sam. He watched Susan's interrogation from the squad room. He remained in the backyard when they dug up the evidence he knew would be there, and he was careful not to be around when they arrested Randall and marched him out of his house. Control was the key to all of it.

I-684 turned into the Hutchinson River Parkway, and the traffic lightened after White Plains. He was moving again, the radio playing a string of hard rock.

Hooper Landsky had been the one disappointment. He'd planned to get both Randall and Hooper to the Andersons' basement and make Randall kill Amanda's lover. Susan had stumbled on Hooper too soon, but Tommy had improvised. And in the end it had all worked out. Mostly.

It was hard to think about how close he'd come to catastrophe. He'd goaded Randall into killing Peter, but he hadn't expected that Randall would want to eliminate everyone who knew about his disorder. The fact that Susan had to go through what she went through made him sick. The kids could've been hurt. Beatrice could've died. It had been his one big mistake, and Susan almost paid the price. He'd never forgive himself for that and could only be thankful that everyone was safe.

———

Tommy pulled into his parents' driveway and shut off the engine. His father stepped out of the front door and waved. Tommy walked around the car and popped the trunk. He grabbed a duffel bag from inside and swung it over his shoulder.

"You made good time," Martin said.

"Everyone's already in for the night. Traffic wasn't too bad. Where's Mom?"

"Taking a bath. She just got back yesterday. She said Florida was nice, but she missed the cold. Come on—I got the firepit going."

Tommy followed his father around to the rear of the house. They walked through a gate that opened into the yard, which was expansive and somewhat private. In the center of the patio, just under the deck above them, was a giant wood-burning firepit he'd helped build a few years earlier.

"It's been going for a few hours now," Martin said, pointing at the flames that reached up into the night sky.

"You think it's hot enough?"

"Oh yeah. It's plenty hot. Plus we have this to help."

Martin grabbed a canister of gasoline and spat some onto the fire. The flames erupted, then calmed, continuing a steady burn.

Martin had been crushed by Lily's death too. Tommy knew he'd loved her like a daughter. He'd failed to see the warning signs of an abusive husband in Gary. He'd failed to see how things might escalate within the Anderson house. And as a cop, he'd failed to listen to his gut when it had told him something wasn't right about Gary. When the original scene in the Andersons' basement had turned out to be so horrific that no cop had wanted to work the case, Martin had volunteered, seeing it as his penance.

But like Tommy, Martin, too, had felt that William Feder should have been held responsible. Should have sacrificed himself rather than harm those women. Helping Tommy was his way of making amends with Rose and Lily.

Tommy unzipped the duffel bag and pulled out the black coat with its oversized hood. He threw them onto the fire, then poured the gasoline over the flames.

Martin's face glowed orange and red. "Miss Adler can ask all she wants about the coat and hood now," he said. "She'll never find them."

"Yup."

"Come on—let's go inside and have a drink. I think we've earned it. And your mother wants to see you."

"Hold on," a voice said from behind them. "Miss Adler actually has a few follow-up questions."

64

Susan walked into Martin Corolla's backyard. Her weapon was at her side, her finger on the trigger. She appeared calm, but she could feel her heart beating rapidly in her chest. The two men looked at her, their expressions of surprise apparent in the glow of the fire behind them. Neither of them moved.

"Step away from each other," she commanded. "One step to the side. Do it."

Martin and Tommy did as they were instructed, their eyes fixed on her.

"What're you doing here?" Tommy asked.

"Solving my case," Susan replied. She could hear her voice cracking. It wasn't the nerves. It was anger. "I guess you're not too observant about being tailed when I'm not driving my mom's Versa, huh?"

"This doesn't concern you," Martin growled. "Get back in your car and go home."

"You're wrong. This does concern me. Concerns my family. My kids." She took a few more steps toward the men, nodding at Tommy. "I knew you had something to do with this. There's just no way you could have a past with Randall or William or whoever the hell he was and not be involved somehow. Like I said before, it fit too perfectly."

Tommy was quiet.

"It was too big a coincidence that you transferred here at the same time our suspect's wife was killed and he started having a breakdown *and* you knew everyone involved. But I admit it took me a while to be sure. What size shoe are you, Tommy? I'd say size twelve or thirteen. About the size of the prints I took from the woods at the Christmas tree lot. Same as the prints in the snow around my house, and the same as the boot print you just left on the floor of the hospital. I checked Randall's autopsy report for that exact thing. Told the ME specifically to measure so I could compare. I'd been so convinced that he was the hooded Sam. But no. His feet were only ten inches. Size eight."

"I don't know what you're talking about," Tommy said. "A boot print in the snow or a boot print in your mom's hospital room doesn't prove anything."

Susan nodded toward the pit. "That coat and hood on the fire do."

"That coat will be burned into ash by the time we're done talking," Martin sneered. "Sorry, miss. You got nothing but speculation and guesses. That's not a case. And even if you took those boot prints and snatched that coat off the fire, it'd still be circumstantial at best. No DA would press charges on what you got. Wouldn't be worth the risk. Not with a cop involved. Not with one of their own. Maybe Tommy found the coat. Maybe it was already burned up when he discovered it at Randall's house."

"Maybe," Susan said. It was hard to contain the adrenaline pumping through her. She looked at Tommy. "But the other day at the campus fire at Quarim, you asked me to grab your recorder from the glove box in your car. It didn't register at the time, but later it clicked. I pushed past a garage door opener to get the recorder. And guess what? You don't have a garage at your house. Neither does your father."

"It's for a garage I rent in Peekskill," Tommy replied. He sounded less confident now.

Susan shook her head. "I had Crosby call in a favor on the drive here. You gotta have some serious friends in high places to get a search warrant on Christmas Eve." She dug into her coat pocket and came away with a plastic evidence bag. The garage door opener was inside. "I was planning on having your car towed and processed, but you left it unlocked. I'm guessing this is going to open Amanda Brock's garage. I mean, it has their address on the back of it."

"That son of a bitch got what was coming to him," Martin roared, his voice carrying out into the otherwise-quiet night. "He tortured those women, and he liked it. I don't care what anyone says about Gary Anderson making him do it. William Feder liked it. Something had to be done. Someone had to avenge those women."

"By killing another innocent woman? And almost killing her lover? That doesn't make sense."

"Collateral damage."

"Dad, shut up," Tommy said. "You have nothing to do with this."

"Wrong again," Susan said. "Your dad is a part of this. He was your partner. He was driving the Subaru Legacy when I found Hooper in Gary Anderson's basement. He obviously wasn't expecting me to be there, so he took off in a rush. When I hopped on the hood of the car, I couldn't see the driver's face, but I did see that giant West Point class ring he wears on his middle finger gripping the steering wheel. You had him checking on Hooper since he was local. Makes sense. Hell, I didn't realize what I'd seen until you left those boot prints at the hospital. As soon as I saw them, it clicked, and just like that, everything fell into place."

Tommy's eyes widened as he looked at Susan. He was dazed and tried to smile. "Okay, but this is just us out here talking now. You may be right. Maybe not. But I know you care about me, and I care about you. I care about your entire family. The kids. Your mom."

"Don't bring my family into this."

"I also know you're a good cop and that you're not going to bring down other cops in a situation like this. My dad's right. Even if we did something like what you're saying, Rose and Lily needed to be avenged. I'm not saying it's right. But I am saying that it needed to be done.

Now I'm asking you, cop to cop, put down your gun, let us walk into the house, and you go home and be with your beautiful family. They need you, Susan. It's Christmas. You don't need to be out here. Go be with them."

Susan tightened her grip on her Beretta. "Your plan almost killed my family. You set Randall loose on them."

"I'm so sorry about that. Honestly. It wasn't what I intended. But you took care of it because you're a good cop. Hell, you're here because you're a good cop. Now I need you to let us go back inside, and when I come in tomorrow, I'll put in for a transfer, and you'll never have to see me again. This can stay between us. No one else has to know what you think you discovered, and we'll all move on with our lives. You think you can do that?"

Susan shook her head slowly. Taking a fellow officer down for the greater good was one of the hardest things she'd ever have to do on the job. "You know I can't. I can't look the other way."

"Yes you can."

"No. Not on a murder."

"We care about each other. Show me you care. Walk away."

"You killed innocent people."

"I did what I had to do. Please. Go."

"I can't," Susan said, her gun aimed at both men. "And even if I could, he couldn't."

Susan watched as both Tommy and Martin looked past her, their expressions shifting from ones of hope to ones of panic and despair. It was over, and now they knew it.

Crosby walked into the yard, followed by a handful of NYPD officers.

"Make it quick," he commanded. "We don't need a perp walk here. Get them in custody and in the cars ASAP. The neighbors don't need a show. I'll talk to the wife."

Susan holstered her weapon and walked up to Tommy as he was being cuffed by one of the officers. "We caught you on a neighbor's security system in Randall's complex. You were coming out of the woods with Randall, and you were putting him in Hooper's Subaru. The wind blew your hood down, and there you were. You gotta be careful in neighborhoods like that. Everyone has some kind of camera these days."

EPILOGUE

Susan sat in the waiting area of Jefferson Hospital's psychiatric unit stroking Tim's hair as he lay on her lap flipping through a pop-up book. The north end of the Philadelphia skyline could be seen out the window on the far end of the floor. Casey was in the corner playing with a dollhouse that Susan would normally deem too dirty to handle, but under the circumstances, she really didn't mind. She'd learned to pick her battles as of late, and prioritizing her life had become her new calling. There was no doubt she loved the job and the high that came from investigating a case, but she loved her family more and had promised herself she wouldn't sacrifice her time with them because the job demanded it. Her kids were just too precious to take a back seat to anything.

It had been two months since Tommy and Martin were taken into custody. They had been arraigned and were currently awaiting trial at Sing Sing Correctional Facility in Ossining, about a half hour north of Manhattan. The judge had considered them a flight risk and denied bail. That had been her first victory. She was looking forward to a few more.

Beatrice was back on her feet but got around slower than she used to. Her body was healing at its own pace, and there could be no rushing such a thing at her age. That suited Susan just fine. It was nice having her mother around since moving her into the house, but they hadn't been anticipating what a project it would be to create a bedroom on the bottom floor. They were still getting their arms around the construction that was to come.

"Mommy, I need a new book."

Susan lifted Tim off her lap and patted him on the butt. "Okay, sweetie. Go get one."

"Can you come with me?"

"It's right there. You can do it."

She watched her little boy carefully shuffle over to the table full of books, glancing back every few feet to make sure his mom was still there. She hadn't fully anticipated the reaction her children would have to being held captive and watching a man die in front of them. At first they had appeared okay. They'd been shaken, but who wouldn't have been? She'd thought they were too young to properly process what had happened and what they witnessed, and Casey seemed to be coping okay. She was her regular self, playing with her dolls and creating things from her arts and crafts kit as she'd always done. Her love of after-school movies never waned, and she slept well almost every night. Tim, however, was having problems. It had begun with questions asked incessantly about the man who tried to take them and the man who hurt Grandma and the man Mommy had to shoot. Susan answered them all the best she could, and he'd seem satisfied with those answers until he'd ask them again and again, and the cycle would reset.

Tim's questions then morphed into nightmares that would cause him to wake up screaming and crying that the bad man was coming to get them. Bed-wetting followed, and it was at this time Susan began searching for someone they could talk to. They'd found a local therapist and had sessions three times a week, but it hadn't helped. Things continued to get worse, and Tim's detachment from his friends at school was noticed by his teachers, who'd made calls home, stating that he'd become distant and his learning was suffering. At that point, Susan knew more drastic measures had to be taken. She needed to dive in and solve this before he passed a point of no return. And here they were.

The elevator chimed, and Susan watched a man step off. He was dressed casually: a pair of tan khakis, a green wool sweater, a bomber jacket and scarf. He walked with the help of a cane, passing the reception desk and coming into the waiting area. When he sat across from her, Tim ran from the book table and buried his face in her lap. That was his reaction to strangers these days.

"I'm sorry," the man said, motioning toward Tim. "Did I take his seat?"

Susan shook her head. "No, that's fine. He was sitting with me."

She studied him out of the corner of her eye as he checked his phone. He looked to be her age. Maybe a little older. Dirty-blond hair that was just a bit overgrown. His beard had a little gray in it. It was attractive.

"Mommy, I can't find a book," Tim whined from her lap.

"Okay. Keep looking. There has to be something there."

"I want you to come with me."

"You can go by yourself. You're a big boy."

"No."

"I think you can."

Tim shook his head. "I can't. You have to come with me."

"Okay, come on."

She got up and walked Tim over to the table. They began pulling out books and studying the covers.

"You're on the job?" the man asked, pointing. "I can see your shield on your belt."

Susan looked down and nodded. "Yeah, I forgot that was there. Came here right from work."

"I used to be on too." He held up his cane. "Not anymore."

"I'm sorry."

"Where are you stationed?"

"I'm actually New York State Police," Susan replied as she cycled through more books that Tim shook his head at.

The man sat up in his seat. "New York? What're you doing down here?"

"My brother got scared when the bad man tried to hurt us, and now he needs to talk to a doctor so he can feel better and be happy again."

Casey was standing on the other side of the man's chair. He spun around and smiled.

"Is that right?"

"Yes. And we don't want him to have bad dreams anymore, so we had to come here so the doctor can make him all better."

"How about you?" he asked. "How are you doing?"

"I'm good," Casey replied. "I don't need to talk to a doctor. Just Tim."

The man turned back around and faced Tim. "I'm here to talk to a doctor too," he said. "Nothing to feel scared about. The people here are real nice. They'll make you feel better for sure. Just like they made me feel better."

Tim dropped a book he was holding and looked at the man, studying him for a while. "Did a bad man try and hurt you too?"

"You could say that."

"And the doctor made you feel better."

"She certainly did."

Tim nodded and finally grabbed a book. Without another word, he walked back over to the chair, climbed up, and started reading.

Susan stood up and made her way back to her seat. Casey returned to playing with the dollhouse. "Thanks," she said to the man. "Believe it or not, I think that helped."

"I wasn't lying," he replied. "This hospital is top notch. He's in good hands. You're doing the right thing."

Susan smiled. There was something about the way he spoke that reassured her she was, in fact, doing right by her son. Tim could have continued treatment in New York, but she'd read so many articles touting the advancements in pediatric psychology at Jefferson Hospital. Philadelphia wasn't that far a drive. If it meant getting their lives back together again, she'd do anything. This was going to work. She could feel it.

The nurse at the reception area leaned over her desk. "Dr. Cain is ready for you."

The man nodded and slowly eased himself up from the seat. "It was nice to talk to you. I hope everything works out. Maybe I'll see you here again."

"Yes," Susan replied. "Maybe." She extended her hand. "I'm Susan Adler, by the way."

The man smiled. "Well, it's nice to meet you, Susan Adler. I'm Liam. Liam Dwyer."

ACKNOWLEDGMENTS

Writing a second book is always harder than the first and can be quite intimidating for a new author. Suddenly, there are deadlines and expectations and contracts as well as sales of the first book that people will compare to the second. It's daunting having a successful debut and having to follow it up with another great story. I hope I've done that for my readers, and I would like to thank the following people who were instrumental in both contributing to the story and talking me off the ledge when I needed it.

First, to my agent, Curtis Russell of PS Literary Agency. Thank you for taking the phone calls when I was at my wit's end and encouraging me to keep pressing forward. I appreciate your ongoing vote of confidence and your true advocacy for my work.

To my editors, Megha Parekh and Caitlin Alexander. Your feedback and suggestions really helped make the story come to life, and your support meant more than you know. I love what we created here and look forward to our continued success.

To Sarah Shaw and the rest of the Thomas & Mercer team. Your enthusiasm for my books is never waning, and that means so much. Again, thank you for everything you do out in the marketplace.

To David Prockter, for planting the seed of this story and getting my wheels turning. You're a great friend and have always been one of my biggest fans. Your support means so much. Thanks, bud.

To Investigator Brian Martin of the New York State Police, Manhattan. Thank you for your insight on the inner workings of the state police and the tour of the Buchannan barracks. I appreciate you answering the random calls and texts to ensure I got my facts straight.

To Martin Farrell (a.k.a. Dad), sergeant, retired, Pleasantville Police Department. Again, thank you for allowing me to pick your brain about police procedures and methods. Your information is invaluable and adds to the authenticity of my law enforcement characters.

To my mother, Mary. You're always there with a tweet or a retweet to help promote my books and spread the word to everyone you can. Thank you for all you do. I love you.

To my family and friends, who supported me with my first book and continue to do so with this one. Your love means so much, and I can only thank you from the bottom of my heart.

To my wife, Cathy. This wild journey is just beginning, and I can't think of anyone else I'd rather experience it with than you. I love you and always will.

To my two daughters, Mackenzie and Jillian, to whom this book is dedicated. Thank you for being the inspiration behind everything that's good, pure, loving, and strong about Susan Adler. When I tell her story, I see you two in my mind. I love you both more than you can possibly know.

Thank you, again, to all of my readers. I hope you continue to enjoy my books and share your reading experiences with me. I write my stories for you, and I'm so grateful you're there to read them.

Finally, a quick note of thanks to Gary Grandstaff, who won a contest to have his name used in the book. When I first started writing this, Gary was only going to be a name mentioned in passing, but as the character became more prominent in the story and ended up being the force behind Randall's relapse, I wanted to give Gary Grandstaff an opportunity to rethink having his name attached to such a diabolical character. In the end, we kept *Gary* and replaced his surname with *Anderson*, but I wanted to at least acknowledge him here since he did win the contest.

Happy reading, everyone. I truly hope you enjoyed this book.

ABOUT THE AUTHOR

Photo © 2017 Mima Photography

Matthew Farrell lives in the Hudson Valley, just outside of New York City, with his wife and two daughters. Get caught up on the progress of his next thriller along with his general musings by following him on Twitter @mfarrellwriter or liking him on Facebook: www.facebook.com/ mfarrellwriter2.